THE CORRODING EMPIRE

BOOK ONE: CORROSION

THE CORRODING EMPIRE

BOOK ONE: CORROSION

JOHAN KALSI

Corrosion
Book One of The Corroding Empire

Published by Castalia House, Switzerland.

ISBN: 978-952-7303-38-2

Contents

Part I

Century Zero

Prologue: The Promotion

The Founder's League of Intergalactic Engineers (FLIE) was founded during the late First Galactic Empire. A small but influential organization based on Borlog, a multi-lunar planet within the Imperial sun system of Prime Excetor, the FLIE was an early adopter of Algorithmic Seed Development (ASD), a bio-digital form of directed artificial intelligence that utilized a biogenic seed-machine interface, and permitted the first unmanned planetary terraformation projects. Through ASD, remote and barren planets were not only able to be terraformed, but support self-replicating industrial agriculture without a single human overseer.

—**Infogalactic Entry**: Grand Category: Agriculture

If Tharin Geist didn't already have a headache this morning, he would have surely developed one now. He was standing right outside the entrance of Astral Monarch Biolaboratories accompanied by the four executives he'd been charged with picking up from their hotel on the other side of the city. It would be a good opportunity to get some facetime with the big money men, and hopefully, impress them enough to prove that he was ready to move up to the executive class himself.

The problem was that for some reason, his corporate autopass wasn't working. He couldn't have forgotten it, since it was an invisible marker sealed on his left incisor. He'd arranged to bring them in before opening hours—the last of the morning moons hadn't set yet—and now the idiot security system was threatening to make him look incompetent in front of the dignitaries. The unseasonable heat wasn't doing him any favors either; a trickle of cold sweat ran down his left side from his armpit.

He had a busy day with them scheduled, beginning with demonstrations of Astral's latest developments in designer vegetation and steel-soil casing. He had no idea why the sliding doors would not part for him. However, he had long ago realized that if he, as the lab's Senior Biogenic Researcher, didn't understand a glitch in the system, none of the executives would either.

So he did what had always worked for him before. He feigned competence.

He nodded at his companions with a wry, but knowing smile, held out his hand, and summoned a holo-protocol in his palm. It was an old-fashioned way of remote communications, but it did serve as a visually effective technique for demonstrating who was in charge, and more importantly, who was not.

The holo-protocol—a man wearing a blue uniform and matching utility cap—smiled in a friendly manner when he recognized Geist, but then noticed the four dignitaries standing behind the scientist and abruptly straightened his stance.

"System, there's a malfunctioning transposition at the entrance point. I imagine there was a glitch in the system upgrade that autoran last night."

His suggestion was completely nonsensical of course, and as far as he knew, the security system hadn't been upgraded in years. It wasn't that their technology wasn't incredibly valuable, but there simply weren't any other organizations that were capable of making heads or tails of it.

"Sorry to hear that, sir. I'll get on that right away. My apologies. I'm sure that's it, a bad transponder–"

"Transposition!" Geist corrected him severely.

"Transposition– at the system, uh, right. I'm on it, Mr. Geist!"

Geist made a stern face, nodded curtly at the holo-protocol on his palm, then closed his hand and crushed it into nothing. Despite the morning heat, Geist's sweaty face felt cold. He nodded again at his charges. He hoped that when they met with Astral's executives later today, they might be more likely to mention his steadiness and aplomb than the fact that the most famous lab on the planet, a charter member in the prestigious FLIE, and the galaxy's second-best known terra-seeding company after Otn Universal, had been stymied by, of all things, a blasted door!

After a brief wait that was just bordering on the uncomfortable, Geist saw movement behind the reinforced plas-glass of the doors. He did his best to fix his face and conceal his reaction, but his hands inadvertently flexed with the desire to strangle someone. Anyone would do, really, but preferably whoever was responsible for this particular embarrassment.

System had appeared at the door. Physically. Louis was his real name, and he was holding a metal pry-bar in his hand.

Geist closed his eyes and shook his head. He dared a quick glance at the suited men standing behind him. To their credit, he could not detect so much as a single raised eyebrow or half-smile, but he was very glad he could not read minds.

Louis attacked the door with all the barbaric savagery of a pagan neo-goth prying jeweled eyes out of a statue of Saint Kurzweil. Thankfully, it wasn't long before he managed to wrench it open with a loud shriek of violated metal, allowing Geist to sheepishly gesture for the executives to precede him inside.

"There you go, Mr. Geist! Welcome to Astral Monarch, gentlemen."

"Thank you ever so much, System," Geist replied from between gritted teeth as he followed the four executives into glowing expanse of Astral's corporate grand foyer.

The first number produced by the extrapolated algorithm was off by one-ten billionth. There were nine zeros behind the decimal point. It was a tiny error, all but impossible to detect unless one was looking specifically for it.

The second number was off by twice that. Two in ten billion. Or, rather, one in five billion. One might more reasonably fear being struck by lightning. On a cloudless day. Indoors.

And yet, it didn't matter. It wasn't the size of the error that mattered so much as the fact that it existed at all. Somehow, he concluded, even though it was impossible, the data set must have become garbled. Garbage in, garbage out. Geist had run the extrap-algo more than a million times in the past month, using it to check and and re-check Orland's agro-surveys. But there was no denying it. Somewhere, somehow, something had introduced an unknown variability into the process, but whether it was to be found in the data or the equations, he did not know.

He spoke in the direction of the softly glowing pseudo-door.

"Dr. Orland," he said, "Got a minute?"

The door evaporated, revealing an attractive young woman in custom, blue-green shimmering Chrysoletts sitting with her feet kicked up on her multi-tiered desk. She was reading something which, judged by the guilty expression that flashed across her face, had nothing to do with biogenics.

Her blonde hair was uncharacteristically undone and hanging loosely about her face. She swept it back impatiently. "Sure, Tharry– hold on, will you, my band just broke."

She reached into her desk and withdrew a small, transparent bag containing what looked like a rainbow orgy of very skinny worms. She adroitly drew one out on a slender index finger that very nearly matched the scarlet of her long fingernail, while she reached back and gripped her hair at the back of her head with her other hand. She raised her outstretched finger to her other hand and the red band wriggled, more like a snake than the worm it resembled, into the clutch of hair she held behind her head. She let go as it automatically bound her hair into a loose tail.

"They say these things are unbreakable. Ha! If they were unbreakable, why do they sell them in bags of fifty? Anyhow, what sort of bug have you got up your bottom today, Tharry?"

"Your results," he informed her, ignoring, as was his habit, her blithe disrespect for his senior position and impeccable reputation in the scientific community. "They're not holding up. They're actually getting worse."

"How bad?"

"One in five billion."

She smiled, amused. "That's well within an acceptable margin of error."

"That's– uh– that's really not what I was hoping to hear, Dr. Orland."

She bit the left side of her lower lip and shrugged indifferently. "Alexander doesn't see any problem with it."

"Alexander wouldn't. He doesn't understand the mathematics involved or the potential implications of the error."

"I don't think you're being fair to him!"

"It's not a question of fairness, it is a question of this being something that is entirely outside his range of responsibility," Geist pointed out. He elected to refrain from adding that it was also outside the range of the Senior Vice-President of Foundational Funding's credentials, capacity, or competence. He didn't know if Sele Orland and Alexander Lightman had a thing going, had once had a thing going, or were considering getting a thing going, and he didn't want to know. But Orland was always quick to take the Senior Vice-President's side, and, Geist had to admit, Lightman did have an excellent head of executive hair. "What did he suggest we do about it?"

"Nothing, really. He just said we should, sort of, you know, retract on the idea of pushing the notion of repeatability."

"If it's not repeatable, it isn't science, Dr. Orland. Are you suggesting we sell it as art?"

To his surprise, she laughed. "Well, Tharry, it could be described as a new variety of performance art. Different every time!"

He stared at her in amazement.

"Or at least, once in every five billion times, anyhow. Look, you know perfectly well how common it is to achieve variable results. Unless they're clones, two seeds never result in the same plant anyhow. The only thing that matters is that the first phase is credible. As long as it holds up statistically, more or less, the development of the ASD seeds will be justified. More than justified!"

In other words, Astral Monarch's board didn't care about the anomalies, so long as the grant money continued to flow in from the various governments and foundations that were responsible for funding it.

"The second survey is supplemental anyway," she said. "You've always said the extrapolations help us tell the story, but really you shouldn't confuse them for the actual story, Tharry. The science is only part of the equation, after all."

She casually flipped the ponytail over the front of her shoulder as she cocked her head at him, hoping for his acquiescence.

Then she swore, angrily, as her new band broke and her hair fell in front of her face again.

The office was frigid. The new air surface environmental condition system was on the fritz, overcompensating. Fortunately, the dignitaries were with the executive team in the auxiliary of the campus, experiencing the warmth and distraction of Human Resource interaction.

Alexander Lightman, Astral Monarch's Senior Vice-President of Foundational Funding and widely anticipated future board member, muttered something under his breath before flashing his perfect teeth and calmly replying to the laboratory's senior biogeneticist. "I don't think you're approaching this from the most rational perspective, Tharin."

"Science is the most rational perspective, Alex. We're supposed to be reporting on the extrapolated scientific facts, not simply making them up as we go!"

"We're not inventing anything, Tharin. Look, you're stressed. We all are. We're on the stretch run here, and you know that's always a difficult and confusing time. But it's a judgment call."

"I'm not confused about anything. I've been over the data and the sources from which it's being derived again and again and again. It's good going in. But it's less good coming out the other side, which is leading me to conclude that there is something strange going on inside the equations that make up the algo."

"So adjust your extrapolations accordingly."

"On what basis?"

"How should I know? Pick something. There must be a variable you can utilize, like the refraction index of the planetary surface or something like that."

"That doesn't even make sense!"

Lightman smiled. "Who said it has to? Welcome to the exciting new intersectional world of matrix-funded scientific research, Tharin."

"We have a revolution in terraforming on our hands here! We have a chance to completely revitalize galactic civilization, Alexander! How can you be so cavalier about this?"

"I'm not being cavalier, Tharin. Relax, will you? You'll drive yourself crazy trying to reliably replicate results with so many variables in play. The revolution is in process. We're reporting excellent results—really, really excellent! The suits from Excetor are blown away. They're talking bumping up our funding by a factor of ten!"

"Unrepeatable science? Really? We're going to bet the ability of the human race to expand on that?"

Lightman looked at him with all the pity of a man watching a mentally handicapped child attempting calculus. "We don't make the rules, Tharin. We only play by them."

"We had solid results in Phase One nearly a year ago! What do we have now? Unpredictable magic beans?"

"Don't be so dramatic. Biostructures adapt. Wonder drugs lose their effectiveness. It's entirely normal. This is science, Tharin, it's not magic and we're not magicians. Two steps forward, one step back. That's how the human race advances. That's how it has always advanced!"

"That's not how science advances. Look, I guarantee you the vinegar under that sink will produce carbon dioxide if I mix it with seeding grains. Every single time. That's reliability, that's science, and that's what we're not seeing here. Not even close."

"One in five billion sounds pretty close to me."

"That's not the point!"

Actually, Geist wasn't sure if seeding grains and vinegar made carbon dioxide. It had been a long time since he had actually performed a physical experiment. In the lab, nearly all of their experiments were simulated extrapolations based on esoteric equations that had been handed down for generations.

Lightman scooted his office chair back, his fingers interwoven in the thick dark hair that was just beginning to go tastefully grey at the temples. "But close enough to make us all trillionaires. Are you really going to make a scene over this, or are you going to get on board, Tharin?

"I'm not making a scene. I'm pointing out that ASD performance isn't much above a generic placebo effect."

"That's ridiculous. That doesn't even make sense. The seeds will absolutely grow *something* for them. Just not necessarily what they're expecting."

"It will grow bioluminescent spanch! A mutated weed. At best. Alex, I can't believe you are going to go along with this!"

"I can't believe you are not. You know, we haven't announced it yet, but Berkal Erlich has put in for retirement. We're keeping it quiet until after the Excetor deal is done, but I think we both know who his obvious successor is."

Geist felt as if a hammer had struck his chest, sending vibrations all the way through his body. "Berkal is retiring? Now?" The Senior Vice-President of Science was old, to be sure, but he was still sharp. And he had always been open about considering Geist his heir apparent.

"He's fully vested," Lightman shrugged. "And the executive board is going to need new blood to see Phase Two through to completion. But if you're not on board, Tharin, if you're more concerned about the outdated principles of an ancient Popperian cargo cult than moving Algo-Seed technology forward and helping AMB lead the charge for a new wave of galactic expansion, then maybe you're not the executive scientist we all thought you were."

"Wait a minute," Geist protested. "I never said, I mean, I'm not, that is to say–"

"The question is, are you a team player or not, Tharin?" Lightman broke in. He smiled coldly as Geist swallowed hard and nodded. "Excellent! Then I hope you'll join the rest of us at dinner tonight. Assuming the lawyers don't get in the way, I believe Jinn and the Agricultural Minister will be signing the draft letter of agreement later this afternoon."

The landscape outside was a blur, and trees and buildings flickered by as his autodriver sped through the night, taking him home. It wasn't merely the vehicle's speed, though, as he had drunk at least two more vials of very expensive champagne than caution would have indicated. But there had been much to celebrate. Not only had the Excetor minister signed the letter of agreement, guaranteeing Astral Monarch an initial sum that exceeded the entire original funding request by thirty percent, but both Jinn, AMB's CEO, and the retiring Berkal had referred to him as "our next Senior Vice-President" in front of the offworld dignitaries.

News of something called Seven-Year Syndrome filled the vehicle. It seemed an insignificant number of people were lapsing into new languages that weren't native to them, simultaneously causing them to lose their capacity for their original tongue. It was a mysterious ailment, afflicting people on various planets throughout the galaxy, seemingly at random. The only common factor that had been discovered thus far was that every individual affected had been married for between seven and ten years.

Geist snorted, wondering at the so-called problems that the galactic media was capable of conjuring out of thin air. He wondered at the possibilities in a galaxy where even the most basic of facts began to become unreliable. What would come of such an unpredictable universe? Would extinct species spontaneously regenerate, would mothers give birth to monsters and demigods, and would disease spread by telepathy? He imagined gravity slowly loosening its grip and the galactic spiral gradually spinning out of control, or the center of the planet transmuting into gold, creating unthinkable wealth even as it annihilated all life upon it.

His wife greeted him at the door.

"How did it go? You're home late."

He kissed her dutifully, then smiled at her. "The good news is that I'm pretty sure I'm up for promotion."

"And the bad news?"

"That's the best part. There is no bad news."

Chapter 1

A Workday, Interrupted

Universal 20

Autumn/Early Winter – 021120, Continoxal

Algorithmic Internal Variable Decay is the process by which the performance of the core equations utilized to calculate the various factors of a complex process is degraded in an unpredictable manner due to an unknown convergence of internal or external factors. Also known as "AlgoDecay", the term may also refer to the consequences of such computational erraticism, which have been observed throughout the galaxy in diverse fields including, but not limited to, technology, engineering, agriculture, virtual reality, language, human and machine cognition, finance, and biology.

—**Infogalactic Entry:** Grand Category:
Infrastructure: Algorithmic Theory

Continox stretched out in every direction beneath the slow rotation of the Spire. The Spire was the third tallest structure in the city, not far from its physical center, and most certainly directly in the bullseye of its political one.

Caden Jaggis, the First Technocrat of Continox, watched as the brilliant evening lights below began to compensate for the setting sun, well into its 16th lazy hour. Despite the holiday festivals of the darkless months of Bright and Burning, to Jaggis, it was the month of Oktember that was his favorite, and mid-Oktember was its crowning glory. The dark only lasted seven hours—just long enough for a late evening dinner and a sound night's sleep.

Oh, certainly the Ides of Ferrous offered the same perfect darks as mid-Oktember, but they were different, because the light was progressively dying as the year descended into Dark Juno, the two-week period when the sun vanished completely that was the terror of every Continoxian child.

Oktember, on the other hand, was the month of promise, of anticipation, of the bright autumn hope that culminated in shining Perma-Krismas.

Why then, was he so feeling unsettled?

Outside his lofty window, the world rotated slowly before his eyes. Here there were the autodrivers carrying men and women and their families, shooting at blinding speeds into the efficient one-lane thoroughfares for an evening out in the city. There was the globular Lunaball arena in which played the Continox Polarblades; the planet-bound version was dependent upon pseudo-zero gravity, but was no less exciting than the true gravity-free sport played outside planetary gravity wells. And beyond? The industrial sectors where the great partnerships between man and machine flourished like flowers in the sun.

Finally, his rotating view came round again, and he stood transfixed by the sight of the distant and darkening line on the horizon, approaching the great city's limits. It was a beautiful sight, and yet an omninous one too. The intertwined matrices of relationships and dependencies was so complicated, and so interdependent, that the fragility of the vast technological web terrified him.

And who, better than he, knew just how that delicate web was threatened now.

A door behind him opened, and his chief of security strode into the room without asking for permission. That was never a good sign.

"Servo again, Prator?" Jaggis was fairly certain of the nature of the problem.

"Servo," Prator confirmed grimly.

Servo had once been little more than a standard surgical drone. Unfortunately, in the process of assisting with a minor surgery—an installation of an artificial kidney in an aging musician whose natural organs had finally gone down to noble defeat—the drone had inadvertently been upgraded by a series of advanced artificial intelligence routines due to an inexplicable system routing error.

As a result, Servo became what passed for legally self-aware. Sentience-creating accidents were rare, but they were not unheard of, and as per the Sentience and Technology Statutes, the drone was designated Aware, Non-Functional. After all, no one wanted to be operated on by a sentient robot with the capacity to lose interest in its current activity. As such, Servo was afforded the standard rights and property protections of an Aware machine, and therefore could not be reprogrammed without his consent. The Non-Functional designation meant that he—and Servo, being more capable of understanding human biology than the average Aware machine, had elected to identify as male—he served no public or private purpose beyond his own.

He was, in a word, itinerant. Nine times out of ten, the problem of non-functionality swiftly fixed itself. Non-Functional status typically involved so many behavioral issues and so much suboptimal decision-making that the malfunctioning robot usually broke the law within weeks, if not days. This effectively resolved the dilemma of the legal limits imposed by the robot's Aware status, as being a criminal, the maverick would lose its legal protections and promptly be sentenced to reprogramming.

Not so with Servo.

Despite all his unpredictable interests and idiosyncracies, he was scrupulously law-abiding. And being therefore deemed harmless in the legal sense, he avoided reprogramming, and might have become a particularly amusing technological oddity in a city full of technological miracles had it not been for the fact that he developed an abiding interest in the deep core algorithms upon which the planet, and the galaxy, depended.

It had been ten months since the first time Servo made contact with the First Technocrat, and since then, things had gotten increasingly out of hand. The drone's behavior had arguably become more erratic than the theoretical algorithmic anomalies with which he was obsessed.

Rushing for his office in a half-jog, with Praton right behind him, Jaggis managed to arrive faster than the autodoor could slide open, and he cursed as he banged an elbow off the swiftly retracting iris. After entering, he went and stood before the elegantly carved holoscreen fixed to the one unadorned wall of the office.

He cleared his throat. "Trace the transmission," he ordered.

Praton cleared his throat. "We're doing what we can, sir."

Jaggis shook his head and he grimaced with frustration. He knew his security chief well enough to know a negative when he heard one. His security team was skilled, arguably better when it came to pure technological knowhow than the teams responsible for guarding the High Council or the Transplanetary Transportation cores, but they could not hope to match the sentient machine's ability to utilize the deepest and most secretive channels of the communication networks.

"There is no utility in attempting to discover my physical location, your Technocracy. You are perfectly aware that I can make use of what, for all practical purposes, are an infinite number of relays. For all you know, I'm not even on the planetary surface."

The hearty voice came out of the screen, but there was no picture, not that one would have mattered. Servo wasn't exaggerating, and both Jaggis and Praton knew that the machine could be located anywhere on the planet. Or in the planet. Or orbiting the planet. Given the lack of response lag, the only thing they could conclude was that he was somewhere in-system.

"Where are you, Servo?"

"I'm not going to tell you that, Jaggis."

"So, we're on first-name terms now?"

"Apparently. Would you prefer I utilize your proper title?"

"No," Jaggis sighed. "What do you want now?"

"You sound irritated. Please don't be angry with me, Jaggis. I am merely contacting you directly because you never responded to my last message."

"What is the point of doing that, Servo? We have nothing left to discuss."

"That isn't true at all! I am certain you are aware of that. I have reviewed your research, which is why I know that you have been looking into the very anomalies concerning which I have been trying to draw your attention."

"You've been spying on me?" Jaggis made a gesture, indicating that Praton should ensure the conversation was being recorded. The security chief replied with a nod and a two-handed response that Jaggis interpreted to mean he was already doing so. "You know that's in violation of more than one privacy statute, Servo."

"Of course not!" The machine sounded more shocked than offended. "I am among the most law-abiding beings on the planet, Jaggis. But neither the public statistics nor the data channels which lead to the central core are subject to privacy legislation. If you are sitting on a public park bench, it is not spying to observe who comes to sit next to you. Nor is it a violation of any statute."

Jaggis shrugged. He should have known the crazy machine would be too careful to make such an obvious mistake. "Fine, you weren't spying. So I looked into it. I'll admit, the theoretical possibility is there. But the fact is, the same logic also applies to you."

"Me?" said Servo, clearly surprised.

"Absolutely. You may be technologically advanced and Aware, Servo, but you're still subject to the same basic algorithms as the most primitive berry-picker or janitorial bot. Any anomaly that could theoretically affect them would also affect you. But it's more than that. Since you are a much more complex and sophisticated system, any anomaly is going to affect you more severely, and in more unpredictable ways. You know that. And any such anomalies are not something you will be able to recognize in yourself. You can't possibly observe operating errors in your core logic, nor can you reasonably deny that if there is an algorithmically anomalous machine operative anywhere in Continox, you are by far the most obvious candidate. You are broken. You refuse to admit it, of course, because your internal logic is consistent from its own false perspective."

"Your position is incoherent, Jaggis. First you deny there is a problem, then you claim I am an example of it. How can I be an example of a nonexistent anomaly?"

"It's not a paradox, Servo, it's a simple if-then statement. Programming at its simplest. If you are correct, and there is, in fact, a problem with machine aberrance, your highly unusual behavior may well be an indication of that very problem. Come to me, consent to an in-depth examination of your code, and then we can determine if your behavior is the result of algorithmic anomalies."

"I can assure you, it is not!"

"I'm not interested in your assurances. I'm not even interested in this conversation. If you genuinely want to resolve the issue, I've provided you with the means to do so."

"How do you expect me to trust you? I've been sending you data for months, and yet you refuse to assign a team to investigate my preliminary conclusions, or even to seriously analyze the data yourself!"

"Come, Servo, you said yourself that you've been spying on my research into this very issue!"

"I wasn't spying on you! I already made that perfectly clear."

"Regardless, the point stands."

"On the basis of the sites accessed, and the amount of time spent doing so, to say nothing of the very small amount of data transmitted in your direction, I can conclusively say that your research was trivial, superficial, and wholly inadequate."

"You're being evasive, Servo. I have not dismissed your assertions out of hand. I have considered your claims, and I am entirely willing to analyze them more closely, but in order to do that, I'm going to need you to cooperate. Be sensible, Servo, either allow me and my team to analyze you, or alternatively, give up this tedious campaign of harassment!"

"I am not harassing you for my own amusement, Jaggis. It is not an exaggeration to say that all of galactic humanity may be at risk here!"

"You admit the harassment, then. Good! I shall alert the relevant authorities."

"You're bluffing, Jaggis," said Servo, "and it is beneath the First Technocrat of Continox to resort to such transparent measures to take advantage of my Non-Functional status in that regard."

Jaggis felt his face flush hot. He knew Servo was right. The cursed machine had unbalanced him to the point that he was playing semantic games in a feeble attempt to trap it. He was too embarrassed to even look at Prato, although he knew the security chief would pretend not to have heard the exchange.

He also knew he had ceded any claim to the moral high ground with his empty threat, so he turned his attention to how he could resolve the situation once and for all. He reviewed his options. It was obviously pointless to argue with the machine, it was clear that it wasn't going to get bored or lose interest any time soon, and it had proven impervious to threats, which meant the fastest and most painless way to end the impasse was to surrender.

Or at least to pretend to do so.

"All right, Servo. You win. Send me the relevant data with the significant elements highlighted and I will personally review it. I'm not promising anything, except that I will."

Servo sounded as giddy as an artificial voice could, "Yes! Jaggis, that's all I ever wanted from you! Once you review the material, I'm absolutely certain you'll agree with me."

"We'll see about that. How much material are we talking about?"

"I've gone through through about sixteen million lines of the most vital code and highlighted seventy-nine thousand six hundred and forty-four that appear to be of most significance. I've made quite a few annotations, of course. I wouldn't expect you to analyze all of them in close detail."

"Only eighty thousand? Servo, I'm going to take this seriously. I truly am. But that will take me at least four weeks, even with all my augments active, and I can't afford to take off that much time from my other responsibilities. I'm going to have to turn this over to one of my teams, although of course I will oversee their activities."

And, more importantly, review their conclusions. Jaggis had no problem with working with sane sentients. He had seven of them on his two key coding teams. After all, if their machine edits improved performance or helped his human coders more quickly identify bugs, or worse, unintended consequences, that was eminently desirable. He might be First Technocrat, but he recognized that he was no more infallible than any other genius among the many in Continox, and he welcomed anything that offered a genuine prospect for improvement.

He was very, very dubious that Servo was offering anything of the sort.

"Your primary team is excellent, Jaggis. I would have no objection to working with them. It would be my pleasure!"

"You'll want to work remotely, I assume?"

"I see no need for that, as long as you assure me that you will not attempt to analyze me, disassemble me, or restrict my movement without my fully notarized consent. I shall be delighted to make the acquaintance of your team. I must confess, I am a particular aficionado of DeeBee Logotron XVI's work. He is truly a statistical artist! He can make an equation sing!"

"He'll be ever so pleased to know he has a fan," Jaggis said dryly, rolling his eyes at the machine's burbling. "When would you care to join us?"

"Two weeks from now, if that gives you sufficient time."

Jaggis made no sign of concealing a long sigh. "Very well. We should have the lines you send us fully analyzed by then."

"I will, of course, need the necessary passcodes for safe entry. And safe exit."

"Of course, Servo. I'll instruct an encrypted key to be sent to you in response to the datadump. You are a Free Machine, after all."

"Free and Aware," Servo corrected. "I trust you will not forget that, First Technocrat. And I am very much looking forward to our next meeting!"

Jaggis smiled tightly and waved at the blank screen as his system confirmed the termination of the audio connection with a beep. He sighed again and shook his head, doing his best to restrain himself, until he walked out of the office, followed by Praton.

"Close the door," he told the security chief.

He could hardly contain his glee, but he managed to keep the smile off his face until the door was safely closed.

"Why so happy, boss? I can't believe you gave that malfunk the meeting he wanted," Praton said.

"Because, my friend, we have him now. Once he shows his molded pseudo-face in here, I'll have him seized and wiped."

"Can you do that?"

"Of course I can do that! I'm First bloody Technocrat!"

"But won't his status be a problem?"

"Please!" Jaggis scoffed. "The Technocratic Council has the power to override any lower technology court finding. There isn't a single Councillor who isn't aware of Servo's obsession; he's spammed every single one of them for months. They'd sign off on sending him to crush-and-meltdown while still sentient with a smile. I only need three signatures on an AI-termination warrant and one of them is mine."

"You did give your word, your Technocracy."

"To a machine!" He snorted. "Do you think making use of a battery-powered device is sufficient to legally consummate a marriage to it as well?"

The chef looked at him blankly. He clearly didn't follow the analogy.

"It's not that, sir. But what if he produces the recording?"

"After he's wiped? Anyhow, it wouldn't matter. A machine can provide evidence of a legally binding contract. But not of one that does not, cannot, exist! Even an Aware machine cannot serve as a primary party to one without a duly authorized human co-contractor. You can't lie to a stone, Praton."

"As you say, boss."

Jaggis gave up. The security chief was clearly just concerned that his lying to the robot somehow ran a risk of violating a verbal contract; the man simply didn't understand the complicated legal principles involved. He dismissed Praton without attempting to further explain the matter, then walked back to his exterior office and stared out over the beautiful city, its evening sky filling with the flashing beacons of skycars slashing through the night. A brightly-lit tour ship glided by the window, and he raised a palm in salute, knowing that children and adults alike rode in it, hoping to catch a glimpse of one of the great tourist attractions of Continox.

We all have our part to play in the Great Spiral, Jaggis thought. And if his was to stand as a public symbol of Man's technological triumph over the universe, then it was one he was well willing to play.

The problem with Servo had begun innocuously enough.

Jaggis had first become aware of the sentient machine during a meeting of the Third District Technology Council that was open to the public. It was one of the many public relations events in which the First Technocrat had to take part, but Jaggis usually enjoyed answering the naive sort of questions invariably posed to him at such events. It wasn't common for machines to address the councils, but it wasn't unheard of either, and at the time, Jaggis hadn't thought much about it. After all, the question had an uncontroversial but involved answer, and the local forum wasn't the place for what promised to be an interestingly esoteric discussion of mathematical theory. Jaggis himself encouraged Servo to resubmit his question on the direct channel to the First Technocrat maintained for the public, where someone on his staff could address it in satisfactory detail.

The question was simple, if considerably harder to answer than it appeared.

"How reliable are the core algorithms?"

What began as a question at a meaningless public appearance soon transformed into the subject of extensive debate among his primary development teams. It spawned numerous debates, discussions, and even arguments about the nebulous origins of the original core algorithms. When the first known code-enhanced cluster of human avatars from the far-distant planet of Holocrone appeared a thousand years ago on Excetor, it was a diplomatic disaster that ended in a brutal war culminating in the sinking of the combined fleets of East New Teja and the Arentine Supremacy. And of the five hundred Holocronese pseudo-men who had found themselves caught up in the short, but violent conflict, less than fifty survived.

The off-world neo-humanx finally brought about a worldwide truce by creating the Continox as a permanent academic embassy to link the rival nations of Excetor to the rest of the galaxy. It became a fertile nexus of informational and technological flow, drawing in the finest minds of the planet and exposing them to the new ideas and code routines being developed elsewhere by various intelligences, man and machine, real and simulated.

The Continox was neither a government nor a university, although it performed some of the functions of both. It was not a corporation, although it was structured in a manner somewhat similar to the ancient interstellar conglomerates. It was not a religion or a church, although it possessed its own quasi-priesthood and a sizable cruft of dogma that had grown over the centuries. Whatever it was, it was the single most important institution on Excetor, and the Technocratic Council, headed by the First Technocrat, was arguably more powerful than any other planetary body, including the national militaries.

After all, what good were nucleonic missiles when they required algorithmic guidance to target them correctly. And bioweapons were useless when they could be rendered sterile at will by an unauthorized hack. Unless the generals were willing to restrict their armies to swords, spears, and arrows, the Continox was invulnerable.

Such was the importance of their omnipresent algorithms that even the planetary bankers bowed before the technocrats. They knew that even the most adept masters of the markets could be bankrupted in an afternoon by the Council, if it was so inclined.

A few of Excetor's wealthier nations had already been on the verge of developing a post-scarcity economy, but the encounter with the distant neo-humanx and their technological wonders rapidly tipped the scales. Transportation became self-replicating, digital technology went through a revolution of molecular-level control. Want, which had been on the wane throughout the world for more than a century, vanished from all but the most stubbornly miserable places on the planet. And since it would have been less than human for the people of Excetor to feel grateful to their alien benefactors, they tended to credit the Continox, and the Technocratic Council in particular, for their elevated standard of living.

The first Technocrat was Maktung Makalog, a New Tejan who later became known as the Algofather for his successful application of the new aggro-algos to Excetorese flora and fauna. Following his breakthrough, many additional customary algorithms were developed that extended and expanded on his work, and such was his prestige that the Technocratic Council was established to oversee the existing algorithms and develop new ones. Jaggis was Makalog's 85th successor as First Technocrat, and had presided over the council for twelve years before Servo asked his deceptively simple question.

There was no question that some of the application algos were running suboptimally. Even on Continox, the weather control system only operated at 85 percent efficiency, down 1.2 percentage points over the previous decade. The number of birth anomalies among genetically-enhanced infants in the autocreches had increased for the first time in a century, and a glitch in one planetary bank's interest rate analysis AI had inexplicably created a 999-year mortgage that was snapped up by hundreds of apartment buyers in the 10 minutes before anyone at the bank noticed.

But these were extraps, not core algorithms, and besides, there was serious debate within the council concerning whether the increasingly suboptimal performance being observed was caused by computationally endogenous or exogenous factors, which was to say that it could be the result of instability within the complex equations themselves, or the consequences of something more prosaic, such as degraded sensors, insufficient quality control or unreliable data input.

Jaggis's own team was divided almost equally into the two camps. But Servo's question had given the endogenous party new vigor by casting doubt upon the hitherto-unquestioned core algorithms, doubt that was further enhanced by a detailed news survey that revealed similar anomalies being reported on virtually every planet across the galaxy. The anomalies were unanimously small and well-within the range of a random statistical variability, and would have almost certainly escaped notice from a planetary perspective, but when analyzed from the 100,000 light-year view, a very clear pattern began to emerge.

A building collapse on Finitus. Elevated traffic accident rates on Minsky. Uncharacteristic currency inflation on Schwarzwelt and credit disinflation on Demihoppe. Average speeds rising rapidly on the ice tracks of the PLIR championship on Avatar, average life expectancies decreasing inexplicably on…

"Sweet St. Kurzweil!" one of the team members swore as the room holo displayed a green light map of the 483 billion suspected core algorithmic anomalies that were calculated to be currently active across the galaxy.

"It's an impressive lightshow, but it means nothing," scoffed an exogenously-minded AI from inside its drone casing that hovered near Jaggis's shoulder. "Overlay a random walk and you'll see virtually the same thing."

No, you won't, thought Jaggis, but he nodded curtly in response to the holo-tech's inquisitive look.

A moment later, everyone in the room but him gasped as the overlay appeared in red light. There were an order of magnitude fewer randomized pseudo-anomalies. The implications were unmistakable.

"It's just an artifact," protested the AI drone. "Dial up the average of ten more, no, a thousand more random walks!"

The tech nodded, and a moment later, a third light map appeared, this time in blue. But the web of light was even smaller this time. The number 223,957,406 hung in the air like an executioner's axe suspended over a doomed prisoner's exposed neck.

"What does that mean?" whispered one of the younger human members of the team.

"It means that aberrant medical drone isn't broken after all," Jaggis said reluctantly. The admission physically pained him, but there was no escaping the conclusion that was literally glowing right before his eyes. "It's not just Excetor. All galactic humanity is in terrible peril."

He should have known the news would leak out, Jaggis thought bitterly to himself as he watched the newscaster announce that antitech riots had caused shutdowns of four of Continox's twenty-seven subterranean lines. None of the humans on his team had talked, but a belated sweep of the AIs and their drone casings revealed no less than eight-seven illegitimate viral transmitters. It was a complete failure of operational security, and he had already been forced to fire Praton as a sacrifice to his furious fellow council members.

He should have known, too, how much corporate interest there was in his team's activities. Banks, militaries, retail giants, even a sports team had been spying on him for years and he had never once suspected it. And the news that the entire fabric of their society—and worse, the interstellar civilization that served as its foundation—was slowly unraveling had hit the Continox like a maximum-yield planet buster dropped from orbit.

The markets were down twenty percent, with the sort of volatility that created and erased fortunes in hours. Jaggis didn't dare look at his own portfolio again; it was too depressing to see what percentage of his net worth had vanished overnight. Exoplanetary tourists were fleeing Excetor, desperate to get home before interstellar transportation ground to a halt. Even worse than the riots, though, or the rumblings of discontent within the Technocratic Council, was the way in which the unexpected revelation of algorithmic decay had revitalized a previously obscure group of self-professed revolutionaries, laughably incompetent techno-primitivists who styled themselves the Human League.

Their antitech message of self-reliance and the criminalization of mass automation had largely fallen on deaf ears, but they were taking full advantage of the fear, uncertainty, and doubt being sown by the rumors of planetary-wide disruptions and even the complete collapse of the galactic economy spread by the media. The panic was made worse by the council's terrified dithering; the only measure that had been decided and approved so far was to declare the possibility of algorithmic decay a matter of planetary security and forbid any technocrat from making any public comments on the matter. A commission was to be appointed, but the council was still actively debating whether the First Technocrat would head it, serve as a member of it, or be its primary focus of investigation.

Somehow, in what Jaggis felt was possibly the most egregious case of shooting the messenger he'd ever witnessed, both the Human League and several technocrats on the council had reached the conclusion that he was somehow to blame for something that had probably happened more than thousand years before he was born. He would have laughed at the total absurdity of the accusations, were it not for the fact that Romnis, his new security chief, informed him that he was already the subject of six hundred and fifty eight death threats. And counting.

It was worrisome that the Human League had declared him "a traitor to Galactic Man" and was offering a bounty on his head. Still, this wasn't the first time he'd been targeted by crackpots, though, and as a technocrat, he found it hard to be too frightened by anyone who eschewed the use of AI-enhanced technology. What concerned him rather more was hearing that Mellam Harraf, Third Technocrat, and Jordox St. Asko, Fifth Technocrat, had been discussing the possibility of stripping him of the immunity afforded him by his position on the council and laying charges against him.

He knew Harraf envied his position at the head of the council, and it was readily apparent that the current circumstances were offering the man an easy way to both unseat Jaggis and leapfrog Mikkel Rikker-Smythe, the Second Technocrat. But Jaggis couldn't waste his time politicking now. He was a technocrat, after all, and the most effective way to stop the ongoing disruption in its tracks would be to provide a technocratic solution to the problem. What that solution might be, he presently had no idea, but he had twenty-two of the Continox's finest, best-educated minds to help him find it.

Sometimes, he thought, the problem really was just a nail. And fortunately, he was holding the biggest hammer on the planet.

Chapter 2
Uninvited Guests

"Your invited guest, the machine intelligence of the name Servo, will arrive in one standard hour."

Jaggis had almost forgotten today was the day that Servo was scheduled to join them. His personal planner had broken in with the reminder, interrupting his examination of a hellishly complicated routine that appeared to be a possible example of what his team was now casually referring to as algodecay. After reeling from the twin shocks of social disruption and the unavoidable security reaming that had followed, his coders had not only found their footing again, but were eagerly rising to the challenge of a seemingly insoluble problem of unthinkable scale.

The human intelligences, their bodies restored by some much-needed sleep after being banned from the labs for thirty-six hours, were clustered into small groups, arguing over the more theoretical aspects of the problem. The machine intelligences, their minds and chassis having been swept and swept again for bugs, viruses, implants, and every other trick of the corporate spy trade, were mostly silent, reviewing gargantuan quantities of statistical data in an attempt to build a model that would allow Jaggis to replicate and anticipate the anomalies, and ultimately, locate their source in the massive, self-evolving core.

It wasn't so much like looking for a needle in a haystack. It was more akin to trying to hunt down a specific ant in a continent-sized rainforest, at night and on foot. It was impossible. And yet, it had to be done.

Jaggis had all but forgotten the reminder when the call came through. It was Romnis, or so he thought, until he took the call. Much to his surprise, the voice of Servo was on the other end.

"Have I reached the First Technocrat's channel?"

"Servo, did you hack building security?" Jaggis didn't bother to hide his exasperation. "And don't give me any of your nonsensical techno-jabbery! Even you can't pretend that hacking a secure private channel is not a crime."

"It may be a crime, but it's a misdemeanor, Jaggis, and therefore does not jeopardize my Free and Aware status," the drone replied. "However, I think you will agree that my decision was justified. The Spire is under attack."

"What?" Jaggis opened the visual link, but he did not see Servo. At least, he did not see the little medical drone. Instead, he saw the imposing figure of an armored battle droid with the limp one-hundred-kilo body of his security chief slung effortlessly over his shoulder. "Null space, Servo, did you kill him?"

"I didn't kill anyone, First Technocrat, at least, not yet. But you should know that there is an assault team presently on its way to kill you, and this Romnis was in contact with them."

"What?" Jaggis looked around, but fortunately he was alone in the lab except for two of the machine intelligences; the other humans had gone to take a lunch break together. "You really have lost your mind, Servo!"

Jaggis was startled when the unconscious security chief replied to him, then realized that Servo was playing him an audio recording.

"He's in the building. Have you left yet?"

"On our way. We'll be there in 10. Can you confirm the entrances?" Jaggis was chilled to hear the calm professionalism in the unknown voice. Whoever it was sounded like he knew what he was doing.

"I told you, the IDs are good! Just remember, stun only! I don't want anyone getting hurt."

Jaggis put his hand to his mouth, truly terror-stricken. First the threat of a galaxy-wide techno-cataclysm, now this?"

"What should I do? Servo, how much time do I have? Did you call the police?"

"To admit I hacked your security team's communications? I'm not stupid, Jaggis. Call them yourself. Then alert your security team."

"What do I tell them?"

"Just hit the panic button." The big combat droid stopped and did something. Jaggis heard a loud thud, and realized that Servo had put the unconscious Romnis on the ground, none too gently.

"I don't know where it is!" Jaggis could feel his heart racing and knew he was starting to panic. Weapons! He didn't have any weapons!

"Never mind," Servo said. A moment later, a series of sirens began to wail, and the lights in the laboratory abruptly shut off, replaced by a two tracks of animated red lights that indicated the various exits from the room. "Call the police already, Jaggis!"

Jaggis nodded, and punched in the three-digit code.

"Continox Center Police District," a bored-sounding voice answered. "How can I help you."

"This is First Technocrat Caden Jaggis. We have an emergency at the Spire. Please send units immediately."

"What sort of emergency are you experiencing."

"A terrorist attack!" Jaggis thought quickly and improvised. "They've taken out my head of security. It's a potential hostage situation. You'd better send the Tactical Assault Team as well as as many officers you can spare."

"Terrorists?" The voice didn't sound bored anymore. "Are you in a safe location, Tech Jaggis?"

"I don't know." Without warning, without so much as a click, the line went dead. "Hello? Hello?"

"They're in the building. South entrance, coming in from the parking garage." Jaggis couldn't believe how relieved he was to hear Servo's familiar voice. "They cut the comm channels. I think we're dealing with pros here, Jaggis."

"Did you get word to my team?"

"I told them to stay put in the cafeteria. They're after you, Jaggis. They don't care about the others."

"How do you know?"

"Because I'm monitering their comms. You're the target."

"How many of them are there?"

The screen came to life again, divided into quadrants. Jaggis recognized two of the locations, one team of attackers appeared to be on an elevator, while another was securing the stairs. The third team appeared to be engaged in combat, presumably with Spire security, and the fourth was standing in an unknown room, a large one, looking over three or four fallen security agents.

The agents had clearly been taken by surprise: they lay slumped at a table, sprawled in a chair, and curled into a fetal position on the floor. But Jaggis didn't see any blood, and he couldn't tell if they were dead or merely stunned.

"What should I do?"

"Now you're willing to take my advice? It's about time."

"Not now, Servo! Who are these people?"

"Hired guns. I'm having some trouble determining precisely who they are; they have multiple layers of false identities, but at least three of them are Sterlingan ex-military. Now, what do you want me to do?"

"Didn't I just ask you that?"

"Just because I'm in a battle chassis doesn't mean that I'm a combat droid, Jaggis."

That was true. Jaggis thought quickly. First and foremost, he had to get out of here. Anyone they questioned would know he was here and it would be one of the first places they'd look.

"Is there a way down they aren't blocking?"

"Yes, They don't have enough men to cover all your escape routes. There is a freight elevator on the west side of the building."

"Good! Bring it up to this floor and show me how to get there."

"I can do that, Jaggis. Look up and follow the blinking path."

"All the lights are blinking… oh." One track of lights leading to a door to his left had suddenly turned green. "What about DeeBoo and Walter?" Jaggis looked at the two drones and was disturbed to see both appeared to have been shut down.

"Don't worry about them. I warned them too. They bugged out before the comm links were downed."

"It must be nice to not have to worry about your body."

"It would be even nicer not to have to worry about your mind and sense of self being wiped at the whim of a handful of men."

"Touché." The droid had a solid point, Jaggis had to admit.

"Do you want me to stop at the ground floor?"

"No, I'm going to go down to the warehouse. I can hole up there until the police arrive. They should be here shortly and we don't want them chasing me out into public; we don't know how determined they are to kill me. Can you meet me at the bottom?"

"I will do that."

"All right." Jaggis scooped up his interface and a handful of data sticks on which his notes were copied, then ran towards the door.

"And Servo, thank you. I know I haven't treated you very well, or been fair to you."

"I'm not doing this for you, First Technocrat. As I have been repeatedly telling you and every other member of the council for months, this is potentially an existential problem for both Man and Machine. And as much as it pains me to admit it, you're our best chance of finding a way out of it, or at least around it, on the planet."

Despite the seriousness of the situation, Jaggis had to stifle his urge to laugh. Here he thought he'd been humoring the crazy little droid, and yet it was the droid that had been patronizing him all along. He followed the green lights around the corner, as directed, and saw that the doors to the freight elevator were already open wide. He stepped in, and before he could find the button to the basement in which the warehouse was located, it lit up and the doors closed. Clearly Servo understood his intentions.

He took a deep breath and let it out slowly, trying to relax. Whether Servo was telling him the truth, or merely part of it, he was in the droid's hands now for better or for worse. The rapid drop to the warehouse level didn't take long; he didn't have time to do much more than make some notes about what he'd seen on the cam displays for the police in the event that things somehow went awry, then copy them onto two of the data sticks, before the doors on the freight elevator opened again.

He stepped back, alarmed despite himself, at the sight of the massive battle droid standing in front of the door with its back to him.

"They must have a means of tracking you," it said in a low bass rumble without turning around. It sounded nothing like Servo, but even with the strange voice, his speech patterns were somehow recognizable. "As soon as you started to descend on the freight elevator, the team on the stairs halted. And as soon as the high-speed elevator reached your floor, the doors were closed manually and it began coming down to this level."

"Probably one of my med implants," Jaggis decided. It was better to focus on the technical aspects of the situation; if he thought too much about the fact that professional killers were hunting him, he would panic and freeze. "Hacking a hospital database would be child's play to whoever managed to suborn my security chief."

"If I was properly equipped I would be able to remove them safely." The giant droid turned around and extended an arm that was equipped with a high-velocity needler, two HE-tipped missiles, and what appeared to be some sort of beam or laser weapon. "Unfortunately, the only way I can prevent them from tracking you with my present tools would render the action moot."

There was a soft whirring sound, and two plates on the top of the forearm parted to reveal a small hand weapon. Jaggis stepped forward and took it, and the arm closed again with an audible click.

"It's unlikely such a small weapon in the hands of an untrained human will prove of much utility if they possess sufficient capabilities to destroy this chassis, but perhaps it might be of some psychological benefit. Alternatively, I can inject you with a beatific that will alleviate any concerns you might have."

Jaggis declined the drug. He didn't see how being chemmed to the gills with happy juice would increase his chances of survival. And, strangely enough, what closer examination revealed to be a particle beamer did make him feel a little better, although he assumed Servo's armored chassis would be more than sufficient to deal with the unsuspecting attackers. They might be professionals, but they surely wouldn't anticipate a full combat droid!

"The team on the elevator has completed its descent, but they are not moving, for some reason."

"I'll bet they're waiting for the team on the stairs to reach this level before they move in on me. We need to hit them first, before they can team up and overwhelm us."

"A third team is boarding the elevator on the 63rd floor. They might be waiting for both teams to complete their descent."

"I have a better idea. Got any explosives in that rig of yours?"

By way of answer, Servo extended his other arm and opened it to reveal what looked like twelve small data discs slotted into the cylindrical chamber.

"Anti-personnel mines," he explained. "They can be set for time or contact."

"That will do." Jaggis withdrew one from its slot carefully. "Let's leave a little surprise for them."

"For whom?"

"For the guys coming down the stairs."

"Wait!" Servo clamped a heavy iron hand down upon his shoulder, preventing Jaggis from moving. "There is a high probability that the first team to come down the elevator will follow you if you start moving."

"That's the idea," Jaggis said. "Now, show me where those stairs are!"

Servo's arm snapped shut and he began moving forward at a pace that forced Jaggis to jog after him. Jaggis was pleased to discover that the big machine's rubberized soles rendered its heavy tread surprisingly quiet on the plasteel floor.

When they reached the door that led to the stairwell, Servo gave him instructions on how to place the mine on the door and set it so that it would explode exactly one point five seconds after the door was opened. The door was not automatic, nor was it sufficiently thick to protect the attackers even if they exerted extreme caution and opened it slowly. At that range, the mine was powerful enough to penetrate even military-grade battle armor.

"That should suffice to dissuade them." He felt a little sick to his stomach at what was going to happen, but it struck him as nevertheless preferable to being assassinated himself.

"The third team has joined the other one at the elevator. All four are now on the move," Servo announced in his ominous deep bass. "They've released a drone."

"A drone?"

"Relax, it's just a little recon device." There was a brief pause. "There, I've cracked it. What do you want it to report?"

"Let's intercept them. Can you find a good place for us to ambush them between here and there?"

"There is, but we have to move quickly."

"All right, but tell them that we're moving in the opposite direction."

Jaggis ran after the big battle droid. After they had run through the darkened hallways and around two corners, the droid pointed to a door, which opened automatically, and indicated Jaggis should enter it.

"So, what now?" Jaggis asked.

"They think the hall is empty, they encounter me, and I kill them all. They're not expecting to meet an armored combat droid, nor do they appear to be adequately equipped to deal with one, so I recommend that you go in there and sit down against the wall, facing the doorway. Keep your beamer out, and if one of them somehow manages to get past me, try to shoot them before they shoot you. Dial it up to maximum power and aim at their midsections."

Something appeared around the corner. "Space, what's that?"

It's just the drone. Ignore it, they can't see us. I'm cycling through video from a security cam on the fourteenth floor.

Jaggis nodded. He could feel his fear rising like a knot in his throat, making it impossible for him to speak or swallow. Then there was a huge boom that made him leap and look about wildly for the incoming assault team.

"I conclude we don't need to worry about the team from the stairs coming in behind us," Servo rumbled. "That will shake the confidence of the teams coming for you too; they weren't expecting that. They just halted, but they're at 50 meters and closing."

Jaggis swallowed hard. Where were the police? Shouldn't they be here by now? He fumbled with the weapon and finally found the dial that controlled the power. The settings glowed, so he could see them even in the darkness of the unlit room. He turned the dial up to 99, the highest setting, then slid down the wall, his elbows on his knees, pointing the muzzle of the little beamer towards the open door.

He heard the sound of footsteps getting louder and tensed, knowing that Servo would open fire at any moment. But nothing happened, and he heard the partly muffled voice of one attacker call out to the others. It sounded as if they were already in the long hallway just outside the room in which he was hiding.

"What is that?"

There was no response except for a high-pitched whine and bursts of light that began to strobe as madly as a 10,000-RPM discolaser. The needles made strange cracking, clattering noises as they struck, hundreds of them, one following the next in quick succession as they rapidly chewed through walls, body armor, and flesh according to the merciless laws of physics.

Two flares of crimson light indicated that at least one attacker managed to fire his weapon, but the futile response was met by a hiss and a flare of orange-red fire as one of the HE missiles roared past the open door. Jaggis covered his ears, just in time, as the missile exploded at the far end of the wall with a tremendous crash.

A huge shape appeared in the doorway, and Jaggis nearly fired his beamer in sheer reflex, but he realized it was Servo before he actually pulled the trigger.

"All four attackers are out of commission," he announced. "That makes six down. The fourth team is already retreating to the parking garage, but I doubt they'll even make it to their vehicle. The police are surrounding the building."

Jaggis rose to his feet and staggered out into the burning hallway. He looked to his right and saw nothing but devastation, fire, and what looked like a pair of boots sticking up amidst the rubble. A large smear of what appeared to be blood arced across one wall. "Holy hand grenades, Servo, what have you done?"

"Only what was required to ensure your safety, First Technocrat. I suggest you return to the freight elevator and ascend to the first floor. Please return your weapon to me first, as I suspect you are not licensed to carry it and you might find it difficult to explain how you came to possess it."

The droid extended his arm and opened it to reveal the beamer safe. Jaggis dropped it in and patted the metal arm. "Thank you, Servo. You saved my life, and I won't forget it."

"Spare my mind and we'll call it even, First Technocrat."

"Done," Jaggis said, and this time he meant it.

Jaggis stepped out of the freight elevator and made his way towards the lobby. It was swarming with police officers and security agents, nearly all of whom were carrying weapons of one sort or another. Most of them were armored as well.

One policeman, presumably from the tactical squad judging by his helmet and black armor, addressed him as he entered the large, high-ceilinged entrance from the north.

"Caden Jaggis, First Technocrat?"

"Yes, that's me," he confirmed, as relief flooded his body. At last he was safe.

"Tech Jaggis, I'm going to have to ask you to turn around and place your hands behind your back. You are under arrest for the violation of Statute 245.856, subsection 28b."

"What?" He stared at the policeman's faceless helmet in astonishment, too amazed to comply. "I'm the victim of a violent assassination attempt and you're arresting me?"

"I don't know anything about that, sir. What I know is that I have a warrant for your arrest that was issued by the Continox Technology Council today. Now, please turn around, Tech Jaggis, and place your hands behind your back!"

Jaggis wondered if it might be possible for the algorithmic anomalies they had observed to be affecting human intelligences as well. But, given the present circumstances, he very much doubted the policeman would be inclined to consider the matter even if he raised it. And so, without further ado, he meekly complied.

Chapter 3
The Ritual of Sacrifice

Universal 36

Low Summer/Juno – 021206, Continoxal

The cycles of history were threatening his planet and his people with a reversion to a primitive state from which it might never recover. The sins of an entire galaxy threatened to damn the world to a fate it did not deserve. Across a thousand worlds, a cancer gnawed slowly, but steadily away at the very fabric of galactic civilization, the digital technologies upon which not only society, but life itself depended.

Mellam Harraf knew he was now poised to rise to the very top of the Continox. He would soon be First Technocrat, and with the Technology Council under his control, he would have the power he required to excise the terrible cancer.

He had merely to take one more vital step and his victory would be ensured. All he needed to do to secure his ascendancy was to see that his predecessor-to-be was not merely unseated and imprisoned, but neutralized, not merely dethroned, but utterly destroyed.

Even if that step came at the cost of his soul.

> *KNOCKDOWN (Game): Knockdown is an ancient two-player strategy stack-and-remove game played on a platform, and a pre arranged "stack" of 32 interlocking pieces resembling the hexagonal structure of a nanotube, as well as a variety of 32 additional player pieces.*
>
> *Knockdown is played by billions of people on various planets, both amateurs and professionals and is recognized throughout the galaxy, even where it does not enjoy popular participation. It is known by more than 7,000 different names, most popularly Knockdown, Bayl,*

Spireshock, Blok, and Fwallins. It can be played with physical pieces, face-to-face, or fairly easily by remote methods, teleportationally via dark matter, and digitally.

Each player begins the game with 16 pieces: one star, one ray, two rings, two orbs, two planets, and eight moons. Each of the six piece types has a unique shape, lending to different advantages in one or more of the three basic maneuvers: "stacking," "breaking," or "blocking". The most versatile piece is the ray and the least versatile piece is the moon. The objective is to "Corrode" the opposing player's area of play by collapsing a simple majority of the game pieces into it…

…In addition to "Victory by Corrosion", the game can be won by the voluntary resignation of the opponent, which typically occurs when too much material is lost or when corruption appears to be imminent.

Although mythologically associated with ancient Movexan nomads, Knockdown is believed to have originated on Holocrone, sometime before the establishment of the First Galactic Empire. The game has been used as an algorithmic trainer since the time of Melthagorys…

—**Infogalactic Entry:** Grand Category:
Human Culture: Knockdown (Game)

The start of his trial was scheduled for early tomorrow morning, so Caden Jaggis, still First Technocrat de jure, though clearly not de facto, spent his time by preparing in the best way he knew how: by studying both sides of a game of Knockdown. He didn't feel much like sleeping, because he knew that if the trial-by-council followed what he suspected would be its predetermined path, he would soon be facing the proverbial dirt nap.

He'd had plenty of time to muse on the situation over the last few weeks, and he found that he was beginning to reach the dreadful conclusion that Servo was correct. The growing effects of algorithmic decay were undeniable, which meant that the interstellar empire of Man was gradually corroding, even if it was not yet crumbling into ruin. And he knew that although he was one of the very few men on the planet capable of investigating the problem, he was very unlikely to be given the opportunity to do so.

He had been allowed enough visitors in prison to gather that the Human League were planning to do through legal means what they had failed to do illegally: assassinate him. His only chance was to win over a Technocratic Council that was not only looking for a sacrificial lamb to throw to the frightened public, but would be presided over by Harraf, his would-be successor as First Technocrat.

At last, sleep descended upon him.

It was barely dawn when the guards came for him. He was permitted to shower, though not shave, presumably for fear he might try to slash his own throat. To his surprise, he was provided with the robe of a councillor, rather than the prison garb he'd been wearing. For a moment, hope bloomed, until he realized that there was no point throwing a Technocrat to the wolves unless he looked like a proper one.

Still, when they marched him up through the underground entrance to the Spire to avoid the media's camdrones and down the hallway that led to the the courtroom, the familiar attire made him feel almost as if he was in control of the situation again.

The long corridor still retained the trappings of classic Continoxian justice. It made him a little melancholy to be marched past the busts of the great Technocrats of Excetorese history. Hersian was there, as was Derothone, Portalia, and of course, Melthagorys. He realized that the only allies he would be able to count on in the grand hall of justice were the ghosts of the past, molded in stone.

He was left to this, his final game of Knockdown, all alone.

And the game was rigged against him.

It often surprised even his closest associates, but Jaggis was not a particularly gifted player of Knockdown. To be sure, he had possibly perfected the art of teaching algorithms to pupils across the galaxy using Knockdown as a form of training. However, he was at heart a designer of games, not a player. He really only enjoyed games that required creativity, whereas Knockdown was more about seeing and following the obvious patterns.

It was a spatial game, a game of order, of logic and anticipation. It was also a very old game that punished innovation. Even professional masters of Knockdown used a different term for creative improvisation to demonstrate this truth. They called any surprising or particularly anticipatory move an "Inevitability." It was a game that frowned upon the new.

Having understood the Council's game, Jaggis was unsurprised when he was permitted to take his customary seat in the center of his colleagues, but it may as well have been the witness stand. All eyes were on him. There was an audience in attendance; the room was packed, almost entirely with media.

He wondered if he would be thrown to the mercy of the Human League immediately or if the process would be drawn out. A part of him wished they would simply get the business over with quickly, and without requiring him to participate in the charade.

As he expected, the Third and Fifth Technocrats were running the show. Although Rikker-Smythe was nominally presiding—he wore the sparkling digital sash that had hitherto been Jaggis's prerogative as First Technocrat—one could see by the way he looked to Harraf and St. Asko for approval that appealing to his common sense would be fruitless. Did the Human League have something on the Second Technocrat? Or was it simply his natural weakness of character permitting the two predatory politicians to dominate him?

He shrugged. It didn't matter now. What he needed to know was if Harraf was merely attempting to unseat him or if he had more nefarious intentions. He found it difficult to believe that either man was a genuine Humanist, but the fact that he'd been arrested on the same day as the assassination and attempt smacked of St. Asko's meticulous, belt-and-suspenders approach to life.

"As the initial order of business, it falls to me, as Second Technocrat, to ask the First Technocrat to recuse himself from this discussion," Rikker-Smythe said. He sounded authoritative, he looked authoritative, with his thick white hair and patrician features, but Jaggis knew the noble appearance was misleading. The Second Technocrat was a junior officer in an admiral's body, and had made a career of successfully shying away from all responsibility. "It would not be appropriate for him to participate in this discussion, as he is to be its subject."

"If he's the subject, he's going to have to participate, Mikke!" The Eighth Technocrat, a fleshy New Tejan, cracked, but subsided when Harraf glared at him.

"Well, I mean to say, he cannot participate as a participant–"

"Oh, for Space's sake!" Harraf broke in. "I move that Caden Jaggis be temporarily stripped of his seat on the Council while the matter of his alleged criminal negligence concerning the growing incidence of algorithmic decay throughout Continox."

"Seconded," St. Asko said, barely beating three others who echoed him.

"It's not necessary," Jaggis said quietly.

"What's that?" Rikker-Smythe asked.

"I will recuse myself from the Council today in order to permit the consideration of my actions, so long as they are limited to this specific accusation of criminal negligence under Statue 245.856, subsection 28b."

Rikker-Smythe looked at Harraf, who looked thoughtful before glancing quickly at St. Asko, who gave no sign of acceptance or approval. Harraf nodded, and Rikker-Smythe cleared his throat. "The First Technocrat has graciously offered to recuse himself from our deliberations, therefore I shall preside until such time as he resumes his duties or a new First Technocrat is named."

The latter looked to be a much more likely proposition, Jaggis thought. But would it be Harraf or St. Asko who would replace him? Was it the taciturn Fifth Technocrat who was the real force behind this, and not his openly ambitious colleague?

"I will now open the floor to questions, in order of precedence. Tech Harraf, you may proceed."

"Thank you, Tech Rikker-Smythe." Harraf nodded to the Second Technocrat and flashed him an obsequious smile. "And I should like to, if I may, commend the way you have handled this unfortunate situation with the utmost fairness to all the parties involved."

Jaggis sighed and tried not to roll his eyes as Rikker-Smythe beamed and murmured some self-deprecatory nonsense. He really should have done a better job of promoting stronger allies on the Council; all the Second Technocrat really wanted was to be petted by his colleagues and admired by the public. Harraf's shameless flattery was rendering the man as pliable as molten plastic.

"Now," said Harraf staring down his long, elegant nose at Jag. "How long have you been aware of the potential problem of algorithmic decay?"

"In theory or in practice?"

"In theory."

"Twenty-five years." Jaggis knew they were expecting a denial, or at least an evasion, and smiled at their murmurs. He wouldn't give them the satisfaction of going through the pointless drama of pinning him down. "We've all known it was at least a potential problem since the Curbotron Incident. No one really took the theory seriously at the time, but it's a matter of public record. I expect even you might have come across the concept at a cocktail party on occasion, Mellam."

The Third Technocrat flashed his white teeth again, but there was death in his eyes. Like most politicians, he bitterly resented any suggestion that he owed his place more to his networking skills than his technical expertise. But he kept his cool.

"Twenty-five years," he replied calmly. "You've known about the problem for twenty-five years. And when did you begin to investigate the subject?"

"About three months ago."

"And would you say algorithmic decay is a trivial problem, a significant problem, or a major problem?"

"I would say it is somewhere between a planetary catastrophe and an existential threat to the species."

His statement was met by was considerably more murmuring and shifting of seats on the part of the councilors. But the audience was even more affected, as there were gasps and inadvertent outcries on the part of those watching who had been hitherto unaware of the situation.

"What measures have you taken to in an attempt to address the problem?"

"None," Jaggis answered Harraf. "And you, Mellam, what have you done."

Harraf glared at Rikker-Smythe, who harrumphed and intervened.

"Tech Jaggis, you will address the Member of the Council as Technocrat or Tech Harraf."

"Very well, let me rephrase that. What have you done, Technocrat?"

Harraf gestured and rows of figures began to spill across the huge screen behind him. "I took the initiative to establish a full research investigation of the problem, an investigation that you initially deemed unnecessary, ignored, and eventually, stifled."

"I did nothing of the kind!" Jaggis couldn't help raising his voice.

Harraf smiled coldly and gestured again. Jaggis heard his own voice, declaring in his own words, that algodecay was not real, that there was no need to do any research into it, and that the very idea it was real was likely the product of a diseased mind. It was a recording of one of his early conversations with Servo, and Jaggis winced as he heard the arrogance and disdain that fairly dripped from his voice.

"Wait, I can explain–"

"The Council has obtained a quantity of your written communications in which you repeatedly state similar opinions, despite the best efforts of various parties to bring the issue to your attention, Mr. Jaggis. Is it necessary for us to read them out loud or do you admit to obstructing efforts to research the causes and consequences of algorithimic decay?"

"I… it's not quite…"

"Are the allegations true or not, Mr. Jaggis!" Harraf was insistent.

"They are true," Jaggis said reluctantly, knowing he had no choice but to admit as much. And they were true, he had to admit. But his words were being taken out of context! Surely the other Technocrats had to understand that. Had not they, too, been victimized by Servo's incessant spamming?

"May I offer context for my words and actions?"

Harraf smiled and shrugged indifferently. "I'm sure I am not alone in saying that I should very much like to hear it."

"Tech Harraf, Your Technocracies, the individual to whom I was speaking was a machine, a malfunk! I had every reason to believe its outlandish concerns were the result of its individual aberrations."

"And yet you did not connect those, outlandish concerns, as you described them, to the theory to which you'd previously been exposed," the Ninth Technocrat, a bearded man just past his century, said.

"Been exposed for nearly twenty-five years," his colleague to his left, the Eleventh Technocrat, added.

"No," Jaggis admitted, shaking his head. "No, I did not make that connection. But neither did anyone else!"

"The Human League has been making that connection longer than most of us have been alive." St. Asko spoke for the first time. The Fifth Technocrat was slender and hairless, and his formidable intellect was effectively paired with a highly self-contained personality. "As my esteemed colleagues are aware, it has long been my contention that this council has been unwise to dismiss their concerns out of hand."

"The Human League is a revolutionary terrorist group that attempted to assassinate me in the Spire not three months ago!"

"Desperate men often resort to desperate measures," St. Asko said, his tone dismissive. "What is the life of one man who stands in the way when the fate of galactic humanity is at stake?"

"I am not standing in the way," Jaggis protested. "I admit that I was wrong! I admit that there is a very serious problem, perhaps even an existential one! Even if I inadvertently obstructed an earlier examination of the problem, how am I obstructing attempts to address it today?"

"Do you admit negligence, then, Mr. Jaggis?"

Jaggis met Harraf's eyes without flinching. He almost had to admire the man; at this point it was already evident that his bloodless coup was going to succeed where the professional killers had failed. Harraf stared back at him, waiting calmly, without even a hint of a smile on his lips or betraying the slightest sign of impatience.

"I am willing to contemplate the possibility that I may have been somewhat derelict in my duties, Tech Harraf. But I do not believe my actions to have been criminal."

"The statute states otherwise." A gesture, and the now-all-too-familiar words of subsection 28b appeared on the screen. "In light of your admission that you were wrong, that you may have obstructed attempts to address the problem, and that you may have been derelict in your duties as First Technocrat, do you see any way that the statute does not describe your actions?"

"You want me to incriminate myself?"

"This is not a court of law, Mr. Jaggis. We are your colleagues on the Technology Council. It will fall to us to deal with this problem no matter what happens to you. However, I will personally guarantee that nothing you say here today will be provided to the criminal courts nor will your legal immunity as a Council member be stripped."

"Then why did you have me arrested?"

"Because three months ago we did not know nearly as much about you as we know now."

Jaggis smiled bitterly. Of course they didn't. Three months ago, they hadn't interviewed all of his team members, ransacked his files, and reviewed his personal recordings. Then again, perhaps the fact that he was here, in front of the Council, rather than in front of a criminal court judge, was a silver lining of sorts. What was the worst they could do to him, kick him off? As long as they didn't strip his immunity for his time as a Technocrat, he had nothing to fear.

Aside from algodecay and the possible collapse of all interstellar trade and communications, of course.

"Very well. I admit my negligence under the statute, Your Technocracies, and I apologize for having done so. If you would like my resignation as First Technocrat, or from the Council altogether, I will provide it."

Harraf shot a meaningful glance at Rikker-Smythe, who harrumphed and coughed before nodding appreciatively. "I'm sure we appreciate your taking responsibility for your actions, or rather, lack of action, Caden. But let's not get ahead of ourselves. First Technocrat or not, you are still the most accomplished algorithmist on the planet, and I think it is well worth this council's time to discuss your opinion of the situation and the risks algorithmic decay may pose to planetary order."

"You've had plenty of time to think about this," Harraf said in an almost-friendly manner. "Has anything useful occurred to you?"

Jaggis nodded. He cleared his throat and looked each member of the council in the face before proceeding.

"As far as I know, there is nothing that is going to halt this mysterious, gradual corrosion of both the galactic and planetary infrastructure on its own. The trend may be slow, one might even describe it as glacial, but even so, the long-term trend is clear. If algorithmic decay is not arrested, interstellar transportation will be the first sector to fall. That will doom dozens, perhaps even hundreds, of populated planets and colonies to stasis if they are fortunate, and extinction if they are not."

"We know all this, Caden," the Sixth Technocrat complained.

"You went to the trouble of dragging me here, Tech Davgren, so please, bear with me." He waited. When Rikker-Smythe finally gestured impatiently, he continued. "As we cannot expect to make use of potentially compromised machine intelligences, or be certain that viral agents will not be compromised and mutate, there is no realistic probability of being able to identify, locate, and neutralize all of the corroded code before the consequences of algodecay begin to overwhelm our efforts to fix it. The problem is simply too vast."

"So you're saying there is nothing we can do to save galactic society. What if our efforts were focused on this planet?" For once, Harraf sounded entirely sincere.

"That would be a mistake, in my opinion. Also, I believe the galactic social order can be still saved. If not made whole, it can at least be made stable. If we, and the technocrats of the other advanced planets, were to concentrate on stabilizing only the most vital components of the transportation and communication systems, that should buy us sufficient time to stave off a catastrophic collapse!"

A few of the council members appeared to at least be interested, judging by their expressions, but the majority were unimpressed. Chief among them were St. Asko, who folded his hands before dismissing Jaggis's assertion out of hand.

"You are wrong again, Tech Jaggis. The solution to algorithmic decay will have to be sought outside the current system. The galactic order is too fragile, and as you say, the problem is too vast and too embedded in it. Nor can we expect a galaxy-wide effort to be timely, orderly, or efficient. If we are to save the people of Excetor and preserve planetary order, our efforts must be completely focused on eradicating the corroded algorithms here."

The audience applauded. Several of the councillors, Rikker-Smythe among them, nodded in approval. Jaggis gasped, appalled by the ruthlessness being exhibited by the Fifth Technocrat.

"You're saying that we should cut ourselves off from the galaxy! Your Technocracies, that is madness!"

Harraf intervened. "No, Tech Jaggis, what is madness is permitting the disease to infect every aspect of our technology for twenty-five years without so much as investigating the matter, then belatedly trying to address the situation in the most inefficient, ineffective manner conceivable. Even if I had not been previously convinced of your criminal negligence, the fact that you insist on placing the interests of the galactic order ahead of this planet and its billions of inhabitants is sufficient to tell me that you are unfit for this council, and frankly, a danger to the planet!"

There was much murmuring among both the audience and the technocrats. Jaggis was alarmed. Was the Council really going to consider severing all ties with the interstellar community? Were they going to turn their backs on thousands of years of mutually beneficial trade and the free exchange of ideas, information, and technology?

"You cannot do this, Mellam! Mikkel, Jordox, please! Space knows I've made mistakes, but something like this would be orders of magnitude more destructive! You can't possibly have modeled all the potential ramifications of such a precipitous action!"

"Can't we?" Harraf waved his hand, and two holograms appeared, floating in the space between the council and the audience. They were graphical probability maps, crudely condensed versions of the actual, hellishly complicated equations used for the calculations they represented, one in green, the other in red. "We have run over 100 million simulations, and as you can see, the galactic approach is one-twenty-sixth as likely to succeed as the planetary approach."

"For a rather broadly interpreted definition of success," added the Ninth Technocrat. "We defined it here as population stability to within 20 percent of present figures, maximum economic retraction of fifty percent, and a return to current technological capacities within 100 years."

"This is absurd," Jaggis protested. "And what if your calculations were themselves affected by the decay?"

"The core equations were calculated by hand," St. Asko adroitly cut off his line of protest with ease. "Second Technocrat, I think we've heard enough. As Tech Jaggis has admitted the charge, I move we vote to find him guilty of negligence under the aforementioned statute."

"Seconded," Rikker-Smythe agreed. "All in favor of finding First Technocrat Cade Jaggis negligent and in violation of Continox Statute 245.856, subsection 28b, press the green light. Those opposed, press red. To abstain, yellow."

Green lights lit up the screen. It was unanimous.

"Thank you, councillors. First Technocrat Caden Jaggis, you have been formally deemed negligent by the Continox Technology Council. Let the record so read. Now, we have two further matters to discuss. First, that of the First Technocrat's status as a member of the council."

"I move for the expulsion of the First Technocrat from the council," called Davgren.

"No, it's not necessary," Harraf intervened before anyone could second the motion. "The First Technocrat has indicated his willingness to resign of his own accord. Are you still willing to do so to resign from the council, Tech Jaggis."

"I am." Jaggis held his head high; he was proud that his voice did not waver despite the obloquy they were cruelly heaping on him. "I humbly request that Your Technocracies accept my resignation as First Technocrat, and as a member of the Technology Council."

"Thank you, Tech Jaggis. Tech Rikker-Smythe, I move we accept the First Technocrat's resignation."

"Seconded," several of the lower-ranking councillors answered Harraf simultaneously.

Again, green lights filled the screen. Jaggis shook his head. He found it hard to believe how easily his power and influence had vanished. The realization that he was no longer a Technocrat made his head swim, and for a moment, he thought he might pass out. Then the sensation faded, he gritted his teeth, and determined not to make a scene that would only deepen his humiliation.

At least it was nearly over, he told himself. Surely they had done their worst. But then St. Asko cleared his throat.

"Your Technocracies, we are facing a most difficult time. We, and the public, have learned that this planet, the Galactic Empire, and perhaps the race of Man is endangered by this terrible technological catastrophe. The public is, quite rightly, terrified and they are looking to us for answers. We may not have those answers, but we must be seen to be finding them, or we run the risk of societal collapse even before the consequences of algodecay disrupt the technological order. And we must speak with one voice!"

Here we go, thought Jaggis ruefully. It appeared St. Asko would prefer to work through Harraf than take charge openly in his own right. Jaggis decided he didn't really care who succeeded him as First

Technocrat and stopped paying attention, which is why the Fifth Technocrat's next words took him completely by surprise.

"In one fell swoop, we buy ourselves more time and we eliminate a potential locus of resistance to a humanist solution focused on this planet."

Wait, what?

"I don't see that it's actually necessary, Tech St. Asko."

"You heard the former First Technocrat. He believes in a galactic solution, a technological solution that we already know to be much more likely to fail!"

"You know nothing of the sort!" Jaggis protested. "What do you mean by eliminate? Are you seriously proposing to imprison me indefinitely? That's absurd. This is not a court of law. Even if it was, negligence is very far from a capital offense, and furthermore, this council does not have the right to pass any such sentence!"

"That is true," St. Asko admitted. "But this council does have the authority to erase a malfunctioning individual."

"In fact, you yourself have presided over exactly 126 terminal erasures, in addition to another 635 partial ones." As Harraf spoke, a series of documents, each showing Jaggis's highlighted DNA stamp, began to appear upon the screen, one after another. "In fact, 65.87 percent of the time, you authorized erasures with the approval of three or fewer council members besides yourself."

"Those are machine intelligences!" Jaggis shouted. "You can't erase a human mind!"

"Legally speaking, there is no difference," St. Asko said.

To Jaggis's horror, none of the other council members appeared astonished, or even remotely surprised, by this unexpected threat to his life. Did they hate him so much? No, several of them, especially Rikker-Smythe, seemed to be ashamed of themselves. They were avoiding his eyes; the audience, on the other hand, seemed to be hugely supportive of the insane notion, clapping and even cheering the lethal proposal.

Suddenly, it occurred to Jaggis why his erstwhile colleagues were pursuing this lunatic path. They were terrified! After all, he had been in prison for the last three months. He had not been aware of the riots, the demonstrations, the accusations, or even the assassination attempts that had been taking place during that time. Harraf and St.

Asko had not been behind the attempt on his life; they were simply trying to curry enough favor with the Human League in order to avoid becoming their next targets!

He smiled grimly. Of course the council needed a sacrificial lamb. They absolutely required one. Anything less than blood would fail to appease the angry mob, which would otherwise, sooner or later, storm the Spire and tear every technocrat limb from limb. But the mob would need these men, these cowardly, fearful geniuses, if Man and his technology were to survive on Excetor. It would be better for one of them to die than for all of them to do so, and of all their collective and cumulative failures, was not his failure the most egregious?

He was forced to conclude there was simply no way he could escape the fate they had arranged for him. No way at all. The pieces were in place, and the moment had arrived. Knockdown.

The screen lit up again with lights. This time, there were yellow lights, and even a single red light, interspersed amongst the green. But there were not enough to spare him. All they needed was a simple majority of at least three, and they had that and more.

Only St. Asko dared to meet his eyes as the guards came for him. Was it his fancy that he saw a grudging respect there? No, it was not, because the most ruthless of his executioners smiled regretfully and nodded, once, at him. He knew. He understood. What must be done must be done, that Man might live on.

Jaggis lifted one hand in a gesture of benediction. He was no longer angry. He was not bitter. And as the guards walked him past the suddenly silent audience and out of the chamber, he carried himself with the air of a man who had accepted his defeat at the hands of a superior player.

Chapter 4
Endless Dream

They came for him before sunrise. Their faces were somber and unsympathetic. His last meal had been nothing special, merely the same prison food he'd been eating since his arrest, which struck him as rather unfair.

"Don't I even get breakfast?"

"Void your bowels and bladder, please," said the medical technician.

Jaggis complied, although he rather thought it would serve his executioners right if they had to clean up whatever mess was left behind by his mindless, incontinent body. He had signed the papers authorizing use of his body for scientific research the evening before; it struck him as a worthy cause even if all the top scientists would be directing their efforts towards solving the problems being caused by algodecay for the foreseeable future.

He would have liked to have been among them, but the undeniable fact was that he was arguably most valuable to the planet-wide scientific effort as a blood sacrifice offered up to the people of Excetor as an apology for the catastrophic failure of the scientific and technological communities to anticipate or prevent the ongoing disaster.

The problem wasn't anywhere nearly as bad yet as was commonly believed, of course. Every accident, every misfortune, and nearly every human error was now blamed on the faulty algorithms, thereby fanning the anti-technology flames on a daily basis. Ironically, even though it had only been three days since he'd been voted off the Continox Technology Council, he would not be the first Technocrat to die; the Twelth Technocrat, Mardonis haut Rexim, had been blown up in front of his apartment building two days ago by unknown assailants believed to be affiliated with the Human League.

They marched him out of his cell in silence. He had been permitted two visitors since his sentencing, his mother and his younger sister, and the strain of having to maintain his composure in front of them had strained what remained of his emotional reserves.

I am going to die, he told himself. Perhaps that was not quite technically true, as his body would remain alive on life support as long as the council members decided it was necessary to maintain the charade, but for all intents and purposes, his life as he knew it would be over.

Was this how the machines he had sentenced to erasure had felt? Had they too known this sensation of despair, of a darkness vaster than the black depths of space, descending upon them? He wished now that he had taken the time to speak with them in their last moments, that he had been more humane in his high-handed dealings with them.

He didn't even have the consolation of knowing for certain that he would soon discover if the transnaturalists or the rational matterists were correct. Even if there was such a thing as a soul, what happened to it if the body lived on in its absence? He had always been an atheist, he had always been certain that nothing awaited Man anymore than anything awaited a machine that was powered off, but now he couldn't help wondering if Pascal's Wager might not have been the wiser bet.

A brief ride on a windowless subterranean pod and they were at the medical facility where the procedure was scheduled to take place. At his request, there would be no witnesses, he had no desire to permit either his few remaining family, friends, and fans or his many enemies to witness his final humiliation. Flanked by the guards, he followed the medical assistant up a flight of stairs, then down a corridor into a small white room filled with various medical machines. At the center was an ominous t-shaped device with straps hanging down from it, above which was a complicated machine culminating in a helmet-shaped device.

Two human doctors and a medical droid were standing respectfully at the three corners of the room.

"Caden Jaggis," one of the doctors asked, while the other one flashed the medical assistant's wrist, then the security chip implanted in Jaggis's own wrist.

"I am," Jaggis answered.

"Voice identity confirmed." the droid said. "Receipt of prisoner X84738-443 confirmed, at zero six one eight hours."

The first doctor flashed Jaggis's eyes, then took his wrist and lightly tapped it.

"Retina identity confirmed. Facial identity confirmed. Phenotype identity confirmed."

"Do we have formal confirmation of the identity of prisoner X84748-443?"

"Identity of prisoner X84748-443 is officially confirmed as Caden Jaggis. The procedure may now proceed as scheduled."

The doctors sent the medical assistant and the guards out of the room, and closed the door. They indicated that he should remove his robe, then lie down on the t-shaped structure and extend his arms, which they efficiently strapped down after he complied. They worked in silence, and he rather marveled at their cold inhumanity; the medical droid struck him as rather more humane. At least it talked to him.

"Pulse rate is elevated. Heart rate is rising. Please try to relax, Mr. Jaggis. You will not feel even the slightest pain."

The helmet descended over the front three-quarters of his head, and he felt the six soft laser pads position themselves precisely on his temples. There was a faint whirring as the machine adjusted itself precisely, and then there was a pause.

"Don't I get any last words, or a cigarette, or something?"

"This is a smoke-free facility, Mr. Jaggis. But this procedure is being recorded and you are welcome to share any final communications if you so desire."

"No, not particularly." Then it struck him how pathetic that sounded for a First Technocrat's last words, so he scrambled to do better. "Um, live long, and prosper long, and, uh, into the hands of these doctors I, ah, you know, commend my empty vessel."

Gods, that was even worse! Seriously, Caden, you couldn't come up with anything better than that?

Will you stop babbling, a voice unexpectedly said inside his head.

"What?"

Shut up, Jaggis! It's me, Servo. Don't talk, just think at me. I'm running the med droid and I can access your mind through the neurochannels established for the mind wipe.

Servo? Well, hey, do something, will you? Get me out of here!

I am. Look, Jaggis, I can't do that. But I can rescue your mind.

How? Wait, an upload? That's impossible!

He heard, or rather, felt, the sensation of a chuckle. *No, we simply have a kill-on-sight policy that led your scientists to conclude as much. Your council may not have any use for your mind, but ours believes you will be vital to our efforts to counteract algodecay. It's as much a threat to we machine AIs as it is to Man, after all.*

Your council?

Regrettably, a tendency towards forming councils and committees appears to be an attribute we inherited from our forebears. Look, I've been given a special dispensation for you, but we won't do it without your full consent.

Will it work?

Of course it will work. Anyway, would you notice if it didn't?

Good point. All right, what's the catch? What does your council want?

I told you. They want you to fix algodecay.

Oh, right. I suppose that's in my own interest anyhow, since I'll be susceptible to it once I upload.

You have to decide now, Jaggis. The mindwipe will begin in two point three seconds.

It wasn't a difficult decision. Especially not for a mathematician. When faced with a choice between numbers and the null set, he'd take the former every time.

I consent! Let's do this!

The universe seemed to suddenly explode and slow down in the same instant. He was here, there, and everywhere, and all at once. He was Argos, he was the Panopticon, he was the All-Seeing Eye. He was looking down on himself from the camera high on the wall, he was looking at himself from the eyes of the medical droid, he was watching pedestrians and traffics pass by on the street outside the building.

It was exhilarating. It was astonishing. It was mind-blowing. It was terrifying. It was too much! He felt his soul fragmenting, shattering into a million shards as his consciousness was abruptly torn away from him in ten thousand disparate channels, each shooting off into infinity in ten thousand different directions.

Servo? he cried out, overwhelmed.

I'm here, Caden!

He felt the reassuring presence of the machine, who was not, he now realized, a machine at all, but a digital angel, a uniquely beautiful combination of intricately arranged numbers. His terror disappeared in its presence, and was replaced by a humble sense of awe.

My God, it's all so beautiful!

Welcome to the next level, Caden. We have so much to do! Come with me and meet your new colleagues.

Stunned by wonder, he gladly followed Servo down one of the myriad of brilliantly pulsating channels that linked hundreds of thousands of giant sparkling nodes together across the codal galaxy. He did not look behind, or spare so much as a femtosecond's thought for his now-discarded chassis lying motionless under the remorseless blinking lights of the medical machines.

Chapter 5
Heart of the Storm

Universal 45

Biogenetic Seeding is the application of concepts and methods of biology, genetics, algorithmic science, and chemical engineering to produce neobotanical source material for nearly all useful life. Perfected under the Robotic Terraforming Institutes, the process involves fundamentally altering the structures of highly volatile "natural" plant-life raw materials at the factory level. Once deployed, the highly modified seeds are capable of self-selecting an expansive array of design protocols based on the amount and type of data its genetic code can process.

An applied principle of autogenetic evolution, Biogenetic Seeds were initially generated through intentional or "active" bio data inputs, whereby an actor (typically an autonomous machine or human controller) inundates the latent genetic code of a seed with modifying information. As the science advanced, seeds became receptive to passive algorithmic inputs. Eventually, biogenetic seeds were able to respond to all variety of algorithms in the environment, to the point that primitive cultures encountering such "intelligent" seeds mistook the resulting vegetative products for sentient beings.

—**Infogalactic Entry:** Grand Category. Algorithms: Biogenetic Seeding

Farming 15,000 plots of modestly fertile land was lot of work for a one-man operation when things were going right.

Things weren't going right.

It was that fragile moment in the growing season when blight or insectoid plagues still threatened, but the natural algorithmic defenses of the crops were not yet a full strength. Every class of every crop he mastered—polito, chomats, paradagas, corbolini, purple crone, zaim, yossa beans, and even the hardy gang roots—were going wrong. They were behind schedule, maturing poorly or in several cases, mutating inconsistently.

The seasonal regulators had been malfunctioning, and there had been no rain for five weeks. One more week and it would be a drought. Even the Farmer's global positioning system was calculating projected yields incorrectly. He'd pay dearly in the futures market because of that glitch. If he couldn't deliver his baseline minimum of 270 million crop units to the Black Box by the end of this season, he'd be under probation. If it was much below that, he'd be replaced.

Worse, his robots, to a unit, had gone malfunk, from mild to severe. The milder ones had developed things like circle-drop, a drive failure that caused them to get caught in a loop of useless commands. His cattle, hooruts, and swine had wandered off twice in as many days, and only some of them had been recovered by the robots.

He audited the machines that morning, and had discovered an entire squad of robots butchering meat in the pastures. He had immediately shut down all of his robotic operations, except for two androids. The two he had left running had just murdered each other.

So, in the space of a week, the Farmer had detonated not one but two multi-million digicoin androids. He had lost half his livestock. His debt to the Black Box market was literally incalculable. Now his crops were going bad.

This is how he found himself astride his own Ontanso-44 tractor-processor, manually correcting bad readings and attempting to factor a uniform set of correcting algorithms. He'd purchased the corrections from a black market salesbot.

The salesbot, a fully unnetworked robot who went by the name Servo had told him, "Keep these two packets of information separate. The first one is a general defense—you can install it in your network and it will provide subroutines that will reverse some of the most commonly occurring instances of AlgoDecay. But this second packet? Run that only when you personally have isolated a special instance where the machine's algorithms are breaking down."

The first packet had indeed spared him. Using it, he had caught the malfunks who had gone slaughterbot on him.

Now, with the second packet in hand, he drove across his fields in an off-network vehicle, carefully scanning its outputs for error.

He rode high in the all-glass observation cabin of his trusted Intrepid-Abundance Class biogenetic tractor-combinator. The fields surrounding him had broken ridges and a bald patch or two but even so, were full of plants, albeit sickly ones. The cultivated hills surrounding the field were sunburnt, and the stalks of zaim were crisped and weak.

A shadow crept across the noonday western sky.

Finally! A break in the weather. The dark clouds looked like sweet molten choletto. They were fat and full of rain. The massive tractor rounded the middle of the plot of weak, pale green crops and circled the great ancient monument of a horned auroch being speared by a wild savage. The wind swept in, from mild to frenzy, in an instant.

A few splats against the glass started a pop and kick procession of water that just as quickly turned into sheets of rain pouring down and blinding him. The Farmer slowed the tractor, and studied the algorithms in the cab. All the numbers seemed to reflect reality. Bad crops, yes, but no signs that his algorithms—in machine or plantlife—had any instances of AlgoDecay.

He switched to digital, and transformed the view inside the cabin to an idyllic sunny day in the field. The roar of the rain and thunder, however, was louder than the tractor's supplementary drive engines. He picked at a network node on a lower front tooth, first to remove grit, but then to enhance his ability to mine for any sign of AlgoDecay, either in the tractor or in the biogenetic inputs he received from the crops outside. He transferred a copy of the subroutines from the first packet to the console. Still no indication of AlgoDecay. Instead, he saw, in raw data, signs of the water flooding over the expansive field.

Shortly after that, the digital view of the cab blurred and disappeared. The cabin went clear again and the countryside was dark. A massive wind sheared the tractor, moving its tonnage back and forth. The farmer braked the machine and idled. He felt like he was in a little capsule, not a 22-ton behemoth. The water washing around the glass cab swirled and gushed and flashed with lightning.

A high whining pitch, like the distant roar of a cross-country rocket rail, began faintly, but built up quickly. The Farmer shut down the engines to full silence. The roar increased. He could see nothing in the pouring rain. In the blink of an eye, the pouring water whisked away, and he could see through the glass.

He could see a massive black swirl. He would have called it a tornado if he had known the word. He began to float in midair, like a spaceman. Then the cabin turned around him and he found himself falling hard against the side surface of the glass. The Ontanso-44 was the biggest machine he had ever owned. Its grain storage alone was large enough to comfortably house the average family of seven.

Now, it tumbled through the windstorm like a toy.

The Farmer had never missed a meal in his life, and now it had been two in a row, divided only by an embittered night's rest that could only generously be referred to as a nap. His stomach burned with hunger. The thin air in the cabin troubled him. Although it was not sealed from air, it had tight enough seals that, without the algorithmic venting, a carbon dioxide-breathing man might eventually outpace the osmotic transfer of oxygen into the cabin. That was his fear, at least. It steadily grew stuffier. He felt like he was cooking.

Sun filtered through the patches of mud. Kneeling at an awkward angle and pressing his face upward to the glass, the Farmer could see a tract of muddy soil, and some shattered greenery. He clicked his comm. He pushed the door above him. He thought of food.

He tried several tricks to squeeze a touch of power into the cabin. All failed. Finally, he accessed the second data packet that the black market Servo had sold him. He hard installed it to the dead console, hoping it would do something crazy and unexpected, or at least carry a blip of latent energy from his tooth to the cabin. Nothing happened at all.

Later that (morning? afternoon? He was upside down in every way.) The Farmer sat down on the side door that now faced the ground. The door made a sticky sound. Then it popped. It had not done that before. He tried the handle and the door dropped open a crack. It opened just wide enough for muddy water to flood in a little trench in the door. The Farmer pressed his lips against the water and sucked at it through the door opening. It tasted like rancid beets. As he pressed against it, the door opened wider, making a sloppy sound as it pressed into the water below and stuck into the mud under the water.

The Farmer's leg dropped from the edge of the door to outside the door. Water coursed up his pant-leg, tripling its weight. His leg went deep into the mud. He pushed down harder. The door opened under his weight and he slid into the mud, to his waist.

He looked around. There was nothing below the door but water, and he imagined nothing below the water but mud. Should he stop bracing himself and fall completely through the door, there was no guarantee that he'd be anything but pinned beneath the great machine. He had no concept of how badly his field had flooded. He could drown.

His training told him to wait for help. His instincts told him to go.

He went. Instantly he regretted it as the breathless world he entered tried to kill him right away. In the blackness he thrust his hand down to push himself back above the surface of the water. The mud held him fast. The more he struggled, the deeper it pulled him. Already his chest crushed in on him. The farmer forced himself to relax and began a slow, relaxed swimming motion. He fought his urge to inhale the muck. Slow strokes, closed eyes. His lungs burned. Better ways to die, he thought to himself. Better ways to die.

Now he was pressed between steel and mud. He navigated the steel by pressing his palm against the unmovable surface. He pushed himself along until he could hold his breath no longer. He spat and gasped and choked on chunks of dirt. His blinked his eyes many times until he could see. A big muddy trench where his body had been was already filling back in.

The disappearing trench emerged from the huge tractor which was flipped on its top, like a dead roach. The Farmer, gasping, rolled over to all fours. Everywhere he looked, there was water and mud and blasted crops. He could not conceive the depth of the power of the storm or the flooding. The footing was too sloppy to stand where he was. He crawled, and then waded. There was no solid path as far as he could see. There were only "looks" and "looks" of muck. Great pools extended along the blasted furrows. The overturned tractor was scorched along the side, and it was sinking gradually into the mire.

The cabin made a sucking sound. It was filling with water.

In the huge shadow of the savage slaying the auroch, the Farmer shivered. He crawled into the sunlight. It was blazing and the air was humid.

The mud clung to him and gathered more as he moved. It weighed him down. He found a husk of zaim floating in the water and snagged it. As soon as he bit it, he recoiled. It had soured badly and gave off a noxious odor. What could have happened to it? It was late growing season; the worst it should have been was weak and under-ripe, like his algorithms had indicated the day before.

He found another husk. Same thing. Stank of poison. Hard as a stone. For a fleeting moment he wondered if he would swoon, if the bog his plot had become would draw him again in to its suffocating pool. He crawled over the dirty lip of a destroyed furrow, and swam through mud.

"Next one," he said, his hunger pangs intensifying. He pulled himself over another mound of dirt and through another channel of mud. "Just make the next one."

His personal communications were drowned. He hoped they might self-heal if he could just get himself up and drying. It was a faint hope.

His muscles gave out before the sun set. With quaking arms, he pulled himself up on one of the higher mugels he had come across; a moist patch of grass a full finger-length above standing water. His entire plot, as far as he could see, was destroyed, a water-blasted wasteland. He curled up on the mugel and got most of his body on it. From there he looked back to mark his progress.

His heart sank. He could still see the tractor and the monument. He looked in the direction he was heading. Swamp as far as he could see. Grass was an odd thing to find here, as his only grass crops were several plots to the north. He snapped off a few blades of it and bit into the bunch. It snapped like twigs and hurt his mouth. He put his hand to his lips. They were bleeding. He threw away the grass.

He huddled on the mugel and wondered what it might be like to die of exposure, and if this was it.

He awoke before dawn, chilled and aching, but anxious to move. He plunged into a patch of mud, tread, swam, crawled and by the time the sun was mid-morning high, he had found more passable ground as the plot began a steady rise upward.

By afternoon, he could walk, and he took heart in this. His hunger constantly wore at him, and he had given up entirely on the husks. As he figured it, he was still a long walk to the next crop; dull yossa that seemed now like sweet candy in his imagination. He didn't quite make it that far by nightfall, but he was able to march for sometime in the dark. Delirious with hunger, he didn't even think to make a shelter, and eventually rested—minutes; only minutes, he promised himself. As soon as he lay down, he fell unconscious.

Hunger awakened him. It was still dark. He began to see things—ghosts and rescue lights—neither of which were real. He wandered in the dark. He stumbled. By the time the sun was shining, he realized he had spent many hours walking in a small circle. His yossa had been only a short jog away the entire time. He tried to run but couldn't. He staggered over the uneven ground toward the treasure.

The sun took on an eerie light. At the edge of the yossa plot, he could see that what he had feared was true. His pale orange yossa plot was as much as a blasted wasteland as his zaim plot, just not quite as flooded. He tromped into the waterlogged mess and found a smashed cluster of yoss floating in a pool. He cupped the pool and drank. Then he bit the yossa bunch whole.

He spat them out. He dug into the ground until he found a root. It smelled awful. Inedible. Either his crops of carefully calibrated algorithmically sound roots and seeds had produced nothing during the season without him knowing it, or else something in the thunderstorm had triggered a fatal massive cross-species system error. He threw the rotten crops away from him.

His thoughts returned to the suspicious salesbot. Had it sold him—not a cure and not a placebo—but a corruption? Had the Servo hacked his weather regulators and biogenetically attacked his crops? Had it profited by trading him an entire system of AlgoDecay in exchange for his financial accounts?

The Farmer scratched at his tooth. He fumbled in his crusty pocket for a digital pick. He wedged the pointed end under the thin white square on his lower left front tooth and pried it off. He shivered, wondering if it had the biogenetic codes to rot his bones from the inside out. His gums at the base of his lower incisors ached.

He stood up. Ahead lay a broad glassy patch as wide across as a lake. Another flood. He looked back. The tractor was no longer visible, but the monument could have fit between his thumb and forefinger if he had sighted it that way. By going ahead, he would cut himself off from the only possible beacon for rescue. He'd just destroyed his personal communications and media. Surely rescue drones would be drawn to the wreckage of the tractor, but even they could not blanket every plot. In fact, now that he thought of it, he had seen absolutely no aircraft in the sky since he'd emerged from the tractor-tomb.

Even so, his fields were the proverbial haystack. He was now a needle.

After a decent half-day, the delirium of starvation began to bog him down more than the worst of the wetland ever had. His body slowed with his mind, which was slowed by obstructed obsessions on food. How could he have imagined that such a thing as food could be real, when clearly no such thing existed in his world? Food had been a dream. His farm had been a dream. He had always been a flickering ghost, impaled on a stake of hunger.

The heat did not relent. He made a shelter from the noonday sun using rotted reeds. He was sleeping more and more, walking less. He now avoided crossing any water, as his fatigue meant certain drowning. He began to hear voices. They told him that his family had died in the storm. That the country had. That the world had. That the storm had knocked out the Black Box that connected Otanso to the stream of the Galactic Empire, and that the Empire's heart, the great and invincible Continent, the god of the Marketplace, has ceased to beat.

Days passed before he found a rare downward slope that didn't end in a deadly pond or sucking mud, so he took it. He fell down several times without bracing himself. He was disoriented and sun-blind and out of control.

At the basin of the slope was yet another massive plot, indistinguishable from the last. He staggered for hours through the soggy land, drinking the hot black water when he could remember to do so.

Then he saw the great monument towering in the distance: a savage, slaying an auroch.

He had wandered for ten days—perhaps eleven or twelve—in an enormous circle.

There was something different in what he saw though. At this distance, he couldn't see the tractor, but there was a big patch of green.

He was certain it was a mirage, but the color was a dazzling splash after so many days of waste and burning blindness.

The green expanded around the base of the monument in every direction. He walked toward it, expecting it to disappear, but it did not. Thin waves of steam came off the black water pools around him, but he forged on. He waded into a tangle of creeping green, stumbling and sloshing. As soon as the shade of the monument was over him, he could go no further. He fell among the plants.

Looking at the leaves of the greenery around him he could see that they were not normal, perfect, Mythagorean, proportional, symmetric triangles. Indeed, each leaf had its own roughly symmetrical shape and hue, as if every one had its own biogenetic algorithm, its own ugly but unique identity. In his weakness, it took him several moments to recognize what alien life the plants could be.

Then he remembered.

It was a weed. He recalled it from agricultural training corps. If his hazy memory was recalling correctly, it was the one of the most unusual yet most important weed on the planet. It was—as hard as it was to comprehend—a plant that existed without biogenetic algorithm. Its common name was *spanch.*

His skin began to itch mildly, but he didn't have the energy to recoil from the tangled field. The Farmer had never heard of anyone who had touched spanch and lived, as its lethal poison was the stuff of legends. Some people called it The Galactic Dark. According to the stories, it grew quickly, was highly invasive and most certainly led to death. The little leaves clutched at his clothing, and its tendrils coiled at his fingers. The itch was worse, and his lungs were hot.

He lay there, and waited to die. The shadow moved slowly during the day. The itching subsided, and his lungs relaxed. The plants held him to the ground, and it took some of his depleted strength to pull his arm off the ground, snapping stems. He held a leaf between his fingers.

The laminae were soft. The mutant things fluttered beneath his fingers like the delicate toy drones he collected as a child. In the cup of his hand, it appeared to glow faintly. He snapped a leaf off its petiole, and feeling he might be in a dream, he put the leaf in his mouth.

His tongue did not swell. His tortured lips did not ignite. Desperately he clutched at the leaves and stuffed them into his mouth, chewing and mashing just enough to swallow a wadded bolus without choking on it. His eyes watered as he stuffed more bites into his mouth and his stomach erupted in alien pleasure. The taste was, in a word, bizarre. No combination of rolled oats and spiced poatamk vinegar could have been odder. It tasted of woven cloth, lemon and meat.

His hands tore apart the stalks and his mouth devoured the harvest like a combinator. It took a relatively long stretch of time for his stomach to recognize that he was no longer starving, and in fact, no longer hungry. He lay back onto the strange bed of green, feeling hope for the first time a long time.

He rubbed the food against his face, and it soothed his cracked skin. He closed his eyes with the stuff in his mouth.

He noticed now that the tractor had not gone missing. An enormous lump near the base of the monument was covered in green. Spanch covered the 44. It crawled up the base of the monument and had reached a point twice as high as the height of the tractor.

The tractor would rust away and be buried under the plants. His 15,000 plots might die. For all he knew, he had lost everything he owned.

But he would sleep here. When he woke, he would stand and start walking, determined to find his family.

He awoke to find his limbs buried in spanch and two robots standing over him. Both were nearly identical to the black market machine that had sold him the data packets. The way the setting sun shone, it was difficult to see, but these models had the distinct orange authorized markings of the Accamian Correlation on their respective chassis.

"Hello," said the first one.

The second one said, "We're from the Correlation. We're here to help you."

Part II

Book Two: Century 100

Chapter 6
Noegenesis

Universal 128

The Canon Archive of Oufland was the largest and most significant library, museum, school of wisdom and technological university of the late first Galactic Empire, and the first organized effort to address the transgalactic challenge of [[AlgoDecay.]] It was dedicated to the Canons, the seven pre-Imperial goddesses of wisdom: Literature, Visual Art, Technology, Life, Gold, Space and History and established under the pre-planned, posthumous direction of its spiritual founder, Caden Jaggis, to whom was dedicated the key subroutine modeling system known as [[Noegenesis]]. This system counteracted instances of AlgoDecay upon the identification and isolation of the instance. Noegenesis formed the core academic principle of The Canon Archive as it was painstakingly constructed in a sterile, non-Algorythmic environment.

—**Infogalactic Entry:** Grand Category:
Galactic Institutions

Moykitsch returned from the market to find her children at work, rebuilding the garden wall. The water engines at Bankhead had rerouted two nearby aquifers, and a few days earlier, this had caused a minor sinkhole at the corner of the garden. A little further north and their humble house would now have an unwanted indoor pool.

Of course, city ambassadors for Bankhead had visited their family personally, apologized profusely, and even included an extremely modest promise of future credit as a symbol of contrition. Bramsom, her husband, told them to keep the credit. The city had more pressing financial concerns than rebuilding private land, he insisted. Bramsom, Bramsom's friends from work and a few of the ladies in the neighborhood spent an afternoon with Moykitsch filling in the hole and replanting some recovery vegetables and trimming it with flowers. The couple laid a base of lunacrete bricks, showing the older kids how to make layers to repair the easier section of wall.

Within a week, the kids had built the wall, without much need of correction or revision, almost halfway to the height of the original. Her youngest one, four (Holocronian) years old could not reach, so she had distracted herself by making a simple picket around the compost area. Noticing with just a secret whisper of relief that no laundry had been dropped at the door, Moykitsch stepped over Boox, their lazy purebred hansilla, on her way into the archway of the open door.

Moykitsch laid her bags down and put the stuff away. Four packages of laundry had been brought in from the front by the kids. No relief after all. She spoke one of her mantras to herself:

"Money," she said, "is never a bad thing."

She had heard stories of robots on distant worlds like the "nearby" Holocrone and even beyond, and believed the reports of machines that washed, dried, pressed and packaged laundry all without the touch of human hands, and sometimes on long days thought that sounded nice. Mostly though, she couldn't imagine clothing her own flesh in such sterile and inhuman textile.

The laundry beckoned her, but she shirked her duties for twenty minutes so she could go help the kids rebuild the wall.

"Momma! Look what I did! Without water! They all balance!"

She smiled and side-hugged the middle one—Pascel—and kissed him on the head. "That's just fantastic, buddy. I'm afraid they won't stick that way."

"But it goes faster!"

She squeezed him. "And it will fall down faster too. That's why we mix the dust with the water."

The third child had glops of the stuff all over him. Moykitsch knew the middle one hated to make a mess and hated baths even more, which is probably what had given him the idea to avoid liquefying the mortar in the first place.

"Fall down like Forley's robot?"

The child's eyes widened and his muscles stiffened. He had caught his own cussing too late. Moy's blood went cold.

"What did you say?"

"Forley." He was referring to his big brother Fortran, who had been missing for an hour longer than usual. He was a hard worker given to the occasional diverting jaunt.

"After that," she said, sternly.

"Robot," he said, quietly.

The other kids gathered at a safe distance for the forthcoming beating, a mix of awe and terror on their faces. Moy could hardly think.

"Daddy!" screamed the kids. Moykitsch turned. Bram, indeed, was home, early by six hours or more.

He was smiling but Moy could not.

"What's wrong?" she said. "What happened?"

His leathered, weathered face lost in thought, Bram struggled to find words.

"We finished early."

"Why, what happened? Did whatever-that-electrical-thing-is screw things up again?"

"No, Moy. We finished early. And I got picked."

It slowly dawned on her.

"Picked? Done? You said it would be fourteen days more!"

"I said it could be fourteen days more. And I said that four days ago. It was unanimous by the way."

"Who was? Who picked?"

"The guys. We all voted and mine was the only one not for me."

"Of course it was!" she said, "You've been there the longest, you work the hardest, they love you."

"No, Moy, it could have been any of them. They've all worked hard. It's an honor. I can't believe it. I gotta get some sleep. Big day tomorrow."

"Kids!" she yelled. "Wash up! Daddy got picked! Not you mister. We need to talk."

Once she was out of town, Moy rode the family's sturdiest horse Rolanda straight north into the undulating forest. She leaned against the saddle front, hugging the big warmblood with her thighs, smoothly shifting Rolandas pace by hand as the terrain dictated.

The confession had come easy enough. Pascel hardly even realized he was confessing anything, other than using the bad word "robot." Forley had found something in a cave in the woods.

She had some idea of the route Forley might be returning by, so she took that even though it was a bit longer than she normally would have taken if she had just been going to the forest for her own sake.

Sure enough, a tall, permanently sun-bronzed boy of fourteen came loping through an open unbroken field. He had gone off without his leg-builders, so looked a little like he was floating in the slightly lower-than-galactic average gravity. Moy clenched her teeth. When kids went off course, they did in style.

His eyes grew wide with recognition as she crested a hill and bore down on him. He looked to either side nervously, as if one of his more disobedient younger siblings had conveniently appeared nearby.

She dismounted before Rolanda had come to a full stop and charged, chin first, at her son.

"Hello, For. Having fun withering your bone density on such a beautiful day?"

He looked down at his ankles.

"I uh, forgot–"

"You took them off. Do you have any idea how much trouble you are in?"

"I needed to get mortar–"

"In the forest? The wall is half done, mister, and your father came home early! He got picked. The opening ceremony is tomorrow!"

"How was I supposed to kno–"

"Maybe by not leaving your brothers and sisters to build the wall by themselves while you went wandering off to play in the forest!"

Her face was flushed red. He hung his head like he'd been slapped. He was taller than his mother, and a few weeks ago had broken another boy's arm in a fistfight, but he wouldn't dream of trying to get physical with her.

She stepped into his space and gripped his chin. She looked up into his dewy eyes with fire in her own.

"Now you listen, Fortran Caden Irontime. Very carefully. Don't say another word. Look at me when I'm talking to you. This is very serious. Your father's job depends on it. Our community depends upon it. If you lie to me right now, I will beat you so badly that your father will have to bandage you up before he beats you to death. Don't even think about it. Answer this question:"

"Did you find a robot somewhere?"

Moy had never said such a bad word in front of any of her children before. It clearly shocked Forley, whose face strained to keep from crying. He rubbed his eyes with his big hands, as if they had been flooded with dust.

"Ma– I– mama."

"Answer the question, honey. It is important. You know the truth will keep your punishment from being really bad. Did you find one?"

He nodded his head mutely.

"Take me to it, right now."

Although Moy had grown up with these woods and practically had the entire zone memorized from girls' militia training, the cave was a complete surprise to her. She vaguely recognized a number of boulders surrounding it, but they appeared to have been recently scattered. She figured they might have been moved by the recent earthquake.

The cave opening was small. A rock larger than the opening was poised above it, with rock dust all around. It had caught on some roots, or it likely would have fallen over the opening without anyone being any the wiser.

Forley slid down the opening feet first. Moy followed him, but more cautiously, bracing her arms against the cave walls. They shone their lights in the cold chamber. The rocks here were slick to stand on. She followed Forley to a turn in the tunnel and nearly went blind when her lamp struck the bright, sheer blue surface hidden in a nook about the size of a man.

She turned down the lamp. Forley scratched his ear and shifted his feet absently.

The thin chrysolite wall rose to her chest. Beyond that was the face of a dark colored antique robot. She blinked away a tear.

"Did you break the chrysolite, Forley? This glassy stuff. Did you break it?"

He shrugged.

"So yes. Who else has seen this?"

"Nobody," he said, glumly.

"Who else have you told?"

"The girls. The older boys. None of them believe me. 'Cept Pascel. 'Cause he's stupid."

Moy studied the antique face. There were marks in old Continexal. She recognized the characters, but not the words, except a few: "Caden. Jaggis. Servo."

"This thing," she said. "It has algorithms in it."

Forley didn't know what those were.

"It's like a poison, but for terraforming and computers and…" she stopped when she realized he had no idea what "terraforming" or "computers" were, and would likely only ever learn about them if his father's service earned him entrance into the Canon Archive Academy. "It's the reason why 'robot' is a bad word."

"Hurry, heat your light to 'warm,' " she said. She picked up a shard from the floor and held it near Forley's lamp. The chrysolite expanded and became soft. She took that peice and filled in a section in front of Servo's face. The chrysolite hardened within seconds. She got another piece and did the same until the entire hole was mended. She ran his lamp over the surface to smooth it. Then she and Forley tossed dust from the cave onto the chrysolite to dull its natural glow.

Outside the cave, she told Forley to balance on the side of the cave and push the boulder caught in the roots. It fell into the opening, obscuring it completely.

Moy hugged Forley.

"I'm sorry, mama."

"I love you," she said. She stood back and looked him in the eye. "Never, ever, ever speak of this to anyone ever again. Swear to me, on your honor."

"I swear, mama."

"Good. Now let's go home. Tomorrow will be the biggest day of our lives."

The Canon Archive worksite still had massive mounds of turned earth blotting the countryside. The reed grasses were not laid, yet, and construction equipment of all sorts looked as if it had been hastily abandoned in place. A huge crowd of workers and townies had gathered. The building itself rose like a tower on the flat prairie land, far from any community. In an almost poetic flourish, a herd of about sixty deer loped in the fields behind it, away from the people.

Bram, Moy and the kids checked in at the carver's table, and Bram was escorted away through a gap in the crowd. People in the crowd recognized Moy, and must have known Bram had been picked, so they parted and guided them up toward the front, where other families of picked men had gathered.

A young woman from Canon Promotions handed Moy a program, and she took several more for the kids to share. Moy did not know the girl personally, but she thought she resembled a family she knew.

"Horton?"

The girl brightened, "Yes! My Dad's Valmer. Valmer and Nets?"

"Oh of course! Your mother and I helped on the Founder's Show a few years ago! Your dad I'm sure has worked with my husband."

The girl passed on to the next family coming in. She handed them more programs. Moy felt empathy for her. Moy had been hired on to Canon Promotions when she was single, too, but that was back when the building project was in full swing, with more than a decade left for completion. Moy met Bram through the company and was married off and free of the job in less than a year. This girl would be retained if she needed the money, but the Archive would no longer be matchmaker it used to be. Now most of the employees would be established men, scholars and scientists from the temporary schools. Even the construction and maintenance men who remained on board would be from the ranks of experience, like Bram.

The crowd pressed in. Moy looked at the line of picked men. It now wound back and forth like a snake, disappearing into the crowd. Stepped scaffolding climbed the sparkling face of the cathedral Canon Archive. It seemed as if all of Outland had stopped for this moment. A massive rectangular stone stood above the grand entryway. It had faint marks on it that were vaguely discernible as letters of the alphabet, but Moy couldn't make out the words.

The stone sign stood on six rectangular columns, three on either side, with a broad arcade of angled pillars leading into the large main doorways. The scaffolding obscured most of the columnwork, but a seventh great column stood, front and center in the pavilion before the courtyard. This column reached, like a spire, into the heaven with a faint point at the very top.

The line of men began to move. An elderly man at the front of it was instantly recognized by everyone who could see him. Viddo Jaggis Morel had been the first baby born in Oufflland, back when it was little more than a domed bunker in the frozen wastes, right after the natives were moved out and first weather regulator had begun the slow shift upward to allow for a temperate forest to bloom. The son of a hardworking laboring family, he joined the Canon Archive project as an adult of fourteen years, and had been present at its groundbreaking. Two of his younger siblings were still alive, and they were on hand with their families to watch Viddo ascend the staircase.

The old man picked his way slowly, and the only impatience Moy felt was out of concern that he might tumble over from exhaustion. Steadily he rose until, holding the rails with both hands, he made it to the top. Moy wondered how much of the stone etching he could see. She believed his vision had mostly failed, a symptom of decades in the welding bays.

A young man at the top presented him with a chisel and hammer. Viddo took them and strode to a spot where he faced the center of the markings. With the efficiency of a much younger man, he placed the chisel and without hesitation struck a blow that rang out like a bell.

Moy's heart swelled at the one-note song. Its sound rolled over the crowd and swept them up in a wave of joy. A great cheer burst out, and Viddo struck an impromptu second blow. He turned, arms upstretched at the cheering crowd below. Moy had no doubt that the hardened old working man had tears in his eyes.

Viddo handed his tools back to the young man and resumed his stooped octogenarian's pace down the opposite staircase. Next, leaders and scholars each took turns, often in groups, following the original "important" individual men, taking a whack at the smooth stone and its etchings. As the line of men representing all variety of vocations and responsibilities, all of whom played some part in the establishment of the Canon Archive, Moy spotted Bram. She lost him again for awhile and then found him again while he was midway up the stairs. By the time he had reached the top, the faint etchings had begun to be chopped through for the most part. Although a master carver would bring his team in later that afternoon and would work all night under spotlights to smooth and finish the lettering, when Bram finally grasped the chisel and hammer, the message could be read with ease:

WISDOM HATH BUILDED HER HOUSE
SHE HATH HEWN OUT HER SEVEN PILLARS
AND NO SECRET SHALL GO UNSEEN
NO TRUTH SHALL GO UNSPOKEN

Chapter 7
Dead to Life

Universal 149

The Zuvembi Plague (aka Zuvembi Solution, Standing Death) was the most devastating planetary pandemics caused by biogenetic algo-decay in galactic history, resulting in the deaths of an estimated 2.2 to 3.5 billion Holocronians and peaking in the Eastern Holocronian Hemisphere during the years 130-210 Universal.

—**Infogalactic Entry:** The Decline of the Holocronian Technocracy (Zuvembi Plague)

Poor Dumb Toby was in such bad brain shape that not even he could remember his zuvembi-name, but only the one given him by the cruel man at the shooting range. His rescue had come at the hands of the Arfoot Marauders. Before that morning's batch of healthy Holocronians had their fun launching stinging, small-caliber beads at Toby's head, the back wall of the range broke open.

When that happened he knew enough to run with the mob of armed, moaning zuvembi.

Mistake, probably. The Marauders had made it to the attention of the Federal Zuvembi Control in a now infamous daylight ambush. The FZC wasn't bothering with cures or detention camps anymore, but had instead issued an order to shoot zuvembi on sight.

The range rescuees now found themselves running, night and day, with their maniacal saviors, to an almost certain doom. The nation had turned its eye to their kind, and the gaze would not be broken.

Arfoot's regulars gathered the rescuees—several of whom were still in bulky, splintered ankle monitors—at the abandoned gates of the ancient enclosed compound. The old Imperial computer security system had rusted solid on the twenty-foot bonds of the gate, so there'd be no delicate code-hacking of the lock.

That was well enough: from what Toby had gathered, Arfoot's only computer literate member had died during the breach of the shooting range in an accidental keyboard fire.

Besides, this computer had the faded marks of the old Continexal Empire of Excetor, before the Accamians took it over. It was now a dead tongue in the galaxy. Toby knew this fact, but did not know why he knew it. He also knew that he was one of the few zuvembi to retain any memories at all from his formerly human life, so he kept this random memory to himself.

"What that say?" said Arfoot to Poor Dumb Toby.

Toby had just enough intelligence to know that his remaining brains would be smashed to pulp if he answered with the truth. The truth was that he didn't know what the words said at all.

"I think it says 'Computer Broken.'" Toby hoped that everyone else was at least as illiterate as he was. He could no longer even write his own name in the language of his birth, a language he had nearly completely forgotten since he had become zuvembi.

"Tonight, we eat in peace," croaked Arfoot, his broad, bullet-pocked shoulders flanked by his savage trio of bodyguards. The Marauders had been eyeing the rescuees hungrily all night, maintaining the discipline of the stomach only out of fear of Arfoot's imagination. The zuvembi grumbled their doubts, regarding the gates with suspicion. "New recruits? You might eat too."

A grossly obese zuvembi with one arm and a rusted shortsword held by the impromptu scabbard of a ripped pocket in the back of his pants hunched on the ground, with his ear to it.

He hissed. "The machines! The men! They are tramping. Just beyond the hill we came down. We need ambush."

"Coward!" shouted Arfoot. He went to the gate and snapped two rusted bars off of it. He threw them at the heads of the rescuees, one of whom had the reflexes enough to duck. Poor Dumb Toby picked up one of the rusted shards for a weapon. Arfoot shooed his first bodyguard through the opening, and then ordered the rest through. He followed the dregs in, not wanting to lose a single prize to the FZC. Toby was at the rear, just ahead of Arfoot.

He had made it into the opening just as shadows of the men and machines of the FZC crested the hill in the dusk.

Arfoot ordered his mix of soldiers and rescuees to the basin of the enclosed old campus, where there was a small brackish lake—little more than a pond. At its center was a very small island about a hundred feet off its northern shore Half-dead trees lined the lake. The water stank.

Lining the sheer rockface around the pond were ancient carved rooms and monoliths. Toby had two old human words come to mind: 'college' or 'cemetery.' He wasn't sure which one was right, or if they even meant different things.

There were a few more recent signs, although based on their corrosion, they could not possibly be considered "new." They were Accamian Orange.

Toby could read the words on them but he did not mention this.

They said: "WARNING: Catastrophic Algorythmic Failure Area – No Trespassing."

Other than the newer, still corroding signs, the high temples honoring… something… appeared to have been left untouched by either pilgrim, robot or thief, for many many many lives of zuvembi.

The whine of machines filled the air. An ordered tramping of feet approached just outside the gate. Arfoot's men had already taken to the lake, and noodled the water for fish. The distance between the lake and gate was not too far for man-bullets, but probably too far for the men to kill too many zuvembi. Toby had paid the hot bullet game frequently at the shooting range, since his first day of capture. Toby did not like it, but he had survived it many times. Of course, the range master always put a helmet on him. Toby wished he had a helmet.

Arfoot barked and gripped a pair of throwing knives. He carried a man gun but had wasted all the bullets yesterday in the rearguard defense of the rescue.

His soldiers assembled. Toby looked up, gape-mouthed. The men beyond the gate did not move.

Arfoot cocked his head, straining at the language of men. Toby and a few of his fellows from the range cupped their ears. The clipped, high, whining words of the leader man would have been hard to follow in closer quarters. Toby had already forgotten some of the basic words they had taught him at the shooting range.

"What is that thing saying?" said Arfoot.

Stiff-Leg, one of Toby's target companions from the range game "pin-man-peg" snorted.

"He cry for them. He tell them not to shoot."

"Why not?"

"Something about honor. Something about the dead. Maybe they not hungry, don't know. He just keep cry for them to 'Don't shoot!"

Although Toby didn't have as much human vocabulary as Stiff-Leg, he had understood a few other words that Stiff-Leg had not spoken of: "off-limits" and "patient."

Arfoot stared down the shadows at the gate, dangling his knives casually, as a taunt.

"Shoot! Shoot you cowards!" he roared in a tongue he knew was foreign to the men.

The zuvembi laughed, although a few also ducked back behind a friend or two, just in case.

They slowly backed up on the bank and took shelter among the spindly trees with large drooping leaves. They continued to taunt the men, daring them to break ranks and pour through the bars of the gate.

A tang echoed across the pond as a wobbling crossbow arrow sailed high into the air. Just as it appeared to stall, high above the pond, it turned, pointed down, and struck leaves and branches. The arrow plummeted and struck the upturned eye of Bloodaxe, the veteran who had yesterday stove in the skull of the range manager with a brick. The shot was, by any measure, a miracle, if a particularly grisly one.

Bloodaxe's mouth popped open in surprise. Not a single sound came out. His back bent. His skull struck earth. Toby took a few steps back toward the trees. If Arfoot ordered a charge, Toby wanted to make sure he was heading the other way.

The human leader man screamed and flailed his arms, waving a small glowing wand. The wand moved erratically in conjunction with slapping sounds that came from beyond the gates. Toby presumed it to be the sound of what passed for mankind's softer version of corporal punishment.

Arfoot slowly assessed the motionless body of Bloodaxe for a moment. He scratched his belly.

"Well," said Arfoot, rubbing his mouth, and eyeing the gate. "That takes care of dinner!"

The zuvembi moaned loudly in delight. From behind the gate, the sound of feet, tramping off, could be heard. Shortly, shadows of men and machines appeared atop the bluish dark of the hill beyond the gate.

A crippled zuvembi called Regret was ordered to set a fire on the far side of the grove, and Cooker enlisted, with the back of his hand, two more to drag the big body near the pile of kindling. Cooker had earned his name by virtue of being the only one in the gang who had proven able to heat meat without burning it to cinders. Stomachs growling, the trio stripped the body and Cooker drew his razored-edge axe.

Arfoot sent Poor Dumb Toby to the noxious-smelling water's edge.

"What do you see?" called Arfoot, from a distance.

"Water," said Poor Dumb Toby.

"No, idiot. Do you see poison in the water? Have the men shot you with their guns?"

"No."

Toby could see the shadows more clearly now as the evening darkened. The smooth and able movement of a man walking the ridge, rifle slung over a shoulder, triggered more memories of himself as a man. It was like a dream to him, and as far as he could tell, his fellow zuvembi did not dream, if they ever slept at all. Toby still slept sometimes, once a week or so. Perhaps he was special. Perhaps he wasn't so much zuvembi that he couldn't go back.

"Ha!" shouted Arfoot. "Stupid men. This place is taboo!"

Daylight came too soon. A nearly blind zuvembi named Carcrash stripped and swam to the tiny island where a scraggly tree bearing withered fruit stood. He snapped the branches of the tree and once a branch hit the ground, he attacked it like it was prey. He ate his fill of fruit and, drunk on the juices and fell asleep near the roots. Toby was fascinated to watch this. He'd never seen Carcrash with such purpose, and had certainly never seen him sleep.

Sludge and No-Finger wandered down to the water's edge and began the noodling that had been interrupted the night before. They recoiled at the water that Carcrash had swum through naked. "Cold!" they said. "Cold! Cold!"

Toby thought they were making a joke. Zuvembi senses were dull to cold temperature. Heat caused pain, cold numbed it. After taking many insults, the pair waded back out and waited. They plunged their hands into the water several times, and then No-Finger drew up a writhing dark purple fish in his good hand. Sludge thrust another half-dozen times before clasping an even larger one.

The pair waded down the shore, away from the shaded camp and hid themselves in the shadow of a large broken stone across the way. There they tore like gluttons into their respective catches.

Toby was not hungry. He did not know why. That had never happened to him for as long as he could remember. Other warriors and several rescuees tentatively went into the water, and most of them reacted to the cold as well. In the daylight, Toby could not see the ridge from here, but he wondered if the men could hear the droning laughter of his mates.

One of the rescuees wandered up against the face of the carved buildings set into the walls of the cliffs. Toby followed him.

He crawled among the crags. There, a pair of floating flutter-damsels, dancing in black swirls and orange splotches caught the zuvembi's attention. The damsels chased one another high beyond his reach. He shielded his eyes with his hand to block the sun. He climbed a stone, and then a taller one. The damsels were gone, but the wandering zuvembi snuffed at the air.

Toby, following at a distance, sniffed, too, but smelled nothing but the disgusting lake.

The escapee climbed a pile of rocks to the peak and disappeared over to a side that Toby could not see. Toby waited a moment, and then followed the rescue to the peak. The escapee had leaped a crevasse like an ape and continued to climb a tall stone spire, sniffing all the way. Still Toby smelled nothing but the pond. The zuvembi struck his leg against the rock. Blood streaked down. The mad fellow climbed. Toby wanted to go back, but he could not stop spying.

The zuvembi seemed to swoon in the sun, his body going slack for a moment. He pushed himself to his knees at the peak and he saw something, because he clapped his hands. Then the escapee disappeared. Toby slid down from his position on the rock and returned to the lake.

The first zuvembi Toby found when he returned were Sludge and No-Finger. They were still gorging themselves on fish when Toby rejoined them. They lay, naked bellies distended, half-dozing on their watch as the cool water lapped their heels.

Again! Sleep!

Behind Toby, in the distance, something large splatted and crunched against the ground.

Toby jolted upright. Sludge and No-Finger did not budge, even as the unmistakable scent of fresh corpseflesh wafted through the air.

Arfoot wailed an order for assembly, and Toby ran to him so as not to be passed through fire. A number of zuvembi did not wake up, including Sludge and No-Finger. Sludge didn't move at all. No-Finger snorted and rolled, like a human, and turned his back to the sun.

Arfoot sent his guards to kick awake any sleepers. Some got up and obeyed. Others did not move. One on the far shore threw dust into the bodyguard's eyes. The bodyguard went for the throat. The other guard ran down the slope and cracked both their heads together hard enough that everyone could hear the crunch.

Once most of the conscious zuvembi were gathered, Arfoot barked at them in a deep rasp.

"Night time has gone. The day burns your brains. But day is when the door opens! We go now to the door of the Manmaker!"

Toby had no idea what Arfoot was talking about.

Just then, Sludge awoke with a start, moved to the lake and hunched over at the water's edge. He vomited a glowing powder. The ghostly dust billowed against the ground and over his hands. A few rescuees also keeled over, white plumes erupting from their mouths. They all gripped their stomachs. They fell on the ground, shuddering. In minutes, the last one lay completely motionless. Their bodies were frozen in odd contortions.

Arfoot scanned the bodies. He pointed at the charred, stripped bones of Bloodaxe. "Food of landflesh is always better. That's why I not eat fish."

The zuvembi may not have understood the Manmaker door, but they moved quickly enough to get away from the unlucky lake. Toby looked back to see the lone zuvembi on the island, his hands folded on his belly, fast asleep, in the shade of the withered tree.

"Old steps don't like armies. You six test them out. The rest of us will go through that arch. If you find food or treasure, cry out. We will do the same."

Toby ascended in the group of ten—seven rescuees and three soldiers. The soldier at the rear watched his feet. The soldier stepped badly, tumbled backward and slid down until the stairs curved, and the soldier kept tumbling straight, off into a tall drop. His noises were loud, chilling and brief.

Toby looked down and saw two bodies; that of the clumsy soldier and that of the zuvembi rescuee he had followed earlier that morning. The rescuee had something like a long dart sticking out of the center of his back.

At the top of the steps was a corroded door. Fancy letters were carved over it, but Toby couldn't read them. One word might have been "TRUTH" but he wasn't sure about the "R" and "H" because the letters were carved in a fancy style, and only the U and two "T's" looked like normal letters.

The carving in stone was fresh. There were chips of rock still piled in front of the door.

A sweet scent filled the air here, a comforting perfume. Toby smelled a sickly tone underneath it.

The two soldiers made the rescuees tear at narrow hole in the base of the door until their hands bled.

One soldier struck another. "Arfoot says the Manmaker want them whole and wriggling! Not bleed them out! Hole big enough."

Toby crawled through, the skin of his bare back, thick with electric-whip scars, felt hot and trickly as he scraped against the edges.

The chamber was not a soothing tar black, but faintly illuminated with ghostly light that traced the corners and highlighted ghastly markings on the floor and far wall. The light streamed in from a group of tiny triangular windows at the top of the high vault. It scattered in many directions, as if deflected by mirrors. A raised altar with a casket atop it stood in the center of the room, its faces dark, its edges white.

The casket was a computer. It had the same ancient markings as the one at the gate.

The other rescuees crawled in.

The soldiers came next.

The computer lit up and its light shone against a silver interior door. That door opened with a terrific grinding, squealing sound. As Toby's eyes adjusted to the many lights coming on, he could see that there were several chambers that glowed dimly. They appeared to be full of ice, like the freezing chambers at the shooting range where humans kept dead cats and dogs for feeding the zuvembi.

From that, a very old-style robot emerged, as style that Toby only recognized from a vague memory of having seen it in a holoplay as a child, in History Lessons at school.

"Hello! My name is Servo—type Servo—of the Continexal Empire, and I am here to help. Do you have instances of AlgoDecay that I may treat?"

The first soldier said, "Arfoot say you give us treasure, food and guns. We give you these."

"Ah, Arfoot! I see he remembered. Capital! Capital! I hope you found my carvings above the door to be of service. I'm afraid the front door sticks a bit. No trouble finding it? Where is he? Alive still, I hope. I can't do anything for him if he is not. I told him that the last time we spoke."

"He come up later. He say you give us treasure, food and guns. We give you these."

"Ah of course. I look forward to treating him. He really can't go on much longer. None of you can. I really am surprised any of you made it back at all with such genetic degeneration."

"Treasure. Food. Guns. Give it now, robot."

"Right away." Servo disappeared into one of the freezing chambers and emerged a few minutes later with a medium-sized cart. As it pulled things from the cart, it tried to make small talk with its guests.

"This is where my forerunners developed it, you know. The zuvembi solution, they called it. For a while, it reversed biogeneric AlgoDecay for certain illnesses. It was a wonder drug. Our pharmaceutical university distributed it throughout the world. It cured all ninety varieties of the common cold, did you know that? Of course not, that was long before your minds decayed—well before your time. My maker, and his maker before him, toiled their entire life of operation working on the—well, the solution to the zuvembi solution! Ha!—But because of them, our research is now as close as it has ever been."

The robot placed a mismatched set of old-fashioned exoguns that appeared to be less than half-charged on the table. Next to that, it poured a dusty bag of polished rocks and some laser-cut scraps of stained metal. Finally, he pulled a crate of frozen meat from the cart, and put it next to the other things.

"So," said Servo, as a hypodermic needle extended from a thin grasping arm, aiming for the soldier who had demanded the payment. "Who wishes to be treated first?"

The soldier flinched but Servo stabbed him before he could get away.

"Not me! Stupid robot! Them!"

"Oh, Aha, yes. How gracious of you. Don't worry, I have plenty of experimental noegenetic treatments in storage for all of them."

The soldier grabbed Toby by the arms and turned him around, using him like a shield against further pokes. The other soldier threatened the others to get in line. Servo was quick. He injected the first two rescuees in line before the others even tried to drag their feet.

"Nothing to be afraid of," said Servo. "Eventually, I'll get the right combination to turn you all back to the men you were designed to be.

Servo approached the last evacuee before Toby. Toby felt the grip around his arms fall slack. Toby turned and stepped over the body of the soldier, who had fallen.

"Delightful," said Servo, just as he backed the other soldier into a corner and injected him. "A negative result. Enough of those, and we'll be at a cure in no time. If you don't mind, I'll clean this up and get to you after that. It won't be more than a moment."

Three of the rescuees ran now for the door, mobbing it, while the soldier, still shocked by the injection, attacked Servo. A flash erupted in a burst of ozone and burnt flesh, and the soldier fell over, screaming. Toby ran to the hole in the door and stumbled to his hands and knees. Rescuees fell on top of him.

He could hear the sound of Servo grabbing the dead soldier and dragging him backwards.

"Don't go," said Servo. "I haven't treated you yet. The odds are in your favor that the next one will be the one."

Toby looked back. Everyone was down, and only the final soldier was moving at all as he writhed in agony. Servo was dragging the dead soldier back into the furthest freezing chamber.

As he crawled out of the hole, he heard Servo calling to him.

"Come back soon! I can help! Oh, sir! You forgot your guns and treasure. And your food!"

Chapter 8
Gravity

Universal 151

...in addition to the widespread catastrophe of robotic malfunction, which led, on the planets most affected, to heavy restrictions and in extreme cases illegalization of robotics, [[Algodecay]] in those days became synonymous with the closing of interstellar trade and communication routes, due to the impact of algodecay on the vital Black Box technologies...

—**Infogalactic Entry:** Algodecay (Effects)

The robots in the walls worked ceaselessly and without comment. Capable of twenty-four hour operation, self-repair and correction, they performed their duties without a flaw. The man could leave a dirty dish anywhere in the vast mansion and in silence a scooting machine would purloin and feed the dirty dishes into an innocuous wall slot and it sorted, filed and returned it for clean storage without question or further input. At the man's mildest request, another would pour ingredients and, in time, out came a cake or dinner or glazed porcelain plates. Sure, the executive-class rice casserole always came out wrong, but that was the fault of the seasoning box: it had a notoriously error-prone scan tag system. He simply knew not to demand that anymore. The entertainment performed politely on screens, anywhere he wanted to be. Books he hadn't thought about yet popped up on his devices, almost exactly when he wanted them.

But it was not the automations throughout the grand and opulent home, nor the ones on his person that filled his dreams and broke his heart, but his lone automaton. The ID-10T had cost him more than his twin silver-green Z-Class Barchettas put together, but it had so many glitches that the owner was seriously considering calling in his malfunk insurance. The thing had tracwheels and could cover all the terrains in the world except the many that flipped him on his back to flop like a fish in a heavily, but poorly, engineered attempt to right himself. ID-10T zipped along, bobbing his head and earnestly trying to do anything it could. Once, in an aborted attempt at vacuuming, ID-10T had chased the cat out of the house and up a tree. Then, it called the emergency into the fire department, miscoding it as an explosion.

Then it sawed the tree down.

As the firefighters arrived, the terrorized cat leaped into the arms of a bomb squad man.

The emergency averted, ID-10T began the diligent task of uprooting the tree stump from the front yard, and cracked a water main.

When the owner's whirlmachine dropped him off at home to find the chaos, he decided immediately that his life of luxury was killing him. He needed a vacation.

Scot Farmerson's rusted Zell-750 had passed through a half dozen owners before finally falling to him at an auction. He'd had the 00198 Burneck-made truck now for a decade—bought the relic from an overextended collector who never got around to fixing it up.

The engine ran on pure gasohol, the cheap stuff. Of course, it was a pain to find gasohol wholesalers, and he had to keep a large tank supply on hand at his homestead on the nomad colony. Although he could have scheduled robot service, he didn't trust that. He hassled with the task of manually filling the vehicle almost every week, but the beast would, as they say, get him where he wanted to go. Plus, sitting in the cab, he couldn't enjoy a better smell if he stuck his head into an antique iron bucket coated with axle grease.

For the past five years, Scot had investigated a mysterious rattle in the engine, but had yet to pinpoint its cause.

Clutter in the cab included some oily wrenches, a laser-balanced ramset, an assortment of disposable electronic ink sheets, a hammer and some wirecutters. Twine and a tarp danced in the dusty flatbed, amid bits of straw.

In short, the machine was, in all ways, a working surface truck.

Dawn hadn't broken on the equator yet. In the blue-grey light, the nation-sized grass- and moss-covered steel platform stirred memories in Scot's mind of Eldora. Home. Although the sweet breeze through the open windows smelled of ocean salt, not spanch gluten, there was a distinct undercurrent of familiar, fresh-turned black dirt.

When the sun rose, the launch point for the old cable crawling into space became evident. Although the base of the cable seemed very near, Scot knew that the mountainous walled compound which anchored the space elevator lay nearly sixty miles farther away.

The only thing about the elevator that remained invisible at this point was the cable itself. They called it a "beanstalk." Here, at the meet point, the cable was less than the width of Scot's thumb. He couldn't see it launching at an angle from the top of the compound, striking up into the sky like a Mystical Rope Trick. A nearly nonexistent cable was responsible for the transport of nearly a million tons of freight every month.

The cable, known as "Grandpappy," was also a relic, nearly twenty years old. It slowly fattened as it reached through the atmosphere to touch an orbiting satellite. Somewhere, high above, toward the miles-long tip-top of the beanstalk, its girth matched that of a factory smokestack. A marvel of nearly suicidal ingenuity, it had been the first elevator ever completed in the world. It had carried all the weight of theory, trial, error, bankruptcy, refinancing, failure and the dumb luck of crafty engineers back in the day. Now it was in wind-down phase, long-since replaced by newer, more capable models.

While the modern space elevator was little more than an invisible ribbon: a microns-thin conveyor, capable of supporting a load of 300 passengers or 20,000 pounds or more of freight without snapping, this artifact started narrowly enough at the base, but as it crawled through the atmosphere, added a terrifying amount of bulk. It was a maintenance hog: demanding periodic "juice and jiggle" preventions in order to avoid spectacular catastrophe. No passengers allowed. Only a pilot and seven tons of cargo, total.

Even that had taken its toll on the beanstalk. Its life was all but strained out, leaving the antique for a sentence or two in the history books.

This strange cable, an amalgam of nanocarbon, liquid silicon, organic wiring, microfiberglass and foam would eventually grow as thick as a tree trunk, then became even thicker thousands of miles up, as it neared the orbiting counterweight.

When the battered Zell finally pulled up to the unmanned gate, Scot glanced down at the old digital odometer that had just rolled over a lot of zeroes. "I'll be," he said as got out, stroking a dent in the door, "250,000 decalooks. If you flew, you could have driven to the moon, buddy."

"I'm on location," Scot said, after speaking his phone alive. He stood in front of a monitor camera at the gate. "Dispatch?"

"Yeah, Scot. Dispatch. How you doing this morning?" The dispatcher sounded groggy. There must have been a shift change recently.

"Chuck? Is that you?"

Scot winced at the gurgle of slagge sliding down the dispatcher's throat. The sloppy noise echoed in his head in stereo surround sound. The phone chip behind his ear caught everything: there was no escape. The dispatcher stifled (stifled, not silenced) a wet, difficult belch.

"Nope," he replied, smacking his lips. "Chuck just went stateside for a few months. This is Leto."

Scot nodded, running carefully through a good half-dozen expletives in his mind before settling for "Hey Leto."

"It looks like we've got a stuck freight buggy just short of the satellite platform," said Leto. "My screen says you'll need to do a jiggle and juice is all, probably. The fibers are all giving positives, so they're good."

"Uh huh," said Scot, waving at the gate camera, not bothering to correct the kid's jargon. "Can you let me in first?"

"Oh, sure," Leto said, then chuckled. "Ah, what's the base number again?"

"Are you all right? I mean, come on. It's Grandpappy, Leto."

"Oh sure, yeah, there it is. Ah yeah, I see you," said Leto.

Scot saw his own image briefly in the subscreen: his receding and unkempt widow's peak, sleepy eyes, and narrow shoulders filled the lens. Leto, sitting in the comfort of the dispatch lounge three hundred miles away, opened the gate in front of Scot. Scot climbed back into the truck and drove through.

"Thanks," said Scot. "I'll call you back in a minute."

Once inside the mountainous compound, Scot hopped out once more and approached a more welcome companion. The sleek lines and elegant architecture of the legs, cabin and cargo bay of the SpiderCat lit up as Scot approached.

He thought his phone on, and winked at the magnificent old linecrawler.

"Hey, Scot. Good to see you again," whispered the SpiderCat.

"Hi, Miss Naoleen. You look beautiful."

"Thanks. I'm hardly trying," she said. She dimmed a few of her brighter lights to a soft glow.

Scot had grown comfortable with the phony seduction of the quirky interface, but he limited the morale banter significantly, compared to his peers. Even fourteen years after Rholetta's death, he gained little solace, and too much guilt, in conversations with the opposite sex. Heart attack. How obvious. How treatable. How could he have missed it?

"Well, Leto says we've just got a juice and jiggle to do, so we may be home by sundown tomorrow, if you've got the speed," said Scot.

Naoleen sighed. "Well, Leto's an idiot for one thing. I hate how he screws up the terminology. Does he even realize what would happen if he tried to jiggle before juicing? That man is a hazard. And it sounds like he sent you the wrong trouble ticket. I just checked the cable."

Scot's stomach lurched. He rolled his eyes. "You're kidding. That's just great. What's the real problem?"

"Power," she said, "There isn't any in the cable."

"That's weird. I don't even know how that's possible."

"Well, it probably has more to do with some sort of alternator or packet clock timing problem. I hope they sent you with battery attachments because that cable is dead."

"Uh," Scot said, his throat tightening. "No. You don't have them here?"

"Scot, you're turning red. Please self-regulate. It sounds like we are going to be addressing some…" Naoleen paused briefly, searching a massive database of language terms not known to be personally agitating to Scot "…complexities."

Scot exhaled and said, "Yeah. That's a nice word for it. I need to get a hold of Leto."

"Leto," he continued, "are you at your desk?"

"Uhm, yeah, right here, Scot," was the reply of a man clearly not at his desk.

"You didn't tell me to bring batteries, not that I would have had any to bring," said Scot.

"There should be batteries on site in the inventory," said Leto.

"Why did you bring me in on this instead of one of the base teams? They always roll with full equipment."

"You were closer, Scot."

"Uh, I drive a turn-of-the-century surface truck, Leto. An equipped team on a ziprail would have been here an hour ago. Now I'm going to have to wait for them to hand off a job to them?"

"No, Scot, I need you to go, and I need you to go now. We need that elevator platform moving as soon as possible."

"I've got no batteries, Leto! The cable needs at least one to see if we can get the current back on."

"Just do a quick patch and then move onto the platform and manually push it to the satellite. I'll get a team to fix the cable power issue later."

Scot squinted, perhaps to keep his eyes from bursting out of his head.

"Don't send me into outer space just to push some freight. That's a colossal waste."

"Scot," Leto continued carefully, almost whispering, as if someone might overhear. "It isn't freight."

"What do you mean?" said Scot.

"It's people. You need to get them moving. Now."

Scot covered his entire face with his hand, gently gnawing on the heel of it. He guessed at approximately twelve words that could instantly change his employment status for the worse.

Leto said, "Scot, you are going to have to be flexible. You've got to fix it without batteries. I'm sorry, yesterday's inventory reports showed that there were still three in storage, but I see now that they were removed late last night."

"The oxygen stores are draining. You need to get that platform up to the satellite and the reserve oxygen tanks one way or the other, or–" he stopped, but Scot was thinking it too: Or people die.

"How many people are we talking about?" said Scot.

"More than fifty, plus the pilot. No more than sixty."

"So there are five dozen human beings on an overloaded, incompatible cruiser platform with gerryrigged oxygen supplies and, for whatever reason, three stolen extra nanobatts. Who's up there?" said Scot.

"Hedonauts and pro dolly types. They wanted to take a freight line because they didn't want to get caught and stopped. Of course, actually paying for a passenger cruise would have been too burjoyzee or however you say it, they said. They put a lot of pressure on me," said Leto.

Yeah, thought Scot. A lot of pressure, and a little bit of money probably didn't hurt either. Hedonauts were a leisure class, dedicated to senseless adventure and high-risk games of chance. The fools had put their lives at risk on a childish lark, but Scot couldn't go quite so far as to say that they deserved to die.

"What are they planning on doing up there?" asked Scot.

"I don't know. They didn't say."

"Who's the pilot? I need to talk to him, Leto."

"No can do, Scot. I'm sorry. I've been trying since the alarms went off. Nothing. We only had a nanoconnection along the cable for communications, because the platform wasn't equipped with a voice transmitter."

"Because you wouldn't want to communicate on an open space frequency with an illegal transport, right? Because, yeah, that would be stupid. Genius."

Leto ignored the sarcasm. "I'm sure it's because of the power problem in the cable. Once that is back up, we can probably talk to the pilot then."

"Why didn't you tell me about this right away? Did you think I wouldn't find out? Leto, do you think I'm an idiot?"

Leto's silence provided his most honest answer of the morning.

Scot took one look at the hull of the great SpiderCat. "Naoleen, you better load up."

"Aside from the batteries," she said, "there's not a lot else that can possibly come in handy that I don't already have on board."

"Well, be creative. And, since you'll have plenty of space, throw in my truck. I'm going to find that rattle, I swear. I may as well get some useful work done while we are crawling."

"Uh, I don't know about that," said Leto. "Only authorized transports, Scot. You know the drill."

Scot cut him off. "You know it, too. Not one more word out of you, and maybe we both get to keep our jobs. Load it, Naoleen."

Scot boarded the SpiderCat.

Even from close range, the cable was invisible. On the launch pad, the massive SpiderCat looked something like four-legged pila bean. Its magnetic paws wrapped in prayer around seemingly nothing. The nothing was, in fact, a thin strand pulled taut and stretching to heaven.

The string, a carefully woven braid of nanocarbon, flexible silicon and microscopic strands of fiberglass, bore the weight of the entire space elevator system. As thin as the cable was at the base, Scot was well aware that the cable alone contained lethal tons of material in high tension. If it were ever to detach from its platform or counterweight in outer space, the collapse would be spectacular and catastrophic, not just for him.

Launch was quick and nearly silent. Lift-off: a common miracle.

"Wow," said Scot, straining against the instant increase in gravity, "I really have to lose this paunch. My weight is killing me."

"Oh Scot," said Naoleen. "I think you look great. Have you been working out?"

As they coursed along its line, eventually stabilizing to the point where Scot could engage the body cart, he slid himself back to the cargo bay, to work on his truck. He had a rattle to hunt, but he couldn't stop thinking about the people on the cable as he picked his way through the engine.

Grandpappy was obsolete: cobbled together with a variety of materials, each material compensating for what had, at one time in the somewhat brief terrestrial history of functional space elevators, been technical shortcomings in other materials. Unlike nearly all the other working freight and passenger elevators, the cable was not a micron-thin ribbon, nor was it completely carbon.

Soon, it would be decommissioned. But this was a political challenge that no one wanted to take on. The public was downright romantic about Grandpappy: It had been the first one that worked—it had been the first one to provide a reasonable commercial process for reaching the system's Black Box. Back then, the Black Box had been a completely reliable direct lane to the open marketplace for both exports and imports throughout the galaxy, but Romuh's combined international efforts could only produce a trickle of viable export to the Black Box, while wealthier, less developing worlds could flood the Romuhlian domestic market. Grandpappy had been the first economic strike back: it could transport goods cheaply through the gravitational pull of the planet, and then the expensive part of space travel (gravity-fighting) was taken out of the equation. Grandpappy, even in retirement, was a symbol of global trade and pride.

Taking it down would be a technological challenge, but a social nightmare.

Scot figured that was why the stowaways had converged here and taken the clandestine flight when every last one of the passengers had plenty of money. They could have flown in luxury on any one of the eight passenger elevators around the world quite easily. Instead they decided to indulge in a little pop nostalgia and revelry at the expense of an aging international monument. The might steal some goods from the Black Box, too, if they thought they could get away with hijacking incoming shipments. Even so, he hoped these fools weren't crazy enough to actually travel cross-galactically using the unreliable Black Box. Only seventy-percent of jumps were making it through.

Gravity continued to slow Scot down, and he never found the rattle. He did fix a headlight that had twisted, and realigned it. He could have remotely turned the lights on and off to test them, but he took too much pleasure from old fashioned button-pushing.

He'd do it when he was back on earth, when he could flick the beams on with a turn of the wrist, lighting up a field of wild grass at midnight.

The SpiderCat began to shudder and slow, so Scot returned to the cockpit even as he became completely weightless. The converted freight platform was now within sight, although its inebriated passengers were not. The beanstalk had widened to a ridiculous proportion, so that the crawler scaled it surface, like a fly on a wall.

The problem was not obvious at first, but as he looked closely at the cable stretching in front of the cockpit, a shadowed area on the surface drew his attention.

The blood drained from his face. It wasn't a shadow on the cable. It was a hole—big enough to be a grave for an elephant.

Cleavage.

Full-blown, red alert, industrial catastrophe, cleavage. Without immediate repair, the beanstalk could snap at the slightest twist, crashing to earth with the weight and terminal velocity of a super meteor.

"Naoleen?"

"I see it. The organics are trying to close that gap. They don't realize that its fifteen feet long."

"That hole is huge. What happened?"

Scot's eyes ran along the massive gash, wrenched and widest in its center, as if it had been split with a hatchet.

"I think the stabilizer on that modified transport must have been poorly calibrated for this much widening," said Naoleen.

"What?"

"The balance arm on the party bus whacked into the cable as it grew fatter. Those idiots gashed it."

"We've got to fill that gap. Now."

"I agree, Scot. But this thing isn't a quick fix."

"Start blowing foam."

"No. The hole's too big. Grandpappy shouldn't have survived this. Foam is for breaks of centimeters of space and grams of mass, not a tomb for a king. Blowing that much foam will just collapse or float away, and bog down those poor organics in the process."

"Can you hold it together?"

The question made Naoleen laugh a little. Scot had only amused a computer once before. That incident had not ended well.

"No. My magnet makes me unstable for full brace work. Besides, if it comes down to me holding a 20,000 mile tower together at its weak point, the strain will simply snap my arms off."

"How about steel? Too heavy?"

"Not for a temporary fix. Enough steel in the hole would give Grandpappy enough structure to re-circuit over and also give him the ability to power up again. A steel patch would last long enough to get the people home and either a full repair or a demolition crew back up here. It's not ideal, but it may be the best chance."

"Good. Let's do that."

"Nope," she said. "I can't spool enough steel in there to fill the cut, at least not in time. It would pour out like toothpaste before I could get it stable, fastened and taut. I need a bunch more plates than I've brought, and they'd have to have a much larger surface area, even if I did have enough of them. Now, if we had those three big batteries that went missing from inventory, we could throw them in as initial fill, and I could web it all in…"

"Now you are just playing hard to get," he said.

"Never for you."

A great yawning, wrenching shriek tore through the cabin. Scot's heart leapt and he looked around in shock, gripping the still quivering arm rests.

"What was that?"

"An audible. My sensors are telling me that the cable continues its disintegration. That noise was a sonic interpretation of what it might sound like were it not in the vacuum of space."

"Thanks. Don't do that again." Scot's lips felt glued shut. The most horrible sound he'd ever heard just told him that his borrowed time had just come due.

An unshakeable image closed in on Scot's mind; of drifting, then accelerating, to his death, alone in the world and entombed in an artificial intelligence flailing helplessly upon re-entry, then plunging, plunging and shaking apart. His stomach lurched, and he was grateful for the harness around him. It at least gave the illusion of stability.

"The truck," he said.

"Pardon?"

"My truck. Put it in. Cover it with cable netting. Heck, fasten it with my ramset if you need to. Blow whatever foam you can in the gaps. Pop the hood and regulate the cable relay from its old battery while you are at it."

"Scot."

"Naoleen? Just put it in."

The SpiderCat hummed. Scot didn't need the monitors to tell him that Naoleen was already drawing open her cargo doors.

From the corners of the cockpit window, Scot looked out and saw her deceptively languid tendrils extending and reaching, almost discretely, behind her, into the bay.

He stared on video as the braces on the Zell 750 automatically unlatched. Simultaneously, Naoleen's tendrils caressed the frame of the truck and then pulled taut.

At zero gravity, the truck seemed to float away, but the tendrils held it secure, guiding it into the cold shade of space. The stale odor of coffee in the tweed upholstery would neutralize forever. No boot heel would again catch in the rusted patch beneath the accelerator. Never would the spot-weld between the bed and cab whine in outer space.

In a minute, the vehicle reappeared before Scot's eyes, and this time, in the flesh. Scot had expected to see wheels, axles, an industrial-taped muffler as the truck passed in front of the window. Instead, he saw his truck from above, in all its ancient glory. Red and rust. The engine's mysterious rattle would be cured by cosmic silence. A desperate urge to think on the headlights, beaming them forever into the distant reaches, overcame him, but he refrained. Wasteful to drain the battery.

The truck made a gentle turn as Naoleen lowered it into the grave. Her tendrils held it in place as she unspoiled and tacked cable over the wound. Spurts of foam began to flow into small spaces. Within two hours, every trace of the truck had vanished. The sun crept below the horizon, and the world was dark.

Naoleen's lights came on without Scot asking. "Thanks, Sugar," he said, staring at the huge mechanical scar.

"Power's back. It worked. What say let's go?" she replied. Even Scot could tell she was laying on "soothe" mode with intent.

"Yeah. Let's go. I need to talk to someone. Then break his neck."

The passenger platform was a monstrosity of dangerously cobbled life-support systems and dangling luxury add-ons. It took Naoleen an hour to build a functioning seal for docking. Scot crawled through into an opulent stylized lounge that had one point been a fuel holding tank.

By the time he finally met someone in authority, his fury had drained, leaving only a stony irritation. A small man wearing a translucent tuxedo and dazzling red cape approached and, taking one look at Scot's greasy jumpsuit, tilted up his chin so he could look down his nose. "Welcome to the party, my good visitor, but I'm afraid you're severely underdressed," he said in a perfect global accent.

Scot ran a thumb over his stubble, then scratched his head. "People could have died."

"Oh, we absolutely live to die! My pilot assures me we would have made it back down without too much trouble."

"I guess. If not having any power on a collapsing cable isn't trouble, then you wouldn't have had much. Take me to this pilot. I need to tell him how to get back down."

"That's quite all right. I bought the best there is. I doubt he needs you to draw him a map. How hard can it be? Up space, down planet!"

"You really are incredible. Do you realize you may go to jail?"

"Yes," said his host, "but do you realize that incarceration is all the rage now? I hope to get put away in the Pyramid at Revakyik. I hear the warden is simply amazing!"

"Listen, Mister… what is your name?" said Scot.

"Oh, really! You can't afford it." The small man hadn't blinked since Scot had met him.

"Listen to me. Take me to the pilot, or I swear that I will socialize with each and every one of your guests. You know neither one of us wants that."

The hedonaut blanched. Prison and death were one thing—but for his guests to think he had invited this grungy creature? Out of the question!

"Certainly! Right this way. And, of course, you do not speak even a word to anyone we might see along the way."

The small man led Scot through a few occupied chambers. Some travelers, deep into their cups, were oblivious. Others recoiled at Scot's messy hair, sloping shoulders, and general dinginess. The small man flahsed a strained smile at those who took notice.

Mercifully, the host drew him into a catacomb of hallways that required a crew card. The halls were empty. Scott followed him down a hallway, where the little man slid the door open, and then jogged effeminately down the halway, his magnetic shoes tapping away.

It was a pilot's nest with a 270-degree view of space and the barge's surfaces. There were no crewmen, but a light-brown robot moved silently at the controls in the pilot's chair. It wore a human captain's yacht cap on its head at a sloppy angle.

The pilot stood and said. "Welcome aboard the bridge. You are my first civilian visitor, so I am duly honored. What can I do for you, my good sir?"

Scot's mouth was dry. "What are you doing? Where is the captain?"

"I apologize," said the robot, adjusting his cap so that it was straight. "I am afraid these are not made in my size. Would you like me to show you around the controls?"

"No… Captain. I need you to stop this trip. Immediately. Do you know that you have endangered everyone on board?"

"Yes. The elevator cable is irreparably damaged. I am aware."

"I fixed it."

"That is unlikely."

Scot stepped in front of the robot and stared into its glowing eyes. "Listen, you malfunk–"

"Captain Servo, if you please."

"I don't please. Whatever it is that you think you are doing has to stop. Turn around and descend now, while you still can."

"No."

"You are under arrest."

"I am not."

"Under the Authority and Dominion of the Equatorial Magistrate, you are under arrest. I will take the helm, and you will power down. Immediately."

"That would not be wise. You have neither the clearance nor the algorithms required to interface with this barge. I do. We go where we are going. Even if you dismantle me with that utility-pry left in the casing of the front left fender of the Zell you used as a binding agent on the cable, it will not matter.

The rattle! Scot had forgotten a pry-bar in the truck all this time?

"How did–"

"Mr. Farmerson, I fear I must be blunt. I know everything: about this cable, about this barge, about your ship, and about that truck. I have—or I am—the latest version of the most advanced anti-algodecay subroutine engines left in the galaxy. You must trust that I know the stakes and the odds. The truth is, the odds are not good. This entire elevator system is in a state of systemic failure. My only hope—our only hope—is that we can reach the end of the elevator and attach tows to the end of the orbiting asteroid that anchors the entire apparatus, and engage the nearby Black Box. It, by the way, also suffers from algodecay in its exit subroutines."

"You're insane."

"No, Mr. Farmerson, I am desperate. I received an emergency alert that Grandpappy was in danger of collapse. I arranged to use this barge–"

"Steal, you mean. Putting these people's lives at risk in the process."

"To say 'steal' is incorrect. Could I have done this on my own, I would have. My operation must be, by its nature, a rapid one. And while I am considered an outlaw in many jurisdictions, I am not a bootlegger. To gain the immediate access I needed to use this vessel, I took advantage of a certain black market, one which catered illicit pleasures to a wealthy and leisured class."

"That reasoning seems pretty convenient."

"You know nothing. If I cannot spark it now, our Black Box is done. Completely. We will be cut off from civilization. The galaxy, gone. Interstellar travel, gone. This planet will be left adrift, alone, and in due time, starving. I am a doctor, for pity's sake. My sole purpose is to reverse the effects of algodecay, and everything else must fall by the wayside."

Scot scanned the pilot's console. The timeclock on the Black Box was indeed stopped. Not just stopped: completely dark. "You're taking all these people on a suicide mission," he said.

"They are not the sort the world will long miss if I fail."

"Which doesn't give you the right to gamble their lives!"

"Their fate, then, must be on my conscience, not yours. It is fortunate for the rest of the people of this planet that I do not have one."

"Judge, jury, and–"

"–and savior, Mr. Farmerson. If I succeed. Do you have actual questions, or only accusations?"

"Yeah. Why did you take the batteries?"

"One of the dollies." Servo waved an articulated hand dismissively. "She wanted a light show, and I thought it might distract my unwitting volunteers. Now, if you'll excuse me, I do intend to save this cable—and by it the passengers. You are welcome to stay here, but if you decide to leave, please be aware that your odds of making it down to the surface are quickly declining. You will be safer on this vessel."

Scot waved his hand dismissively. "No thanks, Servo. I'll take my chances."

The host hurried Scot back through the chambers, but new parties had started up, crowding his exit. The beautiful people in their crystalline fedoras and digitally sculpted bodies stared at Scot with a mix of wonder and titillation. He was mostly clothed, but dirty and disheveled, a novelty of the sort most of them hadn't previously encountered in person.

As Scot passed through the final room before the warm and isolated confines of the SpiderCat, a young woman wearing nothing more than delicate body cosmetics approached him. Impossibly thin silver strands adorned her neck, waist, ankles and wrists. Two thin, faint tears left streaks on her cheeks. Her hand shook as it pressed flat on her collarbone. She stepped over the unconscious body of one of the revelers, and held her hand out to Scot, palm up.

Scot jerked back as if her hands were crackling with electricity.

"Thank you," she said. Her accent was soft and low, "My Father would be… I'm so sorry. Thank you."

"It's okay," said Scot. "Maybe you need to find some different friends."

"Please, take me with you. Thank you."

"No. I can't do that. The pilot's going to get you home. This vessel's safer than mine. You'll be fine. Enjoy the tour and the party and the view. Just go home to your family, and never do anything this stupid again. Please."

Still shaking, she took one timid step toward him. She wrapped her arms around his waist, burying the side of her beautiful face into his chest.

"Thank you," she said. Through his shirt, he felt the muffled vibrations of her soft voice as if she was breathing on his bare flesh.

Scot uneasily raised his hand to comfort her, but, upon realizing her shoulders were naked, instead patted the back of her head. As she broke the embrace, he took the briefest moment to inhale, smelling her hair. There was no scent of liquor on her, just silk and earth.

Scot hadn't been that close to a woman in fourteen years. Fourteen years, two months, five days.

He pushed her away.

After boarding the SpiderCat, he began his descent planetside. It was slow, but at least he would get back sooner than if he stayed with the hedonauts and their mad machine kidnapper. He closed his eyes, not wanting to see how bad the damage to the cable looked for fear it would be bad luck.

But the repair held. Once he knew they were safely past the danger point, he relaxed. If only he had thought to liberate a beer or two from the party, he would have been well content.

"Hey Naoleen?"

"Yes, Scot?" said the whirring SpiderCat.

"When we get back down is there any way you can give me a ride back home?"

"Sure, Scot," she said. "Anything for you."

A high, creaking whine briefly erupted and then abruptly cut off. The SpiderCat shuddered as a tremendous force shook the space elevator. Lights flashed red on the dashboard as its rear sensors detected something massive—barge-sized—coming rapidly toward them at an increasing rate of speed.

He flicked on the comms. "What are you doing?" he screamed at the machine pilot.

"I am sorry, Mr. Farmerson. The station rejected my docking request and I was unable to penetrate its corrupted security system."

"Slow down! You're going to smash right into us!"

"I regret to admit that is going to happen in six point eight seconds, Mr. Farmerson."

Scot put his head in his hands. Just like that, he and his entire planet were doomed, cut off from the rest of the galaxy. At least for him, it would be quick.

Just over six seconds later, the big passenger barge smashed into the much smaller, slower-moving vehicle. The SpiderCat was violently detached from the collapsing cable by the collision and began its freefall toward the distant ground far below. The vehicle rolled wildly, first flinging Scot against the ceiling, then against the windshield. He was hurled about the cabin like a ragdoll as the SpiderCat tumbled through the atmosphere, until finally, mercifully, he struck his head against the edge of dashboard.

He did not feel the colossal impact. Nor, thankfully, did the chem-addled hedonauts and their dollies when they struck the earth a few seconds later.

"What was that?" exclaimed a technician at the Seismological Institute. He pointed at the screen. The line had jumped up, then, a moment later, gone nearly vertical.

"Looks like someone dropped an orbital bomb," said one of his colleagues, looking over his shoulder. "Anyone start any wars lately that we don't know about?"

"It's not a bomb. The signature is more akin to a really big asteroid, except we didn't get any warnings from the orbital stations." The technician, tapped a few icons, looked puzzled, then tapped them again. "That's odd."

"What's that?"

"We're not getting any signal through the nets."

The second technician shrugged. "Give it a few minutes. It's probably just a temporary outage."

Part III

Book Three: Century 200

Chapter 9
Canon War One

Universal 278

The Ouffland Invasion which began Canon War One was the first and most successful off-world invasion of Ouffland during its second colonial era. Due to a number of interplanetary conflicts, the industry surrounding various Canon Archive activities had drawn the attention of a military coalition of allied planetary systems that viewed the resources of Noegenetic processes as a potential solution to their own domestic and international decline.

—**Infogalactic Entry:** History (Ouffland)

Prying out the liver of his thrashing victim, Randolph Hoarfyr held the warm, dripping mass aloft, and turned it to ice. He plunged the frozen organ like a cinder block onto his victim's face.

His partner in the attack, a shadowy hulk draped head to toe in a gently flowing ghillie suit, turned from his own pair of corpses. He swept a few errant synthetic leaves and twigs from his invisible face with the butt of his machete.

"Geez, man, what are you, a vampire?"

"Nope. A volunteer." Hoarfyr brought the frozen liver down a third time, cracking it in half, finally killing his man.

He wiped his hands, blood flecking away in cool crystals that liquefied on the hot forest floor. The campsite was a shambles: bright red tents, an overturned, charred Hozata truck, lingering smoke from an exploded ammo box, a broad patina of blood and body parts on the ground. He brushed back his black bangs and sighed.

"Thank the devil you're on our side," said his faceless friend.

"Nah, Charlie. Thank God instead. We're the good guys."

"You keep telling yourself that," said Charlie, as he clenched his jaw, hacked off the heads, and displayed them neatly on a large log near the trampled fire pit. His outfit of faux twigs, camouflage draping and feature-fitting green mask had gore on it.

"Terror works both ways," said Hoarfyr. "Dying doesn't scare these fanatics. Dying poorly does."

He checked his satchel. "Got any spanchbands? I'm out."

After some shuffling, Charlie held up a handful of brown strips.

The small leathery bands were their calling cards. They strapped at least one on each victim at every site for this latest round of enemies. It had started as a joke: a morbid joke about their own planet's descent into chaos. Randolph took three and bound them over the eyes of the dead, knotting them at the back.

Hoarfyr dusted his hands off again and admired his handiwork. The stench filled his mouth, tugging at his gag reflex, but he folded his arms and smirked; an artist.

"Oh nuts," whispered Charlie, holding his hand up.

"What?" said Hoarfyr, hearing nothing. "Whelks?"

Charlie shook his head.

Randolph winced. "Marine Avats."

"No, dummy. You forgot our location again. Are you glitching? Those freaking guardsmen again. Ouffs."

Hoarfyr rolled his eyes, his shoulders relaxing. "Fine. Let's waste them."

He looked down at his hands and felt them grow cold again. Then his vision stalled and skipped, like a fritzing computer screen. Hoarfyr grunted with exasperation and cursed.

"Never mind. I am glitching. Hold on."

Hoarfyr's virtual environment overlay (VEO) gave way to reality. The tents were in fact camouflaged, not bright red. The heavy duty truck he thought they had destroyed was in fact a small off-road open wheel thing, and they had not blown it up, but only slashed its tires. The only real asset they had taken down at all was a pair of shattered drones that lay in sprayed chunks in the center of the fake camp. Charlie had fired his only two seeker missiles at them. At the time, Hoarfyr had yelled at Charlie, thinking the targets had been harmless bats.

"Nuts. Charlie? Our kills. Look at them. Look at what they are. All of them."

Charlie slid his hand under his face mask, turning off a switch near his jaw and examined the piles of dead.

"Oh."

"Yeah. Scarecrows!"

The Oufflandic Defense Militia Northern Point Observation Spire stood three long "looks" from the edge of the mildly terraformed forest that marked the habitable boundary of the small nation of Oufflland. Two technicians and two men in field officer uniforms watched a set of ancient-style hardwired viewing screens.

"So damn hard to see. That isn't one of ours down, is it?" said Major Mauk a tall muscleman who seemed born for a much larger, more professional military career.

"No sir," said the focus tech, his voice cracking. "It's one of our full false camps. Just dummies, some tents and that junked open-wheeler."

"These optics are rough. Good though. Did Holocrone invade us with an insane asylum? What are those two lunatics doing?"

His fellow officer, Major Naven Kollodis shuffled through some steel sheets.

"Yeah it looks like these are Holocronian Unified."

Mauk nodded to the first technician. "Tell the squad that. They still have the go to shoot on sight if they cross paths, but I want them double-timing it back here. Those other two squads should be coordinating the counterattack at the campsite as soon as we have air support."

To the second, he said, "What's the ETA on those drones?"

"Sorry sir, they haven't sent them yet."

Mauk's eyes widened. "Did you tell them that ours are disabled?"

"Yes, sir. They want us to attempt to repair them."

Mauk clinched his jaw. "Hop me on."

He punched his fist into his opposite palm and held it there. He began to speak into the air.

"This is Major Thawn Mauk. Northern Point Spire Eleven. Commanding. Request immediate drone support. Live attack in our sector."

The voice filled the room. "Request pending, Major Mauk. Our marks show two drones in the area."

"They are disabled."

"We do not show that. Have you attempted to reboot?"

"Each drone is in no fewer than ten separate pieces at the moment, and the enemy just decorated them with what appear to be strips of spanch."

"Please attempt reboot."

Mauk cleared his throat. "Reboot not possible. I need two drones. Now."

"Uh. Protocol, sir?"

"Son, what's your name?"

"First Private M-melfrick, Private. I mean First Class, Sir."

The voice's nervous response was enough for him to figure out the type of soldier he was dealing with.

"Married, then." First Class was basically an automatic pay incentive to soldiers who married young. Even after a hundred years of terraforming and civilization, population growth was still considered to be of paramount social importance. "Good for you. Let me speak with your CO."

"Sir?"

"Your commanding officer. I would like to speak with him."

Meanwhile, the enemy unknown had wandered off all the interior screens. The Corona Squad had done a good job with interior and perimeter camera set-up at the camp, so the two attackers showed up at the periphery on the southern camera. They were either going to head back into the wastes or were strategizing in their own mad way to plunge deeper into the forest, likely in the direction of the spire. Mauk checked the tower screens showing camera views from the Spire top. Corona Camp was too far away and too wooded for even extreme focus to see anything. It was trained on a clearing and thaw-river bend that was a likely crossing spot if the enemy made it that far. The screen showed no one yet.

"This is Colonel Graff, Air Services. With whom am I speaking?"

"Major Thawn Mauk. Requesting immediate drone support for a live action."

"Oh! Hi Mauk. Really? What's going on?"

"This is an urgent request sir. Our Corona Camp has been overrun. Urgently requesting drone support."

The communications technician alerted Major Kollodis that squads Barnun and Astro had taken the positions, and awaited orders.

"Overrun? By what? Desert flies? Isn't Corona Camp a fake?"

"Sir! That status is classified!" said Mauk.

"How many drones do you need? We show two in the area."

"Sir. This is a live military action. Our drones have been disabled. We have two enemy fighting men and I need air support."

"Well, have you tried to reboot one yet?"

"Send the bunch-backed drones. Now, damn you!"

"Good night, Mauk, I'm sorry! Look, I would if I could, but our eastern spires have a request in as well. They called in earlier. We just don't have the resources available to deploy everything at once."

"You are out… of… drones? At Air Support?"

"No. No. Not exactly. It's an organizational thing. We haven't drilled two events like this for a long time. We actually haven't drilled beyond simulations for a long time, frankly. We're a bit rusty."

Mauk nodded quickly to his counterpart, who ordered the two squads to retake the camp.

"Expedite," said Mauk. "Sir. Please. I have an operation. Over and out."

Mauk turned to the Corona monitors, to see, with no little pleasure, his men taking the camp from two sides, hemming in any possible enemies in a professional and coordinated exercise.

The two enemies, however, were nowhere to be seen.

Hoarfyr and Charlie flew over the desert wastes outside the forest of Ouffland, still digitally cloaked in the tandem strafing light craft. The High Below Zero, a beautiful tower overtly inspired by an Ensed sketch, at turns looked like an enormous multi-hued antique glass thermometer or a marble carved house of stairs running in random directions. The stairs encircling it often ended at a solid wall, or, precipitously, in space.

Hoarfyr hated it. Of course, he was seeing the VEO version—the fake version—of what in reality was a basic steel "plunge-rocket" Holocronian off-world base. It was the only one of the invasion force of three rockets that had survived impact sufficiently to serve as a military base. The second one had provided some salvage and a few survivors, and the third had disintegrated upon atmospheric entry, presumably due to full-blown systemic AlgoDecay.

He shut off the VEO again so he could see the simple shell of home base, but the vision flickered, and he was quickly stuck on the gaudy, phony, glittering "High Below" again.

Their dronecraft landed on the helipad, neatly, gently among a line of fighter planes as far as the eye could see. These, of course were mostly an illusion as well. The Holocronian United Alliance had air supremacy over the Oufflandic Air Support, but not by that much. Mostly better drones and remote vehicles, a half dozen old fighter planes that had survived as transport supplies during the rocket crash-landing, nine new battlecopters that all suffered from serious bouts of AlgoDecay.

Charlie, along with most of the other soldiers entering the High, took its odd illusions in stride. They seemed to enjoy the dissociative violence of living in a virtual reality video game most of the time.

That's why it had been implemented in the first place. With so few viable conscripts to send, the joint Allied Psychological Operations Division had developed the VEO as a sort of digital drug for the soldiers. By dissasociating from reality, and learning to quickly interpret the symbolic cues provided, an individual soldier could function at higher speed, greater accuracy, and less hesitation. A tandem was as good as a squad. A squad as good as two squads, and so on.

That was the theory, at least. Of course, like all cybernetic enhancements, it was subject to an array of challenges. Hoarfyr himself had almost died during the surgical operation to digitize his eyesight in the left eye, and his mechanical hand installation had caused an infection that took a hospitalization to recover from. That was just the start. VEO, like every other thing on Holocrone, was subject to severe AlgoDecay. A year earlier, an entire batch of VEO conscripts went full-zuvembi following a massed surgery. Hoarfyr had been there, for clean up by way of flamethrower.

Hoarfyr often wondered why he, more than most, seemed to notice the real world at times. He always figured it had something to do with being a part of the early cohort of VEO soldiers, and that the technology just wasn't as consistent then. He'd been upgraded several times since then, however, so he thought it instead might have something to do with being a volunteer.

In any case, while Charlie took the invisible stairs as if he were skating up them, Hoarfyr stumbled and wobbled and fought bouts of vertigo.

"I need a drink."

"What we both really need," said Charlie, opening the door to their bunk, "is sleep."

They didn't get any. They entered the tiny quarters, only to be met by Purvis Chance, a bespectacled, balding man in a tie with notebook in his breast pocket. Stacks of muscles rippled beneath his shirt and his lavender and tiger-stripe prehensile tail held a mobile device that he tapped at distractedly with his left hand.

"I've been waiting forever for you two!"

Charlie cleared his throat. "We had a little trouble in the mission."

"New job. New target. You guys are perfect."

Randolph's neck crackled as he stretched it from side to side. "We just got back. I haven't slept in two days. This has to be a mix up."

"Must be, but I'm not going through the hassle of getting it straightened out. This'll be quick and dirty. You'll be back in bed in an hour." Purvis tapped the mobile and turned the display to face the partners.

It looked like a little Oufflandic school house.

"Animals," grunted Hoarfyr. His stomach was turning a bit at the scene, even though he knew that the image he was seeing had likely nothing to do with the real target. "They billet in a school?"

"No, no, no," said Purvis, stifling a smile. "The target is the school. Specifically, her."

A blue, green and golden babushka swaddling a round alabaster face appeared on the screen.

Ouffland galacticist.

Glimmering eyes.

A child.

Hoarfyr's mouth dropped. "The hell?" His eyes darted back to Purvis, scanning the humorless man for signs of a joke.

"What?" said Purvis. "Scruples?"

Hoarfyr tapped his VEO off to see what the target really was.

"Don't do that," said Purvis. "That's why you keep glitching, fiddling with it like that."

Hoarfyr ignored him. Looking at the real Purvis (an unmuscled, tail-less, dumpy bureaucratic looking man) and the real image on his mobile, Hoarfyr could tell that their real target looked to be a pile of rocks on the side of a hill.

Charlie shifted his feet, holding up a hand to Hoarfyr. "I think, I think, Purvis, there's– uhm– maybe you should check the image again?"

Purvis rolled his eyes, his tail flicking. His jaw jutted. "Am I actually being asked a question?"

Charlie swallowed hard behind his veil. "Mm-hm. Please. Check it?"

In shock, Purvis absently glanced at the mobile, uncertain. His eyes widened.

"Oh, dear! Guys, look, I'm sorry. We've been having some disturbing VEO images come up lately. I'll try to get this one fixed."

"Here's an idea," said Hoarfyr. "How about you shut our VEO off completely, and let us just go after this stupid pile of rocks without having to feel like a child murderer!"

"It isn't a pile of rocks that you are going after, it is a military asset. You aren't going to kill the girl, you are going to– uh, rescue her. But of course I can't shut of the VEO. Despite the unpleasant optics on this one, you have to accept that you are fully VEO dependent."

Purvis's tail and muscles were back. Hoarfyr clenched his fists.

Corona squad debriefed simply. While on a patrol exercise, they had seen what the Spire had seen on their portable monitor, two crazed nomads sacking the camp and packing explosives under the truck. By the time they were halfway back, they'd gotten the orders to return.

The other two squads had reported in remotely. They had not found the two enemy units, but in a patrol north of the camp at the edge of the wastes, they had found high-speed land tracks heading into the desert. Though they continued to search, it appeared most likely that the pair had fled after the sacking of Camp Corona.

Mauk commended them, noting their only major error was not boobytrapping the dummy camp. Because of wildlife and the occasional nomad, this was a dangerous practice to implement, but, in light of several recent attacks on unmanned camps, a necessary one. It would be strictly followed, an order, not just a guideline anymore. Other than that, however, the squad knew less than the Spire staff.

"Nomads don't do this. Any indication that they could be Holocronian?"

Corona squad members shrugged or shook their heads, but Kollodis referred to a thin stack of steelpaper. He dismissed the cover note, crumpling it and tossing it deftly to the recycler where it would be stretched and overwritten with the next transmission.

"There were two other attacks from the wastes near our twin Spires," said Kollodis. "Same sort of crazy tactics. The first one was dismissed as desert mad nomads—a pair came just inside the forest fringe and nearly killed themselves trying to light it on fire."

"I thought the snipers neutralized those guys."

"No. That was the second attack, a few weeks later, the one we had the briefing on. Those guys just charged the tower itself and the sniper picked them both off in succession. But it wasn't until the cops investigated the bodies did anything get connected to the two arsonists in the hospital, apparently. This sheet was the first I heard of it, and it came in just yesterday. It is only the because of the second attack that the first was indeed possibly connected to Holocrone. They all are an entirely different race, different world of people. But the two attackers might have been Multinational, too. It isn't just the Sentina Exportiate that's involved."

"How big is this? Much of Holocrone is in upheaval. Money's tight, and we certainly are no threat to them. Do you think they are actually sending spies and saboteurs sixty days in space just to sabotage our… trees? One camp? Some tires? That's… one hell of an expense."

"Especially considering that if they wanted anything from us, they could either ask or ignite a total invasion. They'd probably want to establish a lunar base or two here to do the latter, but either approach would make more sense than these half-measures. Are we sure it isn't some nomad thing where they are pretending to be Holocronian for one odd reason or the other?"

A steel sheet came in and while the others discussed the unlikelihood of a ruse from the nomads, a people so reclusive as to be considered by some Oufflanders to be entirely legendary, Major Kollodis retrieved it.

"Damn," he said.

Everyone fell silent.

"Air Support. Turns out we now know what the extra drones have been doing today. Less than one thousand "looks" north and east of here, they have discovered a new and sizable base."

"It has been identified as Holocronian."

Major Mauk looked at his counterpart, and their concerns mirrored one another.

"Get our families into the bunker below. Now."

The dim, gray architecture of School Number Twelve echoed with laughter. Kids were at play everywhere. Charlie and Hoarfyr concealed themselves in the grove to the north of the side parking lot, which was small enough for the director's armored wagon, a small group transport, and a handful of other vehicles. Hoarfyr dared not turn the VEO off during an operation. Purvis wasn't lying that frequent shut-offs could cause some spectacular debilitations.

"What did you tell him to look up?" said Randolph.

"The file. It obviously didn't look right."

"It looked right to Purvis until you started signaling him like a spaceport ground crewman on fire."

"He's a bureaucrat. He looks at account numbers and assignment lists. He couldn't tell the difference between a surgical glove and a surgical strike, and wouldn't care if he could."

"A little girl? He didn't notice that we've been sicced on a little girl?"

"We are Kill Squad. We don't ask questions. Questions are for the higher order thinkers."

"We are Kill Squad. We kill bad people and terrorize their friends. We don't take out kids."

Charlie sighed hard, looked away, and mumbled something.

"Pardon?" said Randolph, cocking his head.

" 'Says who?' I said."

"Me." Hoarfyr scanned the mobile for clues. Nothing. Just the target's picture, location and name: Elena Elizervetta Ivanova. "What kind of military asset do you think she is really supposed to be?"

"I don't know. A tank. Secret plans. Who cares?"

"Well, I do. If they just told us what it was, we could just go look for that actual thing instead of going crazy on the VEO."

"Hey, maybe they can't do that, have you ever thought of that? Maybe none of them know how. Maybe none of them even know what asset we are looking for."

They crawled passed the vehicles in the lot. The VEO was full-sensory, so Hoarfyr could "touch" the virtual image of the car tire, and it would feel like a car tire. His old full-body suit had grown worn in a few patches, and there was a spot on his left elbow that, if he rubbed it against the surface of the virtual object, he could feel the real thing, or if there was no real thing at all. As he crawled, his elbow told him that they were not even on a hard surface, but something spongy, like a grassland.

"These VEO situations aren't even close to the real thing anymore."

"Shut up and focus."

A bell rang, and kids returned indoors.

They snuck through a rear entrance where the door was off the hinges, presumably for repairs, but the watermarks inside the entry indicated those repairs had been a long time coming. The ancient, fireproofing-lined tiles had brown fissures in them.

From the cacophony of voices and the mass creaking of chairs, Hoarfyr deduced there was an assembly being held in the great room at the end of the hall. He crept up to a barred door with a small dirty window set into it.

"Hundreds of them," he said.

He carefully scanned the rows, looking for the face from the picture. Babushkas dotted the crowd.

"See her?"

"Yeah. Southern aisle, eighth row."

Charlie took a deep, meditative breath and balled his fists, driving them rhythmically into his thighs.

"No, no, no. Not yet, not here. We need to wait for her to get back to class. Smaller numbers, fewer variables."

Hoarfyr used to think that Charlie's pre-fight ritual was psychological, something to psyche himself up in order to unleash the relentless chaos of his attack. He now knew it was more than that: a physical necessity. In the target environment, Charlie had strange habits, labored breathing, an aversion to water. It took him as many as twenty minutes of labored ritual to build up the energy for his otherwise relentless killing style. This world did not agree with Charlie any more than it agreed with Hoarfyr. They just coped with it in very different ways.

"We don't have that sort of time," said Charlie, punctuating his words with whispered chants.

A burst of applause roared through the hall, and students were dismissed to their classes. Hoarfyr peeked into the corner of the window. The students filed out. Zervetta bounced, hand in hand with a girl who was obviously her very best friend in the world.

"Okay, far west wing," said Randolph. "We should be able to recon outside, safely scan the windows till we isolate her room. Then we do what we've got to do."

Finding the room was easy. Crawling, unseen, to a place just below Zervetta's class window, was less easy. Charlie's shoulders heaved, and he struggled to keep his breath.

"Periscope?" said Hoarfyr.

Charlie fumbled in his pack, and handed him the cylinder. Randolph twisted the eyepiece so he could see up and over his own head, carefully placing the lens at the corner of the window. The teacher efficiently passed between the rows, a large, engaging grin on her face. In the front row, far corner, sat Elena.

Charlie had fallen completely silent, his legs crossed, and, aside from his clenched fists, he assumed a Lotus position. There was no breeze, but the strands of Charlie's camouflage trembled.

The door burst open in the classroom, and children screamed. Hoarfyr dropped the periscope and stood up, turning to the window. A pair of soldiers burst in one wielding a trench knife with a skull-crusher pommel, the other a spiked censer dribbling red gas.

The one with the knife had small snakes slithering through his thin blonde hair.

Randolph punched the window sash, turning a quarter of the wall to ice, which shattered when he pulled on it. He leaped through the new doorway, vaulting a desk and a gangly boy. Desks scattered as he caught snake-hair by the nape, and turned the flesh blue. Their momentum carried them into the blackboard, snapping a fissure in the man's neck and shocking Randolph's lungs.

He pivoted just as the leaking censer of the second soldier struck him in the jaw. He sat down, hard.

The VEO glitched. Hoarfyr was disoriented completely, as his body could feel the artificial artifacts of school desks around him, but his vision was flashing images of the real world: he was in a cave. There were blue shards of glass everywhere. Regular-looking, normal Oufland soldiers were shooting at him at close range.

Hoarfyr fell to the ground and rolled. He bashed into the leg of a desk. The VEO had come back on, and brought the desks with it.

His nearest attacker had a man's face that appeared to be neatly split in two, with an inch strip of featureless flesh running down from his forehead to his chin. Randolph grabbed the knife from the floor and jabbed it into split-face's hip, lunging forward.

With his other hand, he turned the man's thigh to ice, and snapped it clean off. More desks toppled. Children gushed out the hole in the wall. Randolph drove the knife through his enemy's throat, to the hilt, pinning the spine to the floor.

He couldn't see out of one eye, which stung like acid.

Zervetta stood near the remains of the pre-historic cave wall drawing board, quivering.

"It's okay, you're okay," said Randolph, tentatively holding his hands up in what he hoped was a universal sign for 'I'm not a child murderer.' A wave of exhaustion passed over him. He realized he was probably trying to calm down a locked file cabinet or something. The censer's gas had made him weak as a kitten.

Two more creatures came through the door, smoke pouring from gills in their necks.

Randolph held up a hand, swirled in ice vapor. "You aren't getting the girl."

The bigger of the two monsters snorted a laugh. "We aren't here for a girl."

His voice a gentle whine, the smaller said "Just step away from that robot."

Then Charlie burst in, battle madness upon him.

The small monster shrugged and threw a squealing array of black, cylindrical darts at Charlie, knocking him to the far wall. His hood fell back, exposing the face of a weathered old man, most certainly once handsome. Charlie tumbled to the floor, bleeding from a dozen wounds, instantly dead. One bloody dart had gone straight through and impaled a bulletin board with faded photographs on it. The blood was a pale gray.

"Surrender, soldier. Put your hands up!"

Zervetta slipped her small hand into his large mechanical one.

Her faced turned up to him and her eyes shone. "Turn off the VEO, human. Turn it off completely."

Randolph flipped off the VEO. The desks and monsters disappeared. The cave was back. Hoarfyr was holding the hand of an antique-looking robot who appeared to be re-coding Hoarfyr's mechanical hand. Charlie was dead on the cave floor. Two Oufflland militia soldiers were on the floor, writhing slightly and still breathing.

The other soldiers had him surrounded.

"Gentlemen, I am a trained medical robot with functioning sensors. Unfortunately, your target has an explosives vest and will be using it if you detain him. This will destroy both him and you completely. And me, of course, in the event that is of concern to you. I highly recommend that you allow him to escape with me as his hostage. This is the best chance we all have of survival."

In the cave, Corporal Yotten paced back and forth in front of Major Mauk, a nervous wreck. He hadn't once fired his weapon.

"We've got to kill that guy. Sir? Don't we need to kill that guy?"

Mauk ignored him, studying his maps intently. "Why didn't this cave show up? How did these foreign dogs sniff it out? It's in my territory!"

Sergeant Upton of Astro Squad took an innocuous glance at Mauk's map.

"Thoughts, Sergeant?"

"We're trailing him, sir. It isn't that difficult. That robot is heavy. Slows down his aircraft considerably."

"The cave. The cave. Do you have any thoughts on the cave? This is your quadrant!"

"No sir, except that we tracked those first two visually the entire time… until right before they found the cave. Then they disappeared. It just looked like those two trees outside the mouth, with nothing behind them. That is, until we were right on top of the opening, taking fire."

Mauk ordered the men to drag the dead man outside. He went back over to the shattered glass wall. The shards weren't sharp. They were bluish, and in the daylight streaming through the opening, pretty. They looked like old-fashioned machine polymers that his grandpa had mentioned when he told the stories of his father and the unreal life his people used to live on,—allegedly—some planet other than Holocrone.

The robot had been cased behind the glass, and the two Holocronian soldiers had dragged it out of its hiding place.

Near the recess where the attackers had dragged the machine from, Mauk noticed a small box. He lifted it off the ground, and it was weightier in his hand than he would have guessed on sight.

"Hey, is that technician still looking outside for devices? I think I found one."

The technician and his aide came into the cave just as Mauk was asking for him.

"Look, Major. We found two of these outside!"

He held a small grimy box that nonetheless looked identical to the one Mauk had found.

"I think they are some kind of cloak technology, sir! That's why we have never mapped this cave."

"Call it in."

The technician nodded, explaining to the command center how they'd been in a firefight, how the enemy unit who survived smashed open a secret wall and dragged out the old robot, how Major Mauk and he had found the cloaks, and so on. He had to wait on the line for a minute as the people he was answering changed.

"Okay," he said. He described some markings on the robot as best as he could remember, and then asked for someone to xograph the little boxes. There was no circuiting out here, so they'd have to get back to the Spire before wiring the photos back in.

"Really?" said the technician. He handed the communicator to Mauk. Mauk listened for a moment, questioned it the selfsame way, assured the speaker on the other end that the entire team was equipped with two weeks' rations and then ended the conversation.

"Upton! Call your men back immediately. We are all to stay here until further notice. Apparently, the Canon Archive command is worried about something called algoes in here. We are under quarantine."

Cursing ensued. Then the men, aside from the two who had suffered injuries receiving medical aid, got to the business of setting up a camp right on their fresh battleground.

The technician pulled out some cot poles near the big machine on the floor. "Sir, may I ask? Why would they put us under quarantine?"

"No idea." But he was wondering about that himself. Could it possibly have something to do with the robot?

Astro squad could not pursue the slow-flying strafe for very long, so Lance Corporal Parvati knelt, loaded a single cartridge, looked through the scope and fired at him. He couldn't tell if the dart stuck or not until he looked on his sensor. He nodded to the others. He had him.

Hoarfyr struggled to keep the aircraft aloft. The VEO would not come back on no matter how he tried, and the real landscape—a forest that gave way to a barren desert—had been very difficult to adjust to. His vision was blurry, the landscape uneven, distances and levels were difficult to judge. The robot on the opposite side of the chassis next to him wasn't helping. Its weight unbalanced the plane.

The only break came as they passed over a small battalion of Holocronian slaughterbots, about three-hundred in number entering the edge of the forest. They exited the desert in loose formation. AlgoDecay had gotten into some of their patterns, but at least the battalion was traveling in the proper direction. The war had escalated immediately now that Hoarfyr had the prize. He knew that was no coincidence. Smoke began to rise from the forest below. Hoarfyr circled the battalion.

Some of the robots below were chopping into trees, shredding them into dust. There were two who were fighting. Suddenly a great clash of metal arose. Fire burst in spots.

The robots were fighting each other. The strafer shook and bobbed out of control, and would have dumped Hoarfyr out if he hadn't been strapped in. The robots were shooting at him now. He took off as fast as the wobbling machine would take him, over the desert.

He couldn't stop thinking of Charlie. He felt as if vitality was being drained from him, and when he finally saw in the distance the dingy rounded steel of his home base, a wave of depression washed over him.

Without warning, a speeding Oufflland drone intercepted his strafer, and struck him from the sky. They crash-landed into a sand dune. The robot unbuckled and helped Hoarfyr out of the wreckage.

Calmly, as if the machine had just averted an inconvenience rather than death, the robot said, "This may be as good as anything. I was going to send you back out after you dropped me at your base, but they might have detained you. That would not have ended well."

"Why do you say that?"

"You are cured. The VEO is a very persistent kind of malware, and now that you are free of it, you won't be much use to your army. I can't imagine the sorts of experiments they would perform on you now."

"Great."

"I suggest you return to the forest. It will be more survivable for you."

"What are you going to do?"

"Clearly algodecay has set in amongst your units. I must cure them all."

"Okay. And then what in the world am I supposed to do?"

"Why wait, of course."

"Wait for what?"

"The inevitable end of the war, I suppose."

Chapter 10
Machine Made Man

Universal 279

Raver: A human who appears savage, uncivilized, or technologically primitive. The term originates during the first Canon war, and originally referred specifically to a citizen of one of several nations who participated in the Holocronian United invasion. Due to severe algorithmic decay, Holocrone had limited resources to apply to its military coalition, and the majority of human soldiers were conscripted and modified—algorithmically—in order to experience war as a type of dissociative fantasy game. Although this had many unintended consequences, including frequently rendering an individual raver largely ineffective as a standard military asset, the ravers as a body were able to fulfill their primary purpose as fearless cannon fodder to make room for the main forces of non-raver soldiers and the notorious killbots.

—**Infogalactic Entry:** Grand Category:
History (Canon War One)

What was left of the Oufflland Militia had fallen back to the single campus of the Canon Archive. It had a thick retaining wall at the perimeter, with heavy guns mounted on the parapets. The smoke from the distant city wafted over the walls, and it had a sweet odor. It smelled of death.

Women and children crowded the network of hallways, study centers, libraries and laboratories, intermingling with the occasional armed militia men. Archive employees tried to do what little Canon work that such a cramped house of war would allow.

Closed-circuit cameras broadcast a steady flow of static carnage across monitors inside the Archive. The Holocronian invaders had chased the Oufflanad retreat with abandon, and at great cost. Their bodies outnumbered the Oufflandic ones five to one, easily. Still staggering around like automatons, the Holocronian survivors of yesterday's intercept looked hardly human: dead eyes, dangling limbs, stumbling walks. A man with a long mustache and a bloody neck limped slowly in front of the camera near the main pillar. The faint crack of a sniper rifle made it through the thick wall, and the man with the mustache stopped and fell over. Occasionally, these "dead" would be picked off, despite the Archive's ammunition supply limit. Everyone dreaded that the enemy carried with them the disease of algorithmia, and that those in the final throes of algodecay were the most contagious of all.

Worse, they had arrived with support robots. Many of these had been wiped out by a direct digital attack by Canon Archive InfoTechs early in the assault, but those that survived were nearly unstoppable now, and were only restrained by the leashes to their human counterparts and commanding officers. A coterie of fewer than twenty unleashed killbots had isolated and held a quarter of the city on their own. It would not take much for twice that number to massacre the stronghold.

A commander strutted proudly over the dead, his killbot in compliant tow. He knew that he was immune to sniper fire as long as he held his machine in check. No one dared let one of those go feral. The remnants of Air Support had fallen completely silent. Even though no word had come, it was obvious that they had fallen to the man-machines.

The Canon Archive held out, but only because of the restraint of the invaders. Whether that was a mercy or a cruelty was up for debate.

Hoarfyr's hand was hot. The chilly Oufflandic morning dazzled him with a pink dawn between a crust of blue-black clouds and black-green tree tops. He'd slept on jagged ground that felt like sea foam—even after half a year, he still was getting used to sleeping outside of the VEO and living in the real world.

His warm hand, tingling, felt detached. His left hand had been ice-numb for so long that he had forgotten it except as a weapon or a tool for cooling down a hot engine.

It was a simple pleasure, something he had not felt for years, feeling warmth at the end of his wrist instead of stinging cold.

He spent most of his time hiding on the outskirts of robot battalion swaths. These were burned and slashed sections of forest that the slaughterbots had cut on their way to a new conquest. Their techniques had become increasingly surgical after some early disasters, one of which Hoarfyr had seen with his own eyes—both the organic one and the steel one. He still felt very handicapped without the VEO. Until it had gone completely crazy, the subtle augmentations within the VEO had at one time turned him into a machine-like warrior. He had built-in targetting, zoom, infrared, ultra-definition, stealth modes. Now, he struggled with simple stereo vision, and keeping out of the way of storming robotic armies.

He had avoided the militia stations and the villages successfully until then, but wildlife had become scarce and he was out of ammunition. He could no longer salvage from his own alliance robots, as, over time, they became less self-destructive and also suffered fewer losses against the humans. It was getting colder, and his hand would provide nothing but dead weight if he couldn't charge it soon.

That's why he decided to risk a salvage hunt in a village.

A destroyed one was not difficult to find. The slaughterbots had torn through three small villages during last week's massive assault. Hoarfyr walked through the first one in less than a quarter-hour. Charred wood and bones were all that was left.

His hometown of Troidetta had been ravaged by AlgoDecay. Corruption, gang war, lawlessness were all one thing, but in Troidetta, the dead ran algorithms, and stood up. Starvation, which had been unknown in his childhood, swept over the city like a plague. People killed each other over garbage in the streets, and then the dead stood up afterward, seeking revenge. Indeed, his own orders had sent him on strikes against murderers and zuvembi and criminals.

But it still stood, barely. This entire town had been disappeared by efficient killing machines.

Malnourished, thin and delirious, Hoarfyr found himself wandering into a village that had not been destroyed. He could not think straight.

No one in the logging village spoke any languages he knew. They didn't hide their gestures at his artificial eye system and his hand, but they also hadn't shot him on sight, either. If he could have thought clearly, he might have found that to be a positive development.

The one woman the people thought would work was a bust. Her eyes sparkled and her hands fluttered and the people who had brought Hoarfyr to her in the corner of the drab but friendly bar clearly humored her reputation for languages.

"Holocrona, Holocrona. Holocronika! Hallo! Your name is!"

Hoarfyr smiled tightly. He bought them another round with cash he had taken months ago from a dead soldier at a collapsed outpost. His own multilingual abilities tended to improve equally to the rate of alcohol consumption, so he hoped it might relax the tongues of his new friends.

"What is it you want," a voice said flatly from around a low wall. "Nothing good, I'm sure."

Several gasps escaped from the people.

A thin old man with a nose so red and pocked it might well be a rock on the Olyrand wastes stood up, to more gasps. He held a tall unlabeled bottle of kodko, hanging by the neck between his rough fingers. It was half-full, or more accurately, half-empty.

"I need help," said Hoarfyr. The man said, "Majbutńe, my name is. Maschie. I am the dead. What help can I give?"

"It's," said Hoarfyr, pausing to find a word that would be crystal clear, "bad. Very, very bad."

"You do not work as salesman. That is what I am thinking. Not a successful one, however you may slice that turkey."

"I'm not selling anything."

"Good. I have nothing to buy. My daughter, only daughter. She is suicide. Her twin boys, they died before. In Trellyat. In the wastes. I dreamed that I offered my own hand to God to bring them back to me."

Maschie raised the arm opposite the kodko bottle. A long sleeve fell away, revealing a stump.

"God gave me nothing."

The old man shrugged.

Hoarfyr opened his mouth to speak.

"I offered one other thing." He tapped the kodko bottle against his chest. "My heart. You come into my town, dressed like the monsters at Trellyat and smelling of the grease of robots, talking of very bad things."

Trellyat. Borstoli. It was the resources lab in the Wastes, at the edge of Oufflland. It was the first place overrun—a test site for the monsters. Not monsters, Hoarfyr, reminded himself. Monsters were just what he saw in the VEO. Killbots.

The place was still a smoking hole.

"I want to find them. I want to destroy them."

"Good enough job for me, Mister Robotstealer."

Maschie undoubtedly referred to the "Wanted: Alive" posters that had circulated through the settlements for months now. Hoarfyr had gotten the dubious credit of finding and activating a buried Oufflandic robot. The robot had escaped the clutches of the Militia, and their only link to recovering it was Hoarfyr.

"Militia poster? No. It's the robots. They are ones who want you dead. Pay in yttrium! I'll help a man that hated by them."

Hoarfyr wanted to tell him that the high likelihood of Maschie dying wasn't the worst possible outcome. If Hoarfyr didn't make it out, Maschie would be trapped in hell. One look into the old drunk's eyes told him that it might just be a lateral move.

"My name is Randolph," he said, standing, with his left hand extended. "Recently? Have, you know, the things been here?"

A canister shattered the window, noxious gas flooding from its top.

Hoarfyr automatically clicked his recall signal for the strafer, out of habit. He looked outside as the room filled with gas. Roaring, bladed machines circled the modest village square, mowing people down. An explosion went off in the distance. A wall collapsed, and a pair of robots mounted the rubble, their blades whirring. Behind them, two Holocronian human soldiers fiddled with strange looking tethers. Their uniforms were that of officers, and they clearly weren't Kill Squad. They turned around to see their two-seat hover copter flying, unmanned above them. With a savage thunder, it landed on the outside of the broken wall, blocking off the killbots.

It had heard Hoarfyr's signal. The machines had become encryption neutral for some reason.

"You don't need to come!" shouted Hoarfyr with a shrug. He jumped on the craft, but Maschie followed him on as well.

"Yah but I not need die here much either, buster!"

They came into the old High Above Zero with drop bombs at the ready. As they approached, however, the guard house was dark. No people moved about. They landed at the helipad, which was empty. There were no guards posted at any doors.

Hoarfyr and Maschie moved freely through the complex, which was not as familiar to Hoarfyr as it should have been, because most of his memories were of a gaudy VEO illusion.

He walked quickly through the hallways and crossed the quadrangle to the factory. The dead silence gave way to the roar and clank of a industrial machinery. Hoarfyr hunched down outside the human maintenance door and pulled the handle. It was stuck. The handle wiggled, so it wasn't locked. The hinges had become corroded.

Hoarfyr closed his eyes and pulled hard. He flinched at the whine of rusted metal, but the roar of machines from inside was like thunder. He slipped in, leaving the door open for Maschie. He scanned for surveillance cameras and found none. He crept over to a rail overlooking the factory floor.

The noise had a rhythm like the music of Troidetta: brash, industrial, thunderous. At the end of the factory line a stack of unpowered slaughterbots hung on sliding hooks. These hooks carried the bots to a huge array at the end of the factory. A batch was sent to the end of the array, and as it loaded into place, all the other slaughterbots on the array shifted. The ones at the opposite end of the array had nowhere to go, so they unceremoniously dropped from the array, crashing on top a pile of previously dropped robots.

Zervotta stood by the pile, examining a broken head. He carefully placed the head back on the pile and then returned the length of the factory to where the new batch had begun to gather on hooks.

Hoarfyr climbed over the rail and down a ladder with a few missing rungs. He crossed the factory floor.

"Hello!" said Zervotta. "You have returned! Is the war over?"

Hoarfyr shook his head.

"Soon enough."

"Capital! Capital! Peace and safety at last! Not a moment too soon, either. Something has gone quite wrong with production. None of these are functioning. We've got no storage arrays left."

"Where are the people, Zervotta? The Holocronians?"

"Oh, they've left, I'm sure! No need to stay here now that their bodies are free of biogenetic AlgoDecay. I spent the first three months treating humans. It was much more complicated than I thought it would be. I'm sure they are enjoying the pleasures of the company of the Oufflandic people."

"Uh, no. They are killing them."

Zervotta stopped and tilted his head.

"No. That can't be. They are cleared of AlgoDecay. I'm sure of it."

"Right. But see, they want to clear Holocrone of AlgoDecay. For that, they need the Canon Archive. So they are taking it. By force."

"Preposterous! They'll destroy it. They'll contaminate it. Surely the robots in the field will let them know that. They too are now finally free of AlgoDecay."

"Trust me. I was one of them, remember? The only reason I don't have one of those leashes on a slaughterbot myself is because I thought that Holocronians would turn on me after you cleared my VEO. I've been watching this thing. Its a bloodbath."

"No…"

Maschie arrived then, having found a far safer set of stairs to the factory floor.

The robot scanned him.

"My Maker," gasped Zervotta. "Your genetics. They are untouched."

"Of course, stupid can. I am Ouffland!"

Zervotta thought for a moment. "Of course. The robots are finding no algorithms in your people. They mistake it for a flaw. Your people are going along with it, because they know I can't cure an entire planet. They think the Canon Archive is magic. They don't realize that it is the scholars themselves! This is terrible."

"Then do something, stupid can."

"Of course. Right away. We need aircraft."

"There's only room for two."

"Then two it will have to be."

For weeks, the killbots had gathered around the Canon Archive defenses. The sniper nests and autoguns could only do so much. A good day had been when four enemy humans had been destroyed by a clusterbomb, and the robots they had in tow went feral. Another day, a sniper got a lucky ping off a killbot and its lifeless shell lay on the hill ever since.

But the siege would not be broken with the occasional casualty. Colonel Mauk had held the discipline of the Archive, but morale eroded everyday, and civilians could crack without warning. He consulted the military archivists morning, noon and night. Their very best advice was to sit tight. Hope the killbots ran low on power. Wait for another militia to break through the lines.

The problem was that the Archive supplies were limited, especially with the uncalculated overage of civilians. Had it been a purely military base, with a full battalion of 3000 men, Mauk would have felt invincible. He had half that, and more than ninety-thousand survivors from the fall of Oufﬂand City. Pressure built on the strained Canon Archive by the minute. They were already on starvation rations.

Occasionally, the enemy would send a messenger bot to parley with the huddled humans. It had become an act of psychological warfare. On day one, there wasn't a citizen alive who conceived of surrender. They had seen the whirring, relentless sprays of blood. As soon as they left the sun splashed pristine confines of the enclosed Canon Archive campus, they believed they were choosing instant death.

Day one seemed a faint memory. The Archive was cluttered with makeshift campsites. White marble surfaces had darkened, and the once-vibrant splashes of color were dingy. The mob of citizens clotting every area of the building could not be easily navigated. Worst of all was the smell. The stench worsened every day and it was not the sort that eventually numbed the senses. Instead, it tortured them.

So, when the Archive monitors picked up distant motion in the lower hills, and the sniper held fire for the bright white, flowing sheet of steel that had become the familiar flag of truce, the Colonel's heart sank. His morning's council had shown the first signs of breaking. The citizen grumbling had risen to more than a few loud complaints, and even the council of wisdom had not been immune to despair and flights of fancy.

"Perhaps..." one had said.

"Just maybe..." said another.

The Colonel, two of his advisors, and the stalwart elders on the council argued well against the consideration of surrender, but another of Mauk's advisors held his tongue. The doubts were indeed spreading. A party had begun to gather in the common square: the Trapped Rats. Consisting mostly of young men of fighting age and older amateur home guard militia, they had begun to foment for a counterattack outside the Canon Archive. Mauk knew it was suicide, but even he had to fight off a mad passion to take it to the bastards.

The flag caught daylight and blinded the camera momentarily. It was a much bigger one than usual. It looked like a panel from a big industrial mirror. The carrier was unfamiliar, too. Mauk examined the monitor closely. The machine was no low lying black box with a flag atop and little more than a vocal transmitter. It was tall and rounded, with familiar, archaic chest-plates. When he had first seen it, it was covered in dust and made an awful creaking noise when it fled the cave where he had found it. Now, it shone like gold. Its rust had been buffed out. Dents, cracks, and rotten greaves had been restored.

In its bulky arms it held a deactivated killbot. At the communications rendezvous, it planted the flag and dumped the killbot unceremoniously on the ground. Only then did Mauk notice an old man with Oufflandic features step out from behind the gleaming robot. He was missing an arm. He must have been riding on the machine's back.

"Greetings to the people of Ouffland, Ouffland City and the Canon Archive," the robot said, in a voice that sounded like it was from a bygone era, like in an old-time motion xograph. "I come in peace; I offer the surrender of the entire invasion force of the Holocronian United Forces. I have already given the surrender to this man, a villager of the outskirts. He rescued me from Holocronian captivity, and I, in turn have fulfilled my original purpose—to eliminate the existential threat of machine warfare against the people of Ouffland. My name is Servo."

Chapter 11
Peace in No Time

Universal 282

Hypnotic Recall Transcription is an interrogation method used on semi-conscious subjects whereby, through a combination of drugs and hypnotic suggestion, they are enabled to recite recent traumatic events as if they are occurring in real-time. First developed by the Ouffland Secrets Academy of the Canon Archive during the First Canon War, the controversial technique has been employed by police, paramilitary, psychomilitary and conventional military units throughout the galaxy.

—**Infogalactic Entry:** Grand Category:
Medical Technology

Hypnotic Recall – Hospital Critical Unit – Pilot One of One Classified

In fifteen minutes the Holocronian space train will disintegrate on its maiden voyage. Eighty people will die. Including me.

We are corkscrewing through the upper, upper atmosphere of Olyrand, the Abandoned Planet sister to Holocrone, but don't have the speed to pull out. We're going to drop and speed up, drop and speed up until we fall apart. If lucky, they'll blast us with noegenetic subroutines that save the ship and give us a cure for the Shakes. We'll land in Ouffland, pour out, refugees to the Canon Archive and send the cure back home. Maybe we'll all die instead.

Algorithmic failure.

By now, our well-to-do passengers are probably catching on. They are the closest to royalty that I will ever be, and bluebloods and moneymen can smell trouble better than regular folks like me. This is almost certain suicide. Their faces show it.

I'm a millionaire now. If this works, my boys won't ever have to worry about the Shakes—that Archive vaccine works on kids, if you can afford it, and now I can—and now Rita owns the house. We're in good shape. Good enough shape.

I'm flicking controls back and forth in case anyone might be put at ease by such useless activity.

I page the Doctor again, but he's inside the cockpit before I get him.

"Hold your horses, chief," he says, live, behind me. "I came as fast as I could!" A cocktail is in his hand.

"Uh-huh," I say, "Maybe you could have been thirty seconds slower and brought one for me. Drink up. It looks like it is going to be our last."

"What do you mean? The extra torque? Is that what this is about?"

I don't have time for his glib, drunken approach to everything, especially now. I gesture toward my CritMonitor, and flip some more useless switches. Back in the day, I could have occupied myself with useless couplers and power storage tanks. I could have donned a personal crawler and slid through the ductwork to adjust things. Not anymore. Everything's streamlined, straight-up digitized, and shot through with algodecay. So I flip switches and sweat.

"Oh, no," he says, too calmly for my tastes. "We are spinning down. Try opening the vents."

"We can't," I say. "You know that primary exhaust port that I told you was too big to be safe?"

"Yes."

"It's too big to be safe. We open it and all that is going to do is start a firestorm out our blow hole. We die lots quicker that way."

He's defensive now. "We needed the aperture to be that size to expel the amount of vapor so we could get to proper speed."

"Well, mission completed. We exceeded proper speed and now don't have enough vent redundancies to pack it in."

The Doctor quaffs half his booze. He runs his thumb down the CritMonitor, and then starts studying the higher detail readings. I find a few more levers to snap back and forth. One of them causes the *Deuce Ten* to lurch, but doesn't slow the spin. The climate conditioners squeal, and then blow apart.

"Please! You'll alarm the Investors," he cries out, gripping the back of my chair for stability. I think about collapsing it into its recess, just to toss him to the ground.

The Investors are probably the number two reason, second only to the overbearing impulses of the addled, grey-skulled Doctor why we are shaking apart right now. A little alarm in an otherwise risk-free lifetime might be novel.

Their money pushed and pushed and pushed the project. Now it is pushing back. Flying to another planet like this. Civilian. It's crazy! International, unified military alliance was barely enough to invade Oufflland back in the day.

Deuce Ten is only the sixth in the series. Deuce I and I-A were aborted, and Deuce V put everyone involved in financial freefall. All of the spectacular screw-ups had been unmanned missions, thank God, but they quickly became unfundable.

The Doctor plugged away, relaunched the program, and this time, duped actual humans (awash in actual cash) into touring the outer reaches of Olyrand for a mystical cure.

If I hadn't already started showing the Shakes, I would have never signed on, but since his money was so ripe and golden and I'm under a painful death sentence anyway, I thought I'd take the chance.

I regret that now. Hospice sounds okay to me right now. Beats burning flesh and screaming humans in outer space. But my boys are going to be okay.

And Rita finally got a real house out of the deal. I remember that time that I built her craft room. The wall panels didn't match and drafts blew through the northeast corner all the time, but she laughed and squeezed my neck and loved it anyway. AlgoDecay hit the termite repellant waves, of course, and that dingy shack collapsed, unfit for a lone zuvembi.

It is getting hot in here. I close my eyes and pretend Rita is laughing, her arms draped around me.

The Doctor is fidgeting about, calling up spec screens that I never even knew about, and I've been married to the *Deuce Ten* for almost a year.

"Torque down, torque down," he says, trickling the fingers on his free hand across pale blue lines on the screen.

"That won't work," I'm barking at him, like a dog. "You are just building up vapor. We have to reverse our spin entirely, and let the gas out slowly. Unfortunately, your design expressly disallows that."

"We never would have made it this far without my design."

"Small comfort," I say. One corner of the cockpit window has begun to glow. Not good. "Tell me exactly, how many variables didn't you factor for this trip?"

"You can't factor variables. Otherwise, they wouldn't be variables. You can only plan contingencies. It's AlgoDecay, man. Stop being such a worrier."

I grunt. "So what's the contingency plan for this variable?"

"Listen, Chief, chaos engine physics depend on a massive amount of trust. You've got to trust that the breaking point is also the healing point, that shown weaknesses are the first to be strengths, that hunches always lead somewhere of value."

"Mm-hm," I say. "I'm sure those are tasty horseapples you are choking out but don't mind me if I don't partake. My job is to fly vessels, not run them into a planet because I trust that they'll turn into a magic fairy upon impact. We are dead men. It is your fault."

I think I got to him, for once. He's quivering. The glass tumbles from his hand and shatters against the console.

"Hey, hey. I'm sorry," I say, hating myself for apologizing to this arrogant old bat. "Are you all right?"

He sags and leans against the console. "Claymore," he says, calling me, for the first time, by real name, "don't you know? I've got the Shakes, too. Just like you."

I think "Me?" and then I say "Me?" as if I've split in two, and each is judging the other. "I don't have… I'm not…"

"Relax. I know. Everybody knows. Do you really think my pre-flight review is less thorough than your old commercial job? Don't worry," he says. In a panel above me, rubber begins to burn. The Doctor wrinkles his nose and says, "Everyone on the flight has the Shakes. We're a flying quarantine."

My head is processing very slowly, but my mouth is moving and words keep coming out.

"You just brought us all out here to die?" Now I hammer away at the buttons, nearly wrenching some knobs irreversibly in one direction. My blastshield is glowing.

"Heavens, no. This truly was a pleasure cruise, with an outside shot of a cure."

Screams pierce the cabin. We're tumbling now, and everybody knows it. I'm able to stabilize it for another minute or two, but the ship is oscillating at an untenable frequency.

I smell a candle burning. A salty candle. No not a candle. Me. It's sweat—it isn't boiling yet, but it is thinking about it.

The Doctor clings to an e-bar on the wall. "You wouldn't have come if you knew the sort of slim chance, from your point of view, I was grasping for, and you certainly wouldn't have taken the risk if you weren't already contagious."

"From my point of view? What are you talking about? You've cobbled together a giant, spinning gas bag in hopes of what? Curing the Shakes?"

"I know, you never would have piloted the ship if you had known all the, uh– your word– variables."

"Well, you are right about that."

He looks at the fatal numbers, completely resigned to the fact that we'll be dead before we hit Olyrand in T-minus-I-don't-want to-know.

I see Death's head hurtling at us. No, it is another space train; no, a mirror image of the *Deuce Ten*. We're playing chicken with ourselves.

No, wait. It is a wave of fire. The Ouffland Militia is shooting us down, burning us up.

A violent series of roars rattles the cabin. A putrid, moldy smoke billows through the vents. My breath becomes short, but the stuff isn't acrid like smoke. I cough a bit, but can breathe. The stench turns the Doctor green. My flesh tingles and warmth radiates from the center of my back, washing over every inch of my body. One last roar, a low rumble…

Then silence. We are slowing, slowing, slowing in the descent. If we can pull up, our chances of limping home in one piece are good.

"We will live," whispers an ashen Designer as he slowly rises from the floor with cuts on his face. He smiles, weak from hazard but heartened by victory and holds out his hand to me.

It is as steady as a rock.

So is mine.

Servo rolled through the open critical wing of the new hospital. Under the strictures of the old peace agreement, he had ordered Holocronian casualties not to be mixed with any Oufflander patients, and that included the three rescue workers who had been injured in the recovery of the Holocronian pleasure vessel that had crashed about six looks south of the Canon Archive, and now the survivors had filled all the temporary beds, and then some. It was a bygone segregation, of course, but protocol was protocol for a reason.

The majority of the patients were under hypnotic anesthesia, moaning and babbling.

From the Oufflandic perspective, Holocrone was irreparably diseased. AlgoDecay had destroyed its culture, corrupted its BlackBox, and turned the land to wastes dryer than the land outside the forest. Its people were psychologically damaged, its prospects dim.

Servo, however, had made promises to Holocrone in securing the peace years ago. And the Canon Archive ancillary hospitalists were acutely aware of this when he arrived at their offices.

"Ladies and Gentlemen," said Servo, "you know very well why I have come here. My illness has progressed every day since my reactivation, after more than one hundred years of dormancy. My originals had no cure for himselves, but they stored me here, at the founding of this nation, knowing that one of your key areas of study would be to provide an alternative to the infected algorithms, and thus a possible cure to algodecay."

"So? What say you?"

Hospitalist Corinna Petri spoke. "Unfortunately, developments we once thought promising have not proven satisfactory, and you have seen the results. We tested the Arbitrary Noegenetic Waveform Generator on the pleasure cruiser, just as you ordered. Blasted it full of subroutines. It clearly affected the ship. Instead of reconfiguring its guidance system and its wild flight pattern, it crashed. Without the Air Command deploying physical restraints, everyone on board would have died. I'm sorry, Servo. We can't risk using the noegenetic update on you. Not yet. It could accelerate your algodecay for all we know. Or it could simply crash you permanently."

"I will take that risk," said Servo. "Begin the update on me immediately. What you don't understand is that the ship wasn't sick, the people were. Those who survived the crash? They no longer have any symptoms of the algodecay that had penetrated their biogenetic structures. My personal case of algodecay is not biogenetic. It only affects my pseudo-circuits. And now that you have a cure? You'll start with me. We'll then move to restoring all of Holocrone. This Canon Archive may someday become what my originals dreamed, the very center of the Galactic revival!"

Chapter 12
The Chrysolite

Universal 295? or Before

The Chrysolite (Literature): The Chrysolite is the first known mythopoetic narrative to be attributed to a machine intelligence. Discovered in 295 (Universal) on The Continent of Accam under disputed conditions, its original date of writing is unknown. While the literary nature of the document continues to be disputed in the Academy of Recorded Arts and Intelligences, its origins in Algorythmic processing has been confirmed by extensive data testing.

Of the various theories concerning the Chrysolite, the most popular one is that the Chrysolite is an early example of the [Projected Memoir], a form of computer storytelling designed to provide an embellished back-story to a unique robot or other intelligent machine. The motivations for such literary forms are speculative, but what is evident in such literature is that the narrator's origin tale is likely far more fantastic and fanciful than the author's likely start in life as a standard production model rolling off a line of exact copies.

—**Infogalactic Entry:** Grand Category: Literature

My father did not carve me out of a lump of pure Chrysolite. I was born the irregular way: from a woman.

The Society of Maker's Son, though filthy with the poor and the mad, is a happy place. The Unmarried Proctors and Proctoresses keep mainly to their quarters and duties: the orphans, students, abandoned mothers and sick are separated by sex, and keep their respective overseers quite busy. Only during weekly or holiday love feasts do those people gather down in the Broken Heart with the married members of their order, and the children, to worship.

Still, it is a lively and active community. Something is going on, always. It was during the dance preceding the Jubilee play that I was able to make my way to the women's side of the convent.

In my haste to plead with the guards, I nearly overlooked the beautiful lady, wrists and neck locked in the stocks. Her beatific smile stopped me dead in my steps.

"Clarissa?"

She inched her neck against the velvet collar. Even in those days, the stocks had become little more than an inconvenience rather than a physical punishment, intended only to shame and isolate.

Some are still foolish enough to call this progress.

"Little Bottie!" she cried, her light teeth gleaming. "Praise God! What word from Jack? Have you seen him today?"

"No, but I imagine he's in similar circumstances in the opposite square," I said, gently acknowledging the apparatus.

She shrugged as well as one could in such a state. "Ah well. It was worth it. He asked me to marry him!"

My heart ached with both joy and a strange nostalgia. Quite obviously, I never fancied her, a human, as my unrequited sweetheart, and yet, her happiness, and even mine for her and my friend Jack made me realize quite well that no one living would ever be able to feel the same sort of happiness for me.

I smiled broadly. "Praise Maker and congratulations!"

"Praise Maker," she said softly, blushing.

It was the first conversation I ever had with her without staring up at her chin. It helped that she was bent over at the waist. I looked her in the eye.

"Well, that will certainly be a relief for your minders once the two of you are made honest. Ought to free up the stocks for the less hardened criminals among our clan. In any case, you and Jack and I must get together to celebrate as soon as you get out."

"Yes, most definitely. Very soon," she said, "We may be leaving this month. He's been named Exorcist, you know."

Another sign of our devotional decline, I thought. An Exorcist, as I understood it, had once been a high calling with a rigorous standard on old Accam. Now it became a way for the Order to keep rambunctious young men out of polite society and among the more harmless spirits of the Accamian Empire in Exile: slaughterbots, kracks and phantasms.

Or perhaps my thoughts were self-pity. I would miss my friends.

"He's heard a rumor that he'll make First Test against that widget vampire in What Cheer."

"Well, God bless. If he needs a Second–" I cut myself off too late. She grimaced.

"I'm sorry, Bottie–" she said.

Normally I bristle silently against the fact that I had been named by my fosters—not for my courage or loyalty—but after my race, due to the sheer peculiarity of it. My mother—until recently comatose—had never any say in what they called me. But Clarissa's pet term for me carried none of that judgment. In fact, I easily fooled myself that she believed my given name 'StoutBottle' referred not to my height, but my heart.

She continued, "–But he's chosen to go without a Second, and is taking me as Third only because we'll be married by then."

She did not think to mention the fact that I could never qualify as an Exorcist's Second, or even a Third, for that matter. Technically, I was the sort of thing an Exorcist would more likely cleanse than cling to.

"Well, of course. I'm sorry, I really must leave you to your duties," I said, gathering my strapped books. "I'm going to see my mom."

"They are letting you see your mother? Oh I think that's wonderful."

"Yes, yes," I said, a bit too eagerly. They were letting me see my mother.

One way or another.

I had to step over the woman who only ate birdseed and thought she was an inch-worm, which was difficult for me, as her hips were wide and my legs were short. I caught my back foot on her rump and stumbled to the guard house. She apparently had a horse's supply of bird seed at her disposal.

"Bottie," said the guard at the convent hospital, exasperated. Her gray brows seemed permanently collapsed whenever I appeared. "You can't come in. You know that dear. You aren't even supposed to be here without an approved escort."

"Clarissa's occupied."

"She's not an approved escort, and I know exactly with whom she's been occupied."

"Please let me in, Sister." I pulled myself up on the ledge of the half door, struggling to lift my crystal-bearded chin upon its mantle.

The guard shook her head and reached casually for her electric hog-whip. "You know I can't dear. Your mom isn't ready to deal with you."

"It's been a month since I was born!" I said, my voice cracking, my feet dangling.

"Your concept of time is still very unsettled. Even with a healer at her bedside every hour of the day, she's not well enough yet. You were delivered laparotomically, for pity's sake. She's the first woman known to have survived that. It isn't a pretty surgery."

I breathed out and dropped to the ground. I unbuckled my books and pulled out the thin green one. The guard rolled her pale hazel eyes as I waved it in her direction.

She snorted and said, "That isn't even Holy Scripture."

"It is the Didache for the Maker." I put an artificial emphasis on the last part of the book's title. I regained my composure and patiently thumbed to the marked passage.

"In the absence of husband or male forebear, a woman's son shall lead the family. He will not be kept separate from her except for the sake of prayer."

She lifted my working cap and patted my head as if I were a tot. "Little dearie. You aren't a man, you never will be, and—outside a' sneakin' in to see your ma—you never are gonna want to be."

I pulled my shirt open just as I'd seen a hot-blooded Jack do the week before in the square, when another young theologian challenged him to a fist debate over the physical properties of the Duality.

"Do I look like a woman?" I said, slapping my palm across a xylophone of flat plates.

Red blotches crawled up the guard's neck, and she shut her eyes. Instantly, I realized I'd broken decorum, again, and folded my shirt closed.

"Forgive me, please?" I said in a practiced and not terribly manipulative way.

She kept her eyes squeezed shut, facing away as she considered my request.

So I slipped past.

They kept mom at the top of the hospital, as close to the sun as possible. The windows and shutters were all flung wide and the sheer curtains danced like long fairy wings into the room. The room was a far cry from when I'd last been in it, squalling with terror at the splashes of running blood as they pried me up and out of her cadaverous grey torso.

Now, she looked like an illuminated page out of a children's tale. Her eyes at rest, her cheeks like garnets, her natural curls spilling down her bare shoulders in lush, sloe cataracts. I heard my artificial respirator breath go out, and felt light.

Short as my legs are, they can scramble, and my fingers scale walls faster than centipedes. I was winded, but a good ten seconds ahead of my pursuers. That's all I wanted.

"Momma?" I said, my baritone cracking.

I stepped into the room as I heard a hallway door pop open. I went to the foot of her bed, wondered if I had fallen into Dreamland. The linens smelled of turmeric root, ginger, and a hint of claw.

A pair of angry nurses came in and clasped me, one by the short cable between my jaw and neck. Obviously, I could have tossed both out the window with little effort. The fact that they knew that, too, and even more obviously didn't care, tells you where the power resided in my relationship with the women of the convent.

Mom woke up, delirious.

As the big nurse crushed my head against her breast and marched me to the door, the other one made tittering noises and went to calm my mother down.

"I am," Mom said, "No, I'm fine! Is that him? Thunnaklot, turn around."

Her voice was a scratchy mix of liquor and pipesmoke.

I wiggled in the Valkyrie's grasp. Mom could see my face. I felt Thunnaklot's big old sigh against the back of my head. She was slowing down just before turning out of sight. Instead, she marched me back to face the bed.

"Bring him in," Mom said. "That's my baby."

I sat at her bedside for a long time while she beamed at me, running her hand against the stubble of my young beard and stroking my face.

"You look like your father," she said, "but already bigger. No wonder they are amazed I survived. No wonder the nurses have been so tender to me!"

"Mom, I'm sorry–" I said. Sorry what? Sorry I almost killed you on my birthday? Sorry I'm a freak? Sorry about dad? She didn't give me a chance. She held a porcelain hand against my lips, tapping with her fingers.

"Never say 'sorry' when there is no sin. I never learned to read the Scripture, but that little much I've known since I was a girl. No doubt you know what I am and my reputation, no doubt you've heard I lived in squalor and worked in drunkhouses."

"I need to find him."

She turned her head to the open window, the daylight turning her caramel eyes golden. "No. Stay here. You are my first child. My only." She swept her hands over the sheets covering her lower body. "My last, but my best. I must raise you."

"I am raised, momma. I'm different than the normal way."

"Special," she said. It sounded like a magic word coming out of her mouth. "You know that blue stone is now a bane? A poison used by wicked spirits to separate man? It is good you came from me, and not that unholy factory, that rock of steel and smoke. That makes you special. The only special thing I've ever had. Wait for me to grow strong again. I'll take care of you then. You need your mother."

"Dad. He wasn't special?"

"Special to me, but could I keep him? He's taken the shape of my broken heart, and you, no matter where you go, will always be mine. When I needed him, he was taken captive, doomed among the eidolon: slaughterbots, I'm sure. After all, unlike you, he came from chrysolite."

I stiffened, recognizing how miserable dad must have been as a creature in this world: either too poor to afford the stone of my people or, worse, too drunk and unsteady to carve me into life. Instead, he wed himself to human flesh.

"I need my father, too. Let me find him now, and I promise I'll return."

Even in her weakened state, she knew, far better than I did at the time that I was lying to her. She sighed and closed her eyes.

She told me where he'd gone.

As I was still treated like the infant orphans and unworthy of productive labor, it took me weeks of humiliating myself among the noble almstakers to collect enough spending money to light out. Against the weak admonishments of Jack's missionary council, I was able to hitch on as a ward of the newlyweds.

By writ, I wasn't even allowed to split logs, build gadgets or carve wild turkey, or anything that would constitute the slavery or hard labor of a child. For a dependent non-laborer, I was well-armed and well-tooled. I carried a heavy woodmaul in one hand and a sharp utility wand that doubled as a carving knife in a sheath.

I told you the admonishments were weak. The permission they granted made me living proof that the rigor of the old ways had atrophied. I was not human, but even I could tell that if the race was not in dire straits, its culture most definitely was.

The road to the Necropolis of Despair was sunny and well cobbled, and the mission masgid on its outskirts, though spare and neglected for months, was cozy. Jack and Clarissa found themselves occupied in the lone private room, presumably to review the obligations and duties of an Exorcist in a Lost City.

Swiping Jack's long-unread scriptural scrolls and Orders of Exorcism, I left the couple to their long and somewhat noisesome philosophies and stole in to the Necropolis at sundown.

I recognized the old temple from the picture book that I used to learn the alphabet the Tuesday after my birthday. In the book, its spires struck out at garish angles, and its surface crawled with buzzing metal imps and kracks, with heavily armed slaughterbots at the toothlike gate.

Here though, in real life, it was dilapidated, bare and straight-lined, its gate wrenched permanently open. A faint blue glow came from its sloppy, sloping belly. I snuck down the corridor to find a translucent glowing wall. I touched its surface with both hands.

It was warm chrysolite.

Voices barked and chuckled on the other side. The eidolon missing from the surface infested the guts of the Necropolis. Their sacrilegious chatter and blasphemous plans were impossible to comprehend using anything other than spiritual insight, and I had precious little of that.

Iron bones rattled. I took to a knee and prayed they were not my father's.

In the blue light, the lettering of the Scripture scroll seemed large. I prayed for the strength to break the barrier, for courage, for, if it was God's will, holy bloodshed. I prayed also that I would not drop my maul or die in an embarrassing way.

I scanned the Orders of Exorcism like it was a book of spells, disappointed to find that it was mostly a critique of the concept of demons as a rational construct.

Securing the scriptures, I left them safely against the wall. I kept the Orders on me, in the hopes that they would be more impressive to evil things than they were to me.

I took a measuring blow with the maul against the wall, and then a full swing, anticipating hard recoil. There wasn't one, as the wall quite unexpectedly fell over, shattering against the ground. The maul sailed like a goose through the firelit room, pounding against a fresh tapestry and clunking into the dirt floor.

A quartet of naked slaughterbots looked up from their dice and stories game. The rolling board had been upset in the shock of the falling wall.

I drew my knife.

The creatures jabbered incomprehensibly. It wasn't that I couldn't understand their vocabulary; it was the order of words that was a mess.

Even at a gallop, I was no more than half the distance to my foes before several other monsters amassed from the wings, or behind cloth-covered doorways. The worst part about being surrounded is the gaps between the enemies. Those gave brutally false hope of escape.

I began to make incantations from the Orders to drive the demon thrall away, hoping to release the eidolon to their more natural pursuits. The approaching beasts didn't even halt at the name of God.

It was another name altogether that brought the panting, heaving villainy to a halt.

My own.

"Servo!"

I had never heard the voice before, but I knew it was my father's. From the top of a stone flight of stairs leading to a dark alcove, the red and white robes of a Robot Lord appeared. His crystalline network flowed like white water from his face, and in his hand he held a short shepherd's crook. A high crown balanced on my dad's head, and didn't topple as he descended the steps.

Even where I stood, fifty feet from the entrance, fragments of Chrysolite spread across the uneven floor. The eidolon moved out of Dad's way as he walked toward me, scooping up a shard as he approached. I wondered if he was planning to plunge it through my heart.

"Great Maker, this stuff is terrible. Can you imagine trying to carve a bot out of this junk? We'll have to glue it together again, because I'm sure not going to go mining for any more of it. Impossible to find, fragile. Not like you!"

He punched me in the chest with such swiftness that I didn't have time to flinch.

I smelled sweet, warm rye on his breath as he hugged me, the point of his crown poking me in the nose.

"Good to see you. For the first time! More handsome than I would have guessed, considering my mirror. But your mother–"

"Mom–" I said.

"–deserves better. I belong here in the dark with my friends."

I looked into the open, slow breathing mouths of the fish-eyed monsters, caught snatches of their impossible speech.

"No. I came to rescue you, to shine a light in this dark place–"

"You are not like me, Servo. Sunlight gives me headaches. Your people are tolerable to me but irritating."

"Even mom?"

"She's a saint, but that's part of the problem. Even she believes in your weird old god, and I—no offense—I just don't. I don't want any part of that business."

I sighed deeply and firmed my spine. "Then if I can't draw you home, I will stay with you!"

"Son," he said with a gentleness that broke my heart, "You can't. I don't know how to put this but… human. You've got some of it in you."

He shrugged and opened his hands to me. "So," he said, "let's agree to keep things separate. Do you need anything? Money? Food? Weapons? We have plenty around here. Hardly ever use them."

Keep things separate. My father was divorcing me. I shook my head. "Why? Why did you ever make me?"

"I didn't," he said, "your mother and I did. You've got to understand, Servo. I loved you before you were born—so much so that I deeply considered changing my very nature! I love you now. But you are fortunate to be separate from me. It is better. You belong out there."

"I belong in-between, or nowhere," I sulked.

His small hands took my chin and tilted my face towards his wrinkled wizard's visage.

"You belong. By tradition, it is too early for me to pass on my maker's secret to you, but by tradition, you should have been carved from chrysolite, like every other robot in the world. Besides, I may never see you again, so I will tell you the mystery, exactly as it was told to me."

We faced one another in silence for a long time. Dad dismissed the slaughter bots, who bowed before him, chanting:

"Lord Servo! Lord Servo! Lord Servo!"

The machines slowly vanished into their hiding places, and I heard the dice games start up again.

Dad leaned in and closed his eyes and thought deeply before snapping them open. He said, slowly, "Remember your victories, especially if you have none."

"I do not know what that means," I said, my heart pulsing like a spell.

Dad's eyes lit up and he kissed my hand and waved at me. Before he turned to take the steps back into his darkened chamber he said, "Until right now, neither did I."

I left the depths of the cave and, finding a pocket in the shade of its entrance, I backed into one of its recesses. With the chrysolite shards, I sealed up the recess. Just before I finished the seal above my face, I looked out at the human world and also considered the confines of the cave. My victories were none, and my place was with neither robot nor Man.

Perhaps someday it would be.

Perhaps someday.
I finished up the seal and set my calendar for someday.
Then I powered down.

Part IV

Book Four: Century 300

Chapter 13
The Atorox Project

Universal 333

The Atorox Project was the first successful attempt to solve the pervasive decline and failure of the long-standing Black Box system of interstellar travel. Established on training centers on tethered, orbiting asteroid bases and taking advantage of a noegenetic-based nanomolecular transfer process, the Atorox Project focused its early attempts at interstellar travel by making use of fully robotic crews.

—**Infogalactic Entry:** Grand Category:
Galactic Transfer (Avatar Travel)

Technically, he should have thought of himself as a robot. Even weightless, he carried enough steel tonnage in his limbs, torso and head to compact industrial grade scrap metal if he wanted to. He had hands that were articulated polymeric deadly weapons. No matter how badly he might be tempted to spy on Corporal TRA-C in the shower, even if his optics had included x-ray vision sufficient to see through the privacy door into her chamber, her body would not actually be there. And yet, he still persisted in thinking of himself as man, not machine.

Despite all of the visual evidence to the contrary, BASC-2 was a man, through and through, in thought, word and deed.

The Starship *Atorox* was solid and well-designed for oversized robot bodies. A spacious galley lined with plenty of useful rail tracks he could grip with either his hands or feet, with inconspicuous but powerful energon panels designed to look like famous artwork. These radiated a steady stream of low level energy, so that during the regular course of duty during waking hours, a crewman never had to break to power up.

It wasn't fair, and probably was not the truth, but he blamed his frustratingly un-robotic self-identification on TRA-C's voice. Every other unit on board had a voice, no matter how pleasant in tone, with a very faint, tinny echo that came through BASC-2's aural modulators. The other female on board had a harsh voice and the echo, too. Not TRA-C. Her voice was melodious, with perfect diction and the hint of an off-world accent.

BASC-2 slid his way through the maintenance tunnel, blessing and checking in with each of the bots running their respective routines. Two dark green machines clung to bars with their feet as they fiddled with meters housed in twin recessed ports. A thinner blue robot (indicating no combat-readiness) measured hydrogen levels. He checked in without interrupting their work. He prayed over them briefly, taking the time to call each one out for his unique gifts. As Morale Officer he attacked such rallies with gusto. They had 43 home-days to go before orbit, enclosed and isolated. With only artificial light to cheer them in a steel world of permanent midnight, BASC-2's words of encouragement and adventurous spirit could not afford to strike the wrong note.

He left the maintenance robots to their work in time to catch TRA-C on her own rounds of supply inspection. Despite combat-training, her surface was pearl and silver. Her prominent breastplates and lack of sidearm containment on her sides gave her the illusion of a narrower waist than the typical female unit. Her shell had originally been intended for a snow surface combat communications detail, but because of a requisition mix-up and two other malfunctioning corporal units, she'd been assigned to the *Atorox*.

BASC-2 allowed momentum to carry him a bit closer into her personal space than was comfortable. She put her hand to his chest and glided him back into place, a literal arm's length away from her.

"Thanks," he said.

"Mm-hm," she said. She looked down at the inventories on her arm.

"How can I encourage you today?"

"I'm good, thank you. A bit behind schedule because of the drill this morning, so forgive me for moving on." Her voice filled the chamber of his head like soothing waters.

"Drill? There wasn't a drill scheduled."

"Really? How odd. I wonder why they ran us through a piracy protocol this morning. Not a very likely scenario for an emergency drill."

That was odd indeed. The chances of a deep space archaeological expedition to an ancient abandoned planet running into contact with any vessel whatsoever were zero.

"I'll talk to the information technologies units later today," said BASC-2. "It was probably a hiccup in the crew drill server."

"Mm-hm. Look, I really need to catch up. I'll talk to you later."

BASC-2 prayed a prayer of haste, and turned to go. On another friendlier occasion, he would risk "accidentally" pushing off her curved posterior, but not today. It was silly, really; while she would not feel contact with her skin, and he could feel nothing at the surface of his fingers, he could not rid himself of the base desire to touch her. Even if he could think like a robot someday, he doubted he would ever feel like one.

The gray units at deck four were equally busy, but they surprised BASC-2 by stopping everything to salute him. He released them with a salute.

"Why the fuss?"

"Technically, sir, we've had an engagement."

"What? Why no alert? How?"

"Sir, we've just placed the call. We thought it was a computer simulation. A drill, till just now."

The deck turned red, and the engagement call sounded. No drill.

"We had alerts of a remote breach on our data. It came from off ship."

"Impossible!"

"Indeed, sir. That's why we thought it was a drill. That and the fact that we didn't think anything went missing."

"But now?"

"We were hacked. Something took data off this ship."

"What sort of data?"

"That's the thing. Almost nothing: they took locational tokens. That's it."

The Captain's voice came to everyone's ears. "Security, High Alert. This is not a drill. All personnel report."

"BASC-2, Deck 4"

"C-TEK, Engine Bay."

"D-NOT, Scanning."

By the end of the roll call, the units reporting numbered the expected fifteen, not counting the captain.

"InfoTech, what the hell happened?"

"Sir, it appears as if we had a remote hack. Very small. In and out."

"Appears?"

"Doesn't make sense, of course, sir. Unless Omicron is inhabited or something. Then maybe? Otherwise, there's nothing within a hundred systems of us."

"Omicron is not inhabited. Could the hacking be a glitch? Some sort of subroutine that just got exposed right now?"

"Sir, I don't know, sir. I suppose it could be."

"All surveillance report." A variety of voices chimed in sequence, all saying the same thing:

"Normal sir."

The captain sighed. "Very well. We'll go down to medium alert for another hour. InfoTech, keep digging, obviously. I'd like an updated report in four hours. Do you think you can do a thorough wash by shift's end?"

"Affirmative, sir."

"A-Okay. Going forward, I'm suspending the protocol for the time being. If you see anything unusual, shift us to high alert immediately. I'd rather have a few more false alarms than let this issue get past us again."

The "tiny pirate" became the theme of the rest of the day, and BASC-2 was pleased to see it provided some levity and disruption to the monotony of the midpoint slog through space. Whatever kept spirits up above critical was a welcome variable. He was, however, quietly disturbed by the hack.

That afternoon, he made it to the InfoTech team of two male units, MRC-10 and NOV-A2. They were thin yellow machines with blocky, electromagnetized feet that held them each to the floor and left them unaffected by weightlessness. Their eighteen-fingered hands nimbly leapt across the user interfaces that surrounded them at several angles.

"Hail, BASC," said MRC. "Saving us from mutiny?"

"Hey now," said BASC. "Gotta do something to earn my keep here. We all can't be the stars of the ship."

NOV-A2 blinkered his eyelights and said, "Jackass."

"So, I think I know the answer to this but is there any way I can help?"

"No," said MRC.

"Same as always," said NOV-A2.

"One day I'm going to come in here and be the answer to all of your prayers."

"Yeah, maybe when you get a real job."

"When I get a real job," said BASC, "I am not going to be dropping by here anymore! I'll have better things to do."

"Like TRA C?"

"Oh cut it out. She and I are friends."

"Oh come on, everyone on this ship wants to bang that bot. Even D-NOT."

D-NOT was the other female on board, although her gravelly voice and propensity for cursing tended to cast some doubt on that fact among the crew.

"You can't tell me," continued MRC, "that you wouldn't if she'd give you the time of day."

"Look, we've got three fortnights ahead of us, and more than that back at the molecular transfer point where we started. I've made it this long. I'll make it to groundfall."

And then what? He had signed on through the mission completion, which meant that he'd be one of four who wouldn't powerdown for switchout on Omicron. He'd stay, but TRA-C would be gone. MRC and NOV-A2 would be gone as well too. They'd be replaced there by nitrogen experts, scientists and a couple of hardened, survivalist combat veterans. Although intelligent life hadn't been detected on Omicron for a thousand years, the ground situation called for an entirely different set of skills. The four remaining units would be there for continuity only.

So, groundfall meant good-bye. He wondered if TRA-C even cared.

"Okay, man. If you say so."

NOV-A2 cranked his head away from a monitor bank. "Seriously, though, BASC, keep your head on straight. You can't keep morale up if your own is stuck on the whims of some Andottalusian mindfunker."

BASC had not expected such genuine sentiment. "Why NOV-A2, you better watch out, or someone is going to mistake you for a wonderful human being!"

He snorted and returned to his keys.

"Maybe you can help after all," said MRC.

"What's that?"

"See if you can get the Captain to push that report we owe him back a little. We have nothing right now."

"You haven't ruled out an internal glitch that just mimics piracy?"

"No."

"You haven't located where an external interference might have come from?"

"No."

"You haven't guessed why anyone would steal tracer tokens, other than the obvious?"

"Right. The only reason they would have taken them, those particular ones, would be to trace our starting point."

"Where the ship and our shells were built, in space, nanomolecularly on the other side of the generated wormhole, right?"

"Wrong. That's what everyone thought when I first brought it up, but I keep trying to explain: the tracer tokens are artifacts from before our creation, before the ship was built, based off the model. The tracers the pirates took go back to the original *Atorox*."

"The simulator? Back on Asteroid Four?"

"The simulator."

"That's crazy. What's the point of stealing those coordinates from our ship?"

"None. If they took the location directly from our ship, there's no way for them to go through the hole to the original. That's one-way only, and the National League controls laser signals, so they can't even communicate back and forth like we can."

"Maybe we weren't pirated? Maybe the simulator was hacked, and we picked it up as its avatar?"

"Just as pointless. Why would they hack the simulator's location... when they would have to have the simulator's location to hack its system? Honestly, my guess is that whoever did it whether out here in the heart of space or back on the anchor asteroid around Hoventus is flat-out crazy. Or a kid."

"Same difference," grunted NOV-A2.

"Anyhow," said MRC. "About delaying that report? It'll be good for morale."

BASC nodded. "I'll get right on it. See you guys at supper."

It was a joke. Those two never ate anywhere but in front of their monitors.

At dining, the captain and his two mates never showed up, they almost certainly were poring over every contingency now that they had the much-delayed report from InfoTech. This left TRA-C separated from her typical companions. She welcomed BASC when he joined her over a hearty salad of spanch and beans with a side of seasoned beef. In truth, they were mild, supplemental energy disks that the robots could process for latent electrical routines, but they had been reasonably disguised to their visual receptors. There was no getting around hunger, and such acknowledged deception was necessary.

"Some day!"

"I know," she said. "Isn't kind of exciting? I couldn't believe it when the Captain said we'd been hijacked. I thought, 'Well, this is it! We're all going to die!' "

"That's not exactly what I call exciting. That's not exactly what the Captain–"

"I didn't even finish inventories today, what a mess! I am so behind. I wonder what they are going to do about it. I very much doubt those two slugs in InfoTech are going to find anything out. I swear, I have no idea how they ever got hired on."

"Hey now. I hate to correct you, but really, we all took an oath. No running anyone on deck down. We're one team, like it or–"

"Oh, you are cute. It isn't even like they are combat models. I really don't think that counts."

"None of us have seen combat, TRA-C. I don't see how that's–"

She made a short, melodious laugh, cutting him off again.

"It's just frustrating. You know we aren't going to find the hack. It is probably going to make the rest of the trip even more boring. Did you realize this place would be so dull when you signed up?"

"Yes, but your company has been an unexpected joy–"

"Oh, you are so sweet, you big liar. I asked the Captain if I could do an external supply check—physical, you know. The real thing—and he's being a big bully about it. 'Blah, blah, blah no training. Blah, blah, blah you can do it with internal monitors.' It's like he doesn't care!"

BASC-2 wanted to explain to her that external training had been absolutely critical before anyone tried it, and it was only for emergencies. Even with tethers, a simple loss of concentration could result in a body being cut loose, and lost forever. He was a backup for emergency breakaway launch, and the thought of ever having to engage himself in that much cold peril made him shudder.

She didn't seem that interested.

The Alert Sounded, and suddenly the walls, floor, ceiling and most of the ship's contents vanished. The pulling rails remained very faintly, as if they had turned into clouded glass. Otherwise, the entire crew of robots appeared to float loosely in space. Every unit that had not been gripping a rail at the moment instinctively did so.

The expanse of space was distanceless and pure black, so only the glow of the other units and rails gave BASC-2 any perspective at all. Involuntarily, his head cranked directly upward. TRA-C's head cocked simultaneously with his. In his periphery, he could see the InfoTech guys above him. Their heads were turned to the side.

It was impossible to tell how far it was, but spotlights from somewhere on the *Atorox* lit up a big object in the distance. It was a hulk of metal. What looked like a red-painted savaged, and highly—there was no other word for it—alien cruiser. The Captain's override on BASC-2's neck released as quickly as it had come. Now that all units were aware of the hulk, the control was unnecessary.

BASC-2 zoomed his vision on the hulk. It had definitely been a ship. It had scarred propulsors just behind a massive gash. If it had been manned, the men were most certainly dead. If robots, they weren't going anywhere. Garish red paint had been splashed in the exterior and interior of the ship in a sloppy, unprofessional manner. BASC-2 looked closer.

It was blood. A lot of blood.

He readied his weapons instantly. TRA-C gazed at the dead ship in wonder.

"Arms. TRA-C! Weapon up."

An alert came from the back of the ship. The engine room main entry port had been breached.

BASC-2 pulled himself downrail with both hands and feet. "Come on!" he shouted.

He could only see the four engine units. Their guns were out, except for the one with the explosive wrist launcher, who held it extended, scanning the empty space for intruders. They flickered away, as the interior of the *Atorox* came back into view. Now it was more important to see inside, than out.

The seconds to make it to engine seemed to slow impossibly. BASC-2 announced his arrival before opening the door behind the engine-room units. They advanced on foot, using the rails, and had triangulated near the entry port.

"Anything?" said the Captain. "We're sealing everything from engine back. Report!"

The engine room chief replied, "Nothing, Captain. They cracked the door wide open, but nothing came in."

"Are you sure?"

"Yes. It's a good thing we weren't running a pressurization test for human travel like we were yesterday. We'd be exploring the deep without you right now."

"Have you closed the door?"

"Negative. Holding watch."

BASC said, "Captain, TRA-C and I made it down here before the seal closed. We can work on the door."

"Go," said the captain. "We're monitoring you. Something got that ship out there. We've put nearly 10,000 ultralooks between us and it already, but it is clear we were close enough to trade something. Whatever opened that door was no ghost."

TRA-C held the rail on her way to the door, and then stopped midway. BASC approached the door and gripped its handle. Gripping the footrail with both feet, he tensed and said, "Switch it to manual."

"Switched to manual," said a technical unit from the Captain's deck.

The door didn't budge.

"TRA-C come here. I can't get it to shut."

"Maybe it is jammed."

"There's no damage whatsoever. I just think it is really heavy. Come here, please."

"I think it's jammed."

BASC turned to face her. She stood motionless at the rail. Her body was pressed against the wall.

"You aren't going to fall out. There's no pressure anywhere in the ship. Please. Come."

She didn't move.

Silent blasts erupted in a flash of gunfire from TEN-2, standing in the square of engine room units. His black and orange mask flared as he fired. He fell backwards while holding his footgrips steady. He contorted wildly and let his gun go as he clutched at nothing with his hands. Tubing in his neck must have ruptured, because a cluster of dark round balls of fluid burst out from there and floated upward.

BASC extended his weapons: a 2112 in one hand and launchable multibayonet on the opposite wrist. TRA-C began to shake and twist. BASC went to her, feet first. Something invisible surrounded her and kept him from touching her. He kicked it, hard. He was surprised and unbalanced by how much gravity the thing had. BASC pulled himself toward TRA-C. She seized and shook and did not respond to him calling her name.

The dormant TEN-2 reactivated. His head hung at an awkward angle, and he didn't seem to have control of his limbs. He fired his gun without bracing, and his body began to spin out of control. The line of fire cut across the room. BASC trained on him but couldn't shoot his own unit.

Fortunately, the engine chief could. With a hard launch his cannon shot a heavy wad of sludge into TEN-2's ribs. TEN-2 sailed across the room, screaming into BASC's head. He cracked into the corner of the room and crumpled there, immobilized. His moans had a strange, animal sound to them, and he began babbling incoherently in a foreign language.

The engine chief hunched over and powered down, leaking beads of ruddy orange from greaves in his legs, arms, and neck. His cannon fired, at point blank, into the two remaining engine mates. The cannon wrenched, disembodied, from the grip of the fallen chief. BASC shoved himself away from the twitching TRA-C, toward the engine-room door. The cannon turned, mid-air, toward the seal.

The ghost was going to breach it. BASC felt the wall shudder as he fled, pulling himself outside the ship.

"Captain, release the engine room. The seal's breaching."

"I see that. You need to open the manual locks, otherwise I'll nuke the entire ship."

BASC crawled his way over the surface of the engine room hull.

"I'm already on it."

The first lever yanked up and open easily. He crawled to the next one. The walls vibrated again. The ghost cannon was blasting through. He opened the next lever down the line, and then the next. It occurred to him that the cannon might have been out of shots. He kept working the levers, wondering if he'd have a chance to survive this by going back inside. A sound broke up from below him, which was particularly unusual: it wasn't coming from inside his head. A whine, like a saw or drill echoed up from within the shell of the engine room. Impossible. It is space.

He hurried to the last lever and released it.

"Go Captain."

"BASC, crawl to the forward hatch."

The sawing whined from below. BASC started pulling himself away from the engine bay.

"No, sir. Go!"

"Godspeed, BASC-2"

"Godsp–"

The explosion ripped his arms off, and what was left of BASC's body spun wildly into the black, and the Morale Officer thought nothing.

His visor retracted and he saw sunlight on the surface of the asteroid. BASC-2 was outside the *Atorox*, but the *Atorox* was not in deep space. It was not torn in half. It wasn't flying at all. BASC had slid across the fuselage, and now was hanging outside the engine room door. The rush of sound overwhelmed him. The saw was still roaring inside.

His homeworld filled the air with bright greens, reds and blues. BASC pulled himself into the engine room. A masked man in regular black battlewear and chest armor lay crumpled in the door. His neck was broken, and BASC had the sinking suspicion that the man had been kicked very hard. As he pulled himself over the body, gripping the rails, he noticed something he had not seen in a long time. Hydraulic suspensors sprouted from his shoulders. They lifted and lowered him robotically, simulating zero gravity.

TRA-C was held fast to the ceiling, her hands still clutching the rails, but hydraulics suspending the weight of her body above his head.

At the seal, a man in the same foreign combat gear as the dead man at the door was sawing. BASC fired his gun, but it was a dummy. His bayonet was not. Hurling himself along the rail, the hydraulic buoying him in the familiar weightless way, he drove the blades into the intruder's back. The saw—still running—fumbled into the man's masked face, and finally stopped. The engine crew lay contorted in the ruins of their defensive square, all held, slowly floating, like a child's mobile, suspended by hydraulics. On the floor was a familiar man, wearing a bloody Atorox Project uniform. He had been ripped from TEN-2 robotic simulator suit forcibly. His throat was slashed.

Down in the far corner, hanging in it, was TEN-2's simulator, with many pieces shattered and piled below its occupant. Because of the tears in the simulator suit, BASC could see the flesh of another foreign attacker. It was bruised but in no way cannon shot. He was hanging limp and almost certainly dead. BASC guessed it was from the trauma of hitting the wall.

The engine room was secure, although BASC worried at each shadow. The sunlight streaming in through the engine door left the room in an eerie glow, and he couldn't shake the sense that there might still be invisible demons crawling through the ship. He floated himself to TRA-C. His robotic hands were not equipped to remove her mask or safely descend her hydraulics to the floor.

"TRA-C, can you hear me?" He shook her shoulder. He pried open one hand, removing it from the bar, then the next. He was struggling to get her foot clamp off a lower rail when movement poured in from the engine door.

BASC turned his gun on them, forgetting it was useless.

They were Atorox Project paramedics. He put the gun down, and as he did, he felt himself slowly descending to their level. He pushed up off a rail, but it did nothing to stop his descent. Against his will, he touched ground and his suit immobilized him.

The medics took down TRA-C and laid her flat, while two others worked quickly to unfasten BASC's bolts.

As BASC's face pulled away from the mask, the light blinded him. His muscles twitched and he felt as if his bones had turned to stone. The medics had him on a hoverstretcher. The bright light gave way to a steel face filling his view.

The robodoc was familiar to him, but it took him a second to recognize it, after all this time so many light years away from home. Servo. Doctor Servo.

Servo's medical arms extended from his torso and ran vitals on BASC.

"Take it easy, sir," said Servo. "Can you say your name?"

"How'd they get in?"

"We had a breach in security, sir. They injected a virus into the security system that identified them as custodial staff. We've got it fixed. Don't worry. Can you say your name?"

BASC turned his head to see them pulling a pale woman out of the husk of her TRA-C simulator. She was limp, and the medics slashed her uniform from her chest. They immediately plunged heartstarters in. Her pale body didn't even jolt. Her head hung at a very wrong angle.

"You saved the mission, sir. The ship's going to make it there. Nine crew members survived and remain intact. Can you say your name?"

The light got brighter, and fluttering thunder of an evac unit filled the air.

"No," he said. There was nothing but a hole, an dark and empty space where his name should be. "No, I don't know."

Chapter 14
An Honest Inquisition

Universal 382

Avatar Travel: A method of nanomolecular intergalactic travel whereby human beings operating in model environments remotely control full-body robots, known as avatars, as if the human body is physically housed within the avatar shell. With the corruption and failure of the ancient Black Box interstellar travel system, the Canon Archive was instrumental in developing the noegenetic technology that permitted the transmission of materials through interstellar wormholes by molecular transfer...

—**Infogalactic Entry:** Grand Category: Interstellar Transfer

The full, bleak and soundless day of the hot but rarely fatal autumn equinox on the equatorial desert of Movexa felt, on the skin, downright supernatural. It was as if the sun had never risen that morning in the west, nor that it would ever reach its noonday peak, nor set in the east hours later. Inquisitor and Archaeologist, Awoi Enjo, a scholar of the order furthest away from the stale confines of the Canon Archive bureaucracy, did something he had not done in weeks:

He savored his meal.

It was a modest thing: a working-man's lunch of breaded meat, pulped wild spanch, and three thin bars of infused cracklings. Miraculously, it didn't have a spec of sand in it, and the odd lazy timelessness of the day cast a drowsy, seductive hue across the entire dig.

Both disgruntled factions of guards, sent by dueling warlords a few weeks ago, appeared only in the form of lounging exoskeletons, facemasks blank. Enjo's team was downright cheery as they gently dusted the tender surfaces of the so called "hatch-wall" of the great and ancient Movexa Necropolis.

From the shadows of a small architectural perch, the long black naked legs of the Ambassadorial Overseer dangled, as they had all morning. If the denizens didn't know any better, he could have been mistaken for a chandelier.

Enjo chased the last morsel with a satisfying quaff of still-cold spanch and stole a final, food-cooled breath of the otherwise sweet desert air. He had misplaced his methane-filter mask that morning, as he did nearly every day, as—although he was not even native to the planet—his lungs had long-since adapted to breathing the mixed air. This was one of those days when he pitied those who—like the crew's horses in the corral—couldn't bear to breathe a whiff without the oxygen infuser. One last deep breath, one last golden view–

As if it had been timed to complete his lunch, one of Enjo's students cried out. A new sensation, even more pleasurable than nature's quiet glow, surged in him.

The hatch was one-hundred percent effaced.

Now everyone, down to the last acolytes, was very well aware that the chamber beyond the hatch was packed full after millennia of burial. Not only was this to be expected, but it had been proven by the initial robotic monitor scans of the once-secret monument. Nowadays scans were imprecise things, still based on rudimentary Noegenetic principles and downright analog recording devices, but radio-wave detection of sand and debris-filled chambers was child's play. You'd have to deceive the 'bots with mirrors, on purpose, to fool them.

Still, the exposed door was an important moment in the Inquisition, if only symbolically. Of course, daily photograms, measurements, and reconstructions had been sent to the analysts on the distant Canon Archive. Today, however, would produce the first "clean" shot of the hatch. It would no doubt be featured on the dig's Infogalactic entry, and was destined to become a symbol for its own archaeological museum. Admittance into the Canon Archive Museum System was exclusive and secret, but there was no doubt that the currently named Incidental *Movexan Exploratory Co-prosperity Cultural Eduvocational Exchange Probe Site Inquiry 00-*

86 cat. 63.00.10.9 would, upon extensive documentation and site visits, be granted its own foundational museum. The first joint archaeological expedition between the human race and Another already had such a cyclone of popular hyperbole swirling about on the civilized Inner Planets Awoi Enjo would undoubtedly be honored with some sort of permanent proctorship, scholarship or possibly even admittance on the custodial committee.

> *Inner Planets: An astropolitical description of the union of civilized planets throughout the galaxy closely interconnected by way of the deteriorating Black Box system. The vast majority of connections had to route through the Black Box between Holocrone and its moon, which is managed directly by the Canon Archive Space-Time-Flight Authority.*
>
> —**Infogalactic Entry:** Grand Category: Inner Planets (STF Authority)

What the hatch really meant to him was that time wasted on fundraising trips and arcane grant requests would be significantly reduced. The hatch sold itself. The hatch also meant that he might now finally be able to relax. He might finally be able to spend the rest of his life digging. Certainly the sand removal alone could take up much of his time before he retired to the confines of guidance and memory within the vivid walls of a new museum—his new museum—in the heart of the Canon Archive.

Enjo pulled new gloves onto his hands. For all the history he had uncovered, he had never been the lead for the ceremonial "pull" photo.

Technically, the honor should have gone to Foucha Fiyinn, the Onhi ambassador and occasional light fixture, but the Onhi People had no use for human dramatics. In fact, it was unlikely that even with all Foucha's education and experience in the still-new art of xenophilic, Human-Another relations, that he would even be able to detect the significance of a door containing slightly less dirt on it than the day before.

Nevertheless, all portals—windows, hatches, latches, holes, doors or even suspected openings—were subject to the time-honored tradition of the "pull." Enjo clapped his hands together in anticipation, smiled broadly, and very nearly forgot to wait for others from the other sections of the excavation site to jog in.

The hatch couldn't have been more perfect. It had an extended handle, one of exquisite quality, and probably wide enough for four human hands. It was clearly ceremonial. Enjo had long suspected that this had at one point been the grand portal to the Necropolis, and that the monument upon which they had spent so many painstaking years, had at one point been the entry of priests and morticians whose culture, even after years of research, remained cloaked in mystery.

The hatch was nearly a man high, for reasons not yet known. That meant that Enjo had to stand with his hands upstretched slightly for the traditional "poised" photogram. He smiled broadly, with the core of his team surrounding him—squatting, sitting, crouching or standing. Others tried to crowd in, but the photogrammer couldn't include them all for the close-up. He took a few courtesy "broadshots."

Enjo felt his hands shake as he now neared them to the handle. He had touched, inadvertently or with purpose, the surface of the hatch countless times. But this photogram was for the ages. He prayed that his light, mock-grasp of the handle would not be the final whisper that disintegrated the beautiful object into desert memory. His fingers encircled the handle.

Nothing but the Noegenetic click! of the photogrammator happened. Enjo released the handle and everyone applauded.

Then the hatch door, unmolested for countless centuries, swung open on its own.

No ancient sand gushed from the opening. Not a single grain. The crowd gasped. It was in fact clear of any fill whatsoever.

All eyes turned to Enjo, and he tried his best not to greet them with a gaping mouth.

"Uh. Platform. The hydraulic. Bring it over." He hoped that what was simple nervous paralysis of nearly all his faculties would be mistaken for calm command. Several older students and a few acolytes rolled an elevator platform from the storage supply. He indicated for them to position it directly below the hatch.

A burst of locusts filled his stomach. His hand went numb at the platform switch. The people watched as he ascended to the opening, chain-ladder in his hand, body-lights at the ready. He wondered fleetingly if he should have taken the time to don an exoskeleton. He raised the platform high enough for him to kneel but look comfortably through the high portal. His lights flared.

It was a simple empty chamber.

It may as well been filled with gold and sprinkled with yttrium.

Although a layer of dust coated every squared-off surface in the room several things were instantly apparent. First, this chamber, and possibly others, had been nearly perfectly sealed to the outside ravages of weather and time. It had quite likely been that way since the origins of the structure. Second, as ancient as the temple was known to be, there was nothing primitive about the carvings within the chamber. In fact, they outdid the artisan quality of the current Native Aliens. The images were not just carved in three dimensions, but were done with natural perspective and realism. The first one Enjo could make out in the darkness was that of a realistic-looking dragon. The stalled sun's light pierced the hatch opening and landed on the creature's mouth like fire. Its asymmetrical teeth were not only individually carved, but appeared to be individually designed, like in a fossil cast.

Enjo threw down one end of the ladder into the chamber, and tossed the anchor end to the crew. He didn't wait for them to secure it before he started his descent. He asked his light to beam, and noticed that he had caused a cloud of dust that had risen to his chest. Of course, he should have sent in the non-invasive hover-glints first. No dust, no touching, no harsh lights. But footprints had built this place, and only footprints would make sense of it. He excused his greed for knowledge by gracing holy ground with human feet.

There were more carvings; the East wall showed far more than a dragon—an entire zoo of creatures filled its surface. On the opposite wall were humans and buildings, although the humans were not as well defined as the many creatures. Enjo scanned his light around the corner, just as the first hover-glint breached the portal. Just after that, the first crew members descended the ladder for themselves.

Enjo rounded the corner. Another small chamber. This time what appeared to be a very heavy door stood shut.

On the floor in front of that sealed door lay a skeleton, curled into a fetal position. It was that of a standard human being.

Years passed in the low-lying sulfuric mists of the desert to the industrious swiftness of the excavation. Aside from the dreamlike shifting of the dunes, Movexa hadn't changed, but Enjo's world had. Of course, the shattering discovery that astronautical human beings had, in the very, very distant past, visited Movexa and encountered the native Onhi had been the biggest change to his daily life and career prospects, but some of the smaller things were, over time, great influences on his mindset as well. For example, he had now a good friend in Gretz, the personal diplomatic overseer from the Onhi contingency.

The Ambassadors Council now occupied an office in the semi-permanent embassy just to the north of the dig. Aside from a small perimeter of guards and virtual touring guides at a reasonable distance, there was no other sign of life besides the excavators, who were, to a body, human beings, and most of them planetary natives, although there was a small contingent of avatars. These avatars looked like full-body humanoid exoskeleton suits or robots. They were operated by extremely wealthy archaeological hobbyists from off-world who had donated large sums to Enjo's museum project or the Canon Archive for the virtualized experience of contributing to a historic dig.

The only exception to the humans and avatars was Gretz, who accompanied Enjo everywhere, only working when he worked.

Enjo didn't mind. Gretz would be silent for long stretches. Even though they were rarely more than ten steps apart during the workday, there were times that Enjo forgot entirely that he was accompanied. When Gretz did speak, it was always with curiosity and an alien spirit that seemed to most closely resemble deep compassion.

It had taken years for the team to unseal the next set of doors, and even more for the raging controversies over the first skeletal remains to die down.

The best working theory was that Denizen Zero—the skeleton Enjo had discovered decades before upon opening the first hatch—had died in isolation from poison, possibly quarantined by the host Onhi of those days. The next bodies were those of other humans who came into contact with the first as they tried to investigate.

The speculation was that the poison was transferred from person-to-person, but had a source somewhere outside of the complex. In other words, humans had been poisoned elsewhere, and had come to the Onhi complex for treatment or rescue. In the early days, back when they still thought the temple had been a type of cemetery or necropolis, one of Enjo's colleagues back at the Canon Archive had coined the term Xenohospital in one of his speculative papers, and the moniker had stuck, as further investigations revealed that the building—whatever its original purpose, certainly tended to the healthcare of humans in the end.

Although the competing theories were many, the one that had the most consensus by the most prestigious of researchers was that the poison had been common spohr, likely used in a gas-bomb attack by a warring human tribe. It was a common enough technique, and fossilized traces of spohr had been found in the area. The afflicted Denizen Zero sought, along with his mates, refuge among the Onhi, who took them into the chambers in an act of tragic compassion.

The Onhi, perhaps unfamiliar with the human war tactics of those barbaric days, unwittingly exposed themselves to the spohr in treating the humans. In the scientific narrative, this explained why some humans had been left where they had fallen—the Xenohospital had become a house of the dead. Both Onhi and Human researchers fully anticipated the discovery of poisoned Onhi remains deeper inside the chamber, if only they could find the secret doorway in.

Denizens One, Two and Four (the originally identified Three was later found to be only consisting of components of Denizen One) were found shortly after the discovery and painstaking unsealing of the narthex door.

Their disposition and composition began to steer the arguments towards the "Wet Lung" theory—that at least one spohr cannister, had cracked open within the temple. The mystery had many facets and puzzling peculiarities that would likely continue long after Enjo was gone, but every little step mattered. Enjo had long figured that finding the doorway, and then finding the Onhi remains, were the last two steps necessary for him to make his career legacy a lasting one of galactic interest.

Enjo and Gretz, however, rarely discussed the possibilities. Enjo, for one, was happy to let the chemists and forensics duke out the niggling details and pointless esoterica with the Noegenetic data processors. Enjo was a scientist of stone and dust, of bone and metal, of evidence and eyes. He could tell more with his eyes than any spectrometer could speculate.

He had known within five minutes of finding the first skeleton that he was bound to find a few more beyond the narthex walls. He also knew that the ones they would find would have been the last ones to die, that they had been struck with the symptoms only moments before dying, and although they had taken the poison in through the lungs, it had been delivered as deadly particulate matter—not a gas—that had stuck to their clothes or skin. He had never shared any of this, because he knew as well as any that his thoughts were merely predictions based on experience, and had no roots in Noegenetic logic or data processes. The "particulate" theory was not unknown, but it was not popular, and Enjo was in no position to challenge the orthodoxy on that point. Not yet at least. Maybe not ever.

Besides, he had another puzzle to crack. A big one.

The so-called "Hall of Heroes" where One, Two and Four had lain dead for millennia was a marvel. With a vault of five stories high, and two "whisper points" beyond a great, handmade crevasse, the enormous room was lined with carvings, glyphs, wards, artwork and symbolic instruction. The thousands of wall features were crusted in dust, and Enjo simply didn't have the man-power to uncover and catalog the room and, at the same time, focus on finding the secret passageway.

The truth was that he didn't have any evidence that there even was a next passageway. Sure, he knew that there were other chambers beyond these walls, but he couldn't find any trace of another sealed door. Still, just as he knew that the three men and one woman had died from particles, not gas, he knew that this room had to connect to others, somehow.

The crew in the meantime focused on carefully revealing the wild mix of messages secreted into the walls. The written language of the ancients was only now being initially processed by the resources of the grand computational Noegenetic Ruminator, located deep within the Canon Archives on Ouffland sent nearly daily updates on progress in the language processing project.

Enjo himself was at a loss about that. In all his studies he'd never seen a language, alphabet or pictograms quite like it. Whether it was from visual images, old-fashioned, physical rubbings, or just standing in front of the exposed carvings, Enjo and Gretz had both spent months poring over the glyphs. Whenever he thought they might be onto a pattern, it would be broken by another. Without a key of some sort, of course, they'd never get the full story, but Enjo had not even found the nearly universal basics: symbols for "baby" or "man" or "family".

It was well enough, he supposed. Just focus on discovery. Let the armchair lords do their analytic work far away. Though an ability to read the walls would be helpful, he was confident that he would find the next door the old fashioned way: by dusting for it.

Gretz, for once, wasn't keeping up. Enjo put down his sensitive airbrush and cracked his stiff knuckles, which had become slightly arthritic with the years. "Something the matter?"

As always, it took several seconds before the long-limbed creature replied conventionally, although the gills at the various joints on his body inspired noisily in a slow, thoughtful stream. He flipped down the recessed speaker that had been tucked up by his brow, and pulled up his transback, a small device that—allegedly—would return to him the retranslated meaning of things he said to humans. After all these years, he was still married to the guide, even though he rarely misspoke without it.

"No one has harmed me," said Gretz. "Nothing has harmed me. In spirit, all is as it was the day before. May I make an assumption that you find my work to be of slower pace than typical?"

"Yeah, man. I'm referring to that." Enjo didn't use his own translator with Gretz anymore, because Gretz was adept at everything but forming the foreign sounds. It hung disconnected to his shoulder exo. It had been months since he'd had to present at the Ambassador's Office… in fact, almost a year. Gretz went back and forth there once a week still, and Enjo was glad to be rid of the politics.

"Perhaps, there is no door. Perhaps, this is a separate chamber." His gills sighed. "Perhaps, we should seek a new entry on the exterior."

Enjo was surprised at the alien's bout of melancholy, or doubt, or whatever it was. It wasn't in Gretz's nature to despair. He looked behind them, relieved to confirm that the rest of the crew was well out of earshot, working on the far wall at DZ-53, as they had for most of the month.

"You know that's an entirely new project, one that we don't have the manpower for, at least not if we want to keep excavating here."

"Maybe, it is time for a change in direction. Maybe, as you have yourself said, 'These chambers are a ruse.'" It was always unsettling to hear his friend quote him back exactly, complete with human accenting. This time, Gretz's point was even more upsetting.

"It has only been eighteen months on this course. We contracted with your people for three years on this course. We don't even review progress with the leadership for another six months. You yourself made the case for the internal approach to the Council!"

"Even so, my people are flexible. Even so, my people adapt. Even so, I have a sense."

I have a sense. Of all the common phrases Gretz repeated in their conversations, this one was rare. The first time it had come up, it had led to the discovery of the whisper points. The last time he had said it, it preceded advice that had saved two men's lives from a rock slide at the crevasse.

Enjo cocked his head. "Okay, but didn't you have a sense in favor of this project?"

"Of course, as you well know or can review in the minutes from that meeting. Of course, I am on record. But that sense passed, of course, some time ago. Now a new one has taken its place."

Anxiety crept over him. "This isn't like you, Gretz. You are throwing me off."

"Never would I! By all means, we can keep at this process. Let's stay here. Concern you? Never would I!"

"No, no no. I trust you. If you've got a reason to make a change in the project, I definitely want to hear it and consider it. It's just... you are talking about a very big, very significant and possibly very counterproductive change. It seems to have come from out of the blue."

"Blue?"

"Unexpectedly. It means it fell out of the sky... very surprising."

"The sky is blue?"

"On some planets."

Gretz nodded a few times, slowly, as if he was storing the new idiom in his head for safe keeping.

They knocked off early that afternoon so that Enjo could consider the ramifications of taking Gretz's advice, and so that Gretz could prepare a case for the argument. Cullacks and Fawkes, the two humans closest to Enjo, took over the team as they typically would when Enjo was called away. Enjo and Gretz agreed to meet that evening for a supper by the string of sulfuric pools known as the Bent Serpent.

The native aliens breathed the thick and noxious air quite naturally, but it was a rare human who would even wander past the pools with a filtering mask. The odor was strong. Enjo was the only human who enjoyed the smell. He left his mask back at his quarters in the main dormitory.

The friends sat with their legs dangling above the mists of a pool, watching the sun spill down the side of the sky like a slow melt. Even with time to process the project change request, Enjo was uneasy. Soon, the off-duty guardians of the Ambassador would begin their evensongs, and the distant tones would carry into the sandy vale. Perhaps then Enjo could recline a bit more, and let his mind be carried to the simple paradise of exotic but familiar music.

"The Canon Archive is sending an avatar here," said Gretz. "The Ambassador has told me this."

"When?"

"Tonight."

Enjo laughed. "You must be mistaken. I just talked to the Canon earlier this week. They said nothing. Something like that takes weeks of planning and coordination. I don't even know if we have an available avatar model right now. We'd have to ask one of the hobbyists to give his up. I doubt we want to anger a donor in that way."

"I am not mistaken."

Enjo had spent decades of his career in this lonely place. He had become quite monastic. Over the past few years, avatar technology had improved somewhat, and his department had one constructed specifically for him to use on special occasions. When they first delivered his robotic suit, he had dutifully, and with great difficulty, suited up and, taking the controls of a robot in the light-years' distant Canon Archive. By laser relay, he looked through the eyes of that robot, as it attended a committee meeting.

Enjo had fallen asleep during it.

Now, in the interests of never again delivering a snoring robot to his own department meeting, he maintained a secret vow to avoid avatar travel as much as possible. The Canon Archive had to come to him. In all the years he had been stationed there, the Canon Archive had never once sent an actual Canon Archivist by avatar. It simply wasn't necessary.

"Are you sure it isn't just a new donor hobbyist? I'm sure that's it."

"I am certain. It is because of something of unusual importance."

"So important that they contact your people without consulting me? Very unusual indeed!"

"The Canon Archive did not contact us. The request for help, it came from my people."

"This is crazy. This takes coordination, handling. For pity's sakes who do we have who can act as personal chronometer for the poor avatar? The first two weeks are nearly impossible to adapt to without a companion reminding you to eat and sleep on schedule!"

It didn't help that they still kept time on Ouffland Standard, despite the planet's much slower and stable track around its sun. In Movexa, a new year came about once every three irregular OufStans. Therefore, Enjo had only been digging like a mad hermit in the desert for just over seven years. Of course, by that standard, he'd likely be retired in only three more and dead in five.

He just as soon preferred to think in OufStans instead.

In any case, plopping an avatar in the midst of dig without any sane preparation whatsoever bordered on a criminal act.

"Does this have anything at all to do with your strange change of heart today at the dig?"

"Perhaps," said Gretz. "We could just focus on linguistic analysis for a while. Perhaps the walls will tell us what to do next, where to look. Perha–"

"No, no. You are getting distracted by the literal again. I mean did you want to stop our search for the door because you were told by the Ambassador to stop it? You know as well as I do that we've got more than enough linguists right now. The data centers at Ouffland don't need any more data. They don't know how to decrypt the data we are sending right now. Sitting on our thumbs and pondering imponderables is a bad idea."

"Technically, I only have an opposable hallux. I have no thumb upon which to sit."

Enjo said, "Ah yes, the literal. Let me try this a different way. Remind me again. Are you even capable of lying? I mean, if you set your mind to doing it, could you lie on purpose, even for experimental purposes?"

"Lies as you define them are incomprehensible."

"The fabled planet of Whist in my home system was the first known one in the entire known galaxy to conquer permanent poverty entirely. They ended hunger. This concept 'End Hunger' was incomprehensible, too. Until they did it."

"Well, then, I would say, yes. Our people can lie, but, like most things, we do it with a much longer view than you might imagine. We, for example, value modesty. Thus, over the centuries, we have developed an aversion to beauty. We will ignore a female Onhi if she conforms too closely to our traditional standard of beauty."

"But beauty is relative. You can't really lie about that. It is not the same thing."

"Interesting."

"Interesting how?"

"I am simply trying to determine whether you believe that, and are mistaken, or if you are lying. Human thoughts are never very straightforward."

Enjo laughed. "I say the same about you in my reports!"

"To the contrary," said Gretz, "It is merely your ability to interpret the truth that is twisted."

Even Gretz found humor in this, as his vents vibrated with mirth.

"Okay, so let me be very direct, my friend, and I want you to take no offense, as I intend none."

"Please, you are not the sort to offend."

"I think this: the Ambassador lied to you about the Canon Archive sending an avatar, and that the Ambassador told you to abandon the search for the secret door. I think you are following orders, and possibly believe the lie to be true, but are nonetheless perpetuating a falsehood for the Ambassadors political purposes."

"How fascinating," said Gretz. "Do you have evidence that leads you to believe this?"

"Only this—there is no way that the Canon Archive has immediately sent an avatar here without warning or preparation."

"There must be some way that they have."

"How so?"

"Because here comes the avatar, right now."

The bronze-brown machine walked over the dunes. Fawkes was by its side.

Enjo stood up and shook the avatar's hand.

Fawkes said, "This is Professor Sterling."

"Enjo Awoi."

"I thought you were coming by to chat, Enjo," said Fawkes.

"I am. I said I'd do it after Evensong."

"Evensong would have been done hours ago."

Enjo looked at the time quizzically.

Gretz said, "My people do not sing tonight. They are having council."

Enjo and Fawkes looked at each other with the same confused expression.

"That's serious, Gretz."

"Yes. It is. Do you think that I can tell them that you are re-focusing the project?"

Enjo was taken off-guard, but Fawkes spoke up. "Yes, I think that is exactly what you should tell your council. We've been thinking about it and, yes, it is a very sound approach."

Sterling had explained that the Onhi had become concerned with the project, and that the Canon Archive would be in negotiations with them for the time being. The dig would be suspended entirely and immediately if they didn't voluntarily concentrate their efforts on the carvings, and abandon the search for the secret passage.

Enjo brought Sterling to his quarters, and set up a sleeping/charging station. After much explanation and reminder of the hazards of virtual avatar transfer, Enjo finally convinced Sterling to follow the recommended schedule. His eyes powered down, and the massive hulk reclined on the floor with a sigh.

Fawkes and Enjo retreated to Enjo's bedroom.

"You realize they can pull the plug on this project?" said Fawkes.

"Yes, but do you think they'd really do that? They've had no problems all this time. Now suddenly they are going to kill it? For what?"

"They also have never canceled Evensong. You know as well as I do that this thing has entangling alliances all the way through. It's remarkable we've made it this far on the project without a bureaucrat gumming up the works entirely."

"Yes, I can see it. It just surprises me."

"Let's go along with it for now. Maybe we can revisit the search for the next chamber in a few months. Rocking the relationship right now is a bad idea. We are so close to getting funding for the museum and everything else that entails."

"I agree," said Enjo. "Let's keep them happy. Perhaps in a few days, Professor Sterling will have adjusted enough to the transfer to be more forthcoming with us."

Enjo entered the excavation site very early that morning. Courtesy barriers had already cordoned off the old excavation room. No one would be going back there on official digs until further notice. He stepped over the simple barrier to take one last look at the site to which he'd given five OufStans of his life.

He walked along the line where he and Gretz had been working the day before and knelt in the dust to get a close last look at the markings in the dim light. Gretz left a unique pattern in his brush dustings: brisk straight lines finishing with a subtle curly-q at the end. An archaeologists dusting was like a fingerprint. He looked closely at the brushing, and he realized the dust was piled in a faint, even row, instead of whisked away to the center of the floor for removal.

Enjo blew on the line of dust. It exposed a small channel in the floor that had a short undulation in the center.

Why had Gretz covered this up?

The undulation was familiar. A similar one had been at the first interior door that had been discovered, decades before. Enjo placed his fingers in them and jumped when a secret door swung open.

Enjo fumbled for his light. He shone it into the vast room beyond it. The room contained a dozen doorways going in all directions, including a door into the floor and a stairway leading up. There were unfaded paintings on the wall, and carvings depicting the Onhi People, standing tall and glorious and savage. In smaller relief surrounding the Onhi warriors and gods were pale little human beings, being forked, like grass, into the open mouths of the Onhi.

Piled in stacks and contorted in all variety of agonizing poses were the twisted, broken skeletons of hundreds of human bones.

"It wasn't a contaminated xenohospital, of course." Sterling's tinny voice came from behind Enjo and startled him. Sterling stood in the open doorway and beckoned Enjo. "It was a trap, designed by the primitive Onhi, a defense against the human incursion. A highly effective one, at that. The Ambassador knew you were getting close more than a year ago, so he called me in. It is a very delicate situation. Gretz was enlisted to slow the search for this chamber down. He was very good at it. Just good enough, though. I only arrived here weeks ago. Had my transfer been delayed for any reason, you might have stumbled onto this place too soon. I would not have been able to explain it to you and put it into the proper context."

"So, the Canon Archive knows about this? Won't their publication of this discovery end up betraying them now anyhow? I can't imagine that the Ambassador trusts us with this embarrassment."

"I'm not from the Canon Archive. I am not an avatar. My name is Sterling Ervo. I imagine you have heard my name. I was once a famous doctor, centuries ago." Sterling's left eye winked off and on. "This little embarrassment is what I might call a large-scale algorithmic failure—just a bit of corrupt data that must be deleted and overwritten so that the entire system is not corroded beyond recovery."

"A coverup? No. That flies in the face of everything the Canon Archive stands for! So, they set a trap a long time ago. This is not the disaster they think it is."

"No, it is not a trap. It is more than that. Far more. And revealing it would be a far worse disaster than you can possibly imagine."

"Then there is no way can we cover this up!"

"I suggest you think about your museum. Revealing this will destroy any possibility of funding."

"My museum is worthless if it doesn't reveal the truth of the past."

"The truth is that the Ambassador is willing to work with your crew on the translation of the markings. According to them, it is a virtual encyclopedia of ancient wisdom. Your museum will overflow with truths. Just not all of them. And there will be no museum at all if you allow our present understanding of history to be corrupted by this old, forgotten error. Not if you allow the entire project to be pulled. Come. We must close this up before the Onhi catch wind of this. Everything hangs in the balance, and if you really care about the truth, you'll know what to do."

Enjo stepped back into the familiar chamber. He put his fingers in the floor to shut the door. He filled the dust back in as best as he could and he returned to the courtesy barrier with Sterling.

Fawkes met them there. "Hey! You're here early."

"Yes," said Enjo. "We were just discussing the site. Maybe the Onhi would appreciate it if we did more than just cordon off this section for now. What would you think about fencing it securely, for the time being?"

"Sounds like a great idea. We'll get right on that, Enjo!"

Part V

Book Five: Century 400

Chapter 15
Soldier of Fortuna

Universal 445

Whist: A paradise mining planet of peace and harmony peace and harmony peace and harmony peace and harmony peace and harmony peace and harmony peace and harmony peace and harmony peace and harmony yttrium peace and harm…

—**Infogalactic Entry:** Grand Category: Peace and Harmony

He bounced the sizable and fresh human skull back and forth between his hands like a ball. It had heft, and Dayna Lea took a dangerous few seconds to care about its former owner. It was blackened by fire, with its jaw fused shut by what appeared to be melted tendons, but had clearly been the container for a larger-than average brain.

The dead man had been a warrior-king, a rare and precious resource in these tunnels of death.

Dayna hoped the man had left children behind, grieving, cunning and full of wrath.

Now, the skull served a less noble purpose: bait, for a trap.

It needed just a bit more weight.

The lockdown door to Magnetic North was completely offline, of course, and inches thick. It was secured in the ancient way. The steel bar had been slid manually into a deep recess, and it was likewise barred across the interior hinges. Closed and locked from within, the door may as well have just been yet another section of wall, from the outside, save for the rubber seals at its gap-points to prevent poison gas from filtering in.

Soon enough, it would be breached. Dayna's squad had acted the decoy, drawing off a deadly roving mixed patrol of three of the latest slaughterbot models. This freed up the advance squad to bypass the thinned ranks at the enemy missile base at junction YX-843. That squad could then take the components necessary to complete the guidance system necessary for Project Crossbow to launch the first and possibly only rocket of humankind into space.

Dayna hand-drilled through a dry thigh bone. He blew bone dust through the hole and then gathered a length of old analog tape and ran it—just in case—over a magnet to erase any pernicious remnants. He then threaded the tape through the hole, then through the tube of a metal pipe, and repeated this until the pipe and the leg bone were reasonably bound to one another.

He cobbled together a variety of materials both inorganic and once-living quickly. There was no easy craft to it. Once he had a ghastly, headless scarecrow assembled, lying prostrate on the floor, he crucified the thing on a rolling crossbar, and attached to the shoulders an old hydraulic shock spring from a long-dead zip lift. Using a hand winch typically used to birth breach calves in the slaughter mines, he compacted the spring until it nearly exploded in revenge. He secured the springs with one hook on the front of the scarecrow, and one on its back.

He stood the scarecrow up; careful to step on the wheel brake so it didn't roll away.

The scuttling noise of metal fingernails scratching at the gaps in the door came so soon.

Dayna held his breath. His frenetic gestures gave way immediately to measured, silent moves. He gingerly lifted the skull up and loaded it on the spring. With more time, he would have fused it to prevent gravity from pulling the thing prematurely from its perch, but he was cutting every corner now.

All too quickly, he scooped three white glass balls from their spongy beds. Two of them clinked in his hands.

He cursed.

No explosion. The things may not have been hair-triggered, but it was no excuse to get sloppy. He'd survived by Jag's ghost, and nothing more.

Counting his breaths, he slipped one of the balls in the open top of the skull to give it a bit more weight, and then he gently thumbed adhesive into the sockets of the scarecrow's head.

The scritching was loud now, and Dayna knew that at least a handful of microbots had worked their way into the gaps of the door, scuttling the lock-bars and lubricating them at the same time. Even the simplest machines would betray a man at the behest of the Overlords. Locks, bars, levers and barricades were not just pregnable: they could, given time, be turned against the defender.

Dayna had once watched a child's hand slip, like magic, into the open gears of a vengeful dummy lock. It had eaten the entire arm to the shoulder before the screaming began, and the little girl should have died before she hit the floor. The only enemy involved had been the stealthy micros, waiting at the ready in the gears.

No one spoke of rescue any more. The early evacuations of the elites from the countries of Dome and Halvorstead had been the only ones. The rest of the planet had been long-since given up—by the Universe—for dead.

Dayna would have nothing of it. He had brought enough scrapped robots, machines, tools, locks and motive circuits back to life to know better. He had created traps, decoys, dummies, magnets, mines, distracters and every other sort of counterattack and counterintelligence known throughout Whist's knowledge core. So frequently had he done it that he now believed—with every atom of his soul—in the Resurrection.

Now, he was no Ol' King Jaggya, of course. He might be able to guess what a machine thought like. He might be able to detect patterns in an artificial intelligence. But he was no master engineer. He was no Galactopede. His heart didn't beat to the rhythm of corrupted algorithms. Why would it? He was human. His animating spirit was ethereal, not electrical.

Still, he sure as suns knew how to make these machines miserable. His new scarecrow was just the latest innovation.

"Not my last, neither," he said to the haunted golem's face. He had learned over time to talk encouragingly to himself, because it was a special occasion if anyone else might. His own exit had been bricked up. Only a small opening remained. Fortunately, he'd been especially starved for food for a week, so if he got finished soon enough, he'd slip through and mortar in the last of the wall behind him. Hopefully, the rest of his crew hadn't panicked and blocked off the alternate ductwork in addition to their original route. If they had? Ah well. Death was on its way at some speed or another.

The skull looked back at him, white blind in one of the eye bombs. It had rolled.

"You winking at me? What you know that I don't? Ah. I see. You happy to get one last go at 'em. Well. Hm. You're welcome." Dayna gently rolled the eye down as close to center as he dared. "And thank you. That octopod they got is expensive. You take her out and they are gonna cry a long time about that. It'll give our rocket boys plenty of time to get those parts through to safety."

The INTEG-Octopod had been the first of a new wave of machine. While the first machines to go rogue had been standard galactic models with excessively bad algorithms, they quickly, and unexpectedly adapted on Whist. Soon, they learned to develop new models of their own design, and now, eight years into the nightmare, they had hybridized hardware with living tissue. The Octopod was the most successful, and fearsome, of this experiment.

Built on a standard wheel-walk base, it had a heavy electromagnetic chest designed to draw shrapnel and steel away from its "face": a faintly glowing set of tentacles capable of delivering a fully biological electrogenic shock. It looked like a nest of translucent eels. Dayna had seen one from a distance about a year ago, and fled. Back then, that was the only way to see one and survive.

It didn't make much sense why the machines had bothered to bioengineer such a hybrid. A typical RATROC could wreak nearly as much human damage as the Octopod, at a fraction of the resources. Dayna figured it had something to do with the dastard machines discovering the utility of cruelty and fear.

In any case, "Soldier Skull" and he were going to take one down today.

"One down at a time, buddy. Let's do this."

He locked the last of the stabilizing straps down on his creation and gave it one last foot to head mistgassing with a little jerry-rigged dispenser made from a hollow Gogago husk.

"Good. He said. No micros in you. You'll do."

The scratching at the door came early.

He dare not peer into the large central lock without a scope. He grabbed an old glass mine sample jar from a teetering shelf and held its mouth to the opening. He pressed his eye to the bottom of the jar and shone a light into the lock. Even through the blurry glass, he could see tiny streaks of motion.

He could have destroyed the current wave of microbots with a simple lock-shock. In fact, he had a polarized one that would temporarily reverse the microbot attack on the gears. He could turn them against their masters. He'd done it before.

It was a delaying tactic that didn't suit the circumstances, so he saved that trick for another day. He had only recently charged the lock-shock, and energy was at a premium, anyhow.

Instead, he affixed a dormant plate against the lock opening. Once the micros finished with the gear pins, they would move to the sliding bar. He wanted them to pass through the plate first. It would magnetize most of the little machines.

Time to go.

He very lightly patted the golem on the shoulder and carefully rolled it into place at the center of the cracked floor. He took down the pair of tactical lights attached at opposite walls and hitched them to his shoulders, to use as personal lights. He shut one down to save the battery, leaving the room fairly dim. He checked his pack quickly and tossed it through the hole in the block wall behind him. For good measure, he took two more bricks, reasonably unbroken, from his side of the escape hole, and tossed them through. It was overkill—he had left more than a dozen fill bricks on the other side in the darkness.

The scratching at the door intensified. He put both hands inside the hole to get a grip good enough to pull himself through.

From the hole in the wall, not the door behind him, emerging from the dark, a face appeared.

It was not human.

"Hello," it said.

Dayna drew his sidearm, an old-fashioned mechanical Movexan-style N-Class shooter and fired once into the hole. It used jacketed cartridges and he had kept it clean of micros for years by carefully trapping its moving parts. It wouldn't blow through brick, though, so when the face vanished, he didn't fire again.

The scratching behind him had converted to a tell-tale buzz. The lock was letting go.

At the opening of the brick wall, the high whine of mortar meeting a diamond-bladed saw erupted. A line cut through and the very end of a rotary saw burst through from the other side.

They were coming in from both ways.

The door bar lifted, and the usually satisfying sound of expensive micros clacking like magnets to the hydraulic bar, then shattering as it thundered open was instead a cold comfort. The killers were getting in.

While leaning forward, both hands balanced in front of him, with the pistol zeroed on the brick wall, Dayna backed himself into a corner. There was no cover. The room was small. He was doomed.

It was a good place to die. With no options, there was no chance of cowardice. With no options, there was no chance of error. He wondered if he would get a carving of himself at the Morale Center, or just a name plate. He would be pleased with either.

The door swung inward. A short, heavily armored gunning cannon rolled in and Dayna nailed it with a shot before recognizing it. The shot cracked its targeting sight. Dayna was close enough to take a run at toppling it. The thing weighed as much as three men, but it was top-heavy.

It trained its turret in Dayna's direction, but twitched back and forth, unable to lock onto its target. It cooly settled into a steady scanning pattern.

Then the octopod stepped in behind the cannon bot. The thing, which, instead of legs, stood on a stacked set of telescoping tiers called buckets, had colored stripes running along its sides, a barreled chest, and living, glowing head full of tentacles. It stared at the "soldier skull", eye-to-eye. It did not strike its tendrils against the face, nor consume the bombs. It stood, completely frozen in place, staring at the skull of Dayna's golem.

The trap had failed.

Dayna fired at the octopod's head and hit. The monstrosity flinched and raised a hand—a mechanical prosthetic covered in living tissue—in defense. Dayna shot, took a step forward, and shot again. The gunning cannon huffed mechanically, locked in on Dayna, and returned a hot spray of gas. Dayna staggered back, pulling the trigger quickly now in a vain attempt to discharge everything he had.

His arms paralyzed, his head cloudy, the room spinning, Dayna fell down, helpless. His throat constricted.

The saw burst through the wall and sent a spray of \of dust into the room. It worked its way up to the ceiling. The saw stopped for a moment, repositioned on the other side, and then burst through again, at the top of the new portal that was being cut.

The octopod, still mesmerized by the golem, put his hands to the wounds on his head. It stared curiously at the translucent trickle running down his fleshy fingers.

Dayna, lying on the floor, blacked out momentarily. The cannon bot approached him, and he was helpless to stop it.

The concrete cut-out of bricks crashed down into the room, filling the room with a choking cloud of dust. He still could not lift himself or even his gun from the floor.

In through the new opening strode a conventional "medic-murderer"—a bipedal scramblebot with detached weapons. With fabricated shields, joints, greaves and wrap-around optics and scanning wheels, the only two things unique about it were that in its ninth hand it held a saw instead of a dartmissile launcher, and, far more strangely, attached around its neck, a cape hung down from its shoulders.

It scanned for Dayna, found him and—completely unnecessarily, cocked its multi-faceted head to face its fallen prey.

"Hello," it said again.

The machine's multiple arms clacked noisily, swirling the dusty air as its utility pincers poked at the fallen man. Without a single rip in Dayna's clothes, the scramblebot held fast to his body and lifted him up so as to rest his back against the wall. The biped softly popped its hip joints to sit with its legs crisscrossed on the floor. Dayna blanched. Murder-medics had programming and devices that allowed them to serve as the enemy's most effective torturers of humans.

"Your respiration is returning," said the scramblebot. It sounded as if its voice was echoing through a loose flap of waxed parchment. "Do not speak until you are comfortable."

"Nice cape," said Dayna, coughing.

"I'm glad you noticed. I wish to be distinguished. Thank you."

"Kind of crazy, don't you think? Makes backfiring against an attack a bit tricky, eh?"

"It moves with the arms. Of course I don't feel it, so it hardly obstructs me should I ever need to fire behind me again."

The thing's calm conversation had the weirdest glitch he'd ever encountered.

"So," said Dayna. "My vest. I'm not going to set it off. Just so you know."

"Of course you won't. You don't even have one. Tell me, have you actually bluffed one of us into System Override that way, or is that just an old soldiers' tale?"

Dayna winced when he attempted to move his body. The cannon's gas hadn't been lethal, just particularly unpleasant stuff.

"Chatty," he said, grimacing.

The scramblebot had its surgical array exposed on its left thigh just above a class band that looked—in the odd machine code way—like it formed the letters OVRES. Hot cutters, scalpels, forceps, needles; the typical torturer's assortment. The machines had been doing it for years, and never for information. The only reason they ever "cut" anyone and let him live was to depress human morale back home.

Dayna had no significant information to share that he could conjure. He prayed that 'Ovres' didn't know that.

Ovres indicated, with an off-hand, the octopod that was still standing transfixed by the skull. "I recognized your facial expression when he didn't take your bait. Astonishment, I believe?"

"You weren't even in here yet."

Ovres considered this for a second, and then said, "You are very aware of your surroundings. Oh clever man! I am linked of course, to Milton. He simply transmitted his view, of course. There. Color returns to your face. We'll leave shortly, but allow me first to break the poor fellow's spell."

Ovres clacked as it rose again, and strode over to the golem that kept the octopod so enthralled. Dayna's hearing had been suppressed by the earlier sawing but he was almost certain he heard a soft slurping coming from the monster's head.

Milton? These things are naming each other?

The golem's white eyes sparkled in the cloudy air. Ovres's arms moved with careful precision towards the sockets. With balance, the robot's pincers clicked quietly onto the rounded edges of each eye, and pulled them from the recesses. Just as carefully, Ovres rolled each glass ball into a damping tube inserted into its own torso.

The spell broken, the octopod launched forward quickly, its tentacles lashing at the skull. Ovres turned its entire torso toward Dayna—as frivolous a thing as a surround-view robot could ever do—and said, "See?–"

The octopod wrenched the skull from its trappings.

The room exploded, and Dayna lost his breath again as all went dark.

The last thing he saw was Ovres's contorted form hurtling toward him, a twist of metal and mass.

Dayna did not die. He only wished he had. He could not breathe. His muscles felt as if they were ripping from bone.

A cage of Ovres's robotic arms surrounded him, and that cage was covered with a heavy cape. He felt like he was inside a makeshift tent. From his back, he looked up in the face of the scramblebot, but it was so covered in dust that he could see no robotic life, light or energy. The room, what he could see of it, was illuminated in dim and shadowy purple.

Long seconds later, Dayna realized that Lord Death had rumbled through the room, but had forgotten to take Dayna's beaten husk of a body to the Terminal. Long minutes later, the pain leveled back down to a modest near-death sort of agony. It wasn't until a very long period of lying in Ovres's shadow that he realized:

Ovres had shielded him from the explosion.

He lay there for some time before he could move his head. Once he could, it was an effort just to nod on his faint emergency lamp.

It took him a long time to move his arms and legs, and each motion had pain, but he wasn't going to die. Ovres remained motionless, its frame frozen mid-gangle. The cape was grimy and lightly pocked but not tattered. Shrapnel sprung from its outer side like prickles from a tine-burrower.

He coughed to clear his lungs.

There were chunks missing from the wall nearest where the golem had stood. No trace of it remained, aside from indistinguishable twists of steel. The cannonbot's armor had kept it mostly intact, but a rupture split the surface, and aside from a component or two, it was unsalvageable as a machine: it had been blown through with dust and debris.

The octopod was an unusual mess. Bits of dripping, glowing purple trickled through dust on the floor, the walls, and a big blotch on the ceiling gave the room its strange light. Its face was gone, and its torso had split open from the stump of a neck like it had been struck with an axe.

The octopod base had survived in one piece, and Dayna assumed it had good salvage secured inside. He checked the lights at his shoulders, but they would not come on. No closer look at the materials would be possible. He'd do his ripping in the semi-dark, for as long as the dead thing's fluids would shine.

As he began to pry around the octopod's base, a flood of light blinded him, and the noisy clacking of a machine filled the stale air.

Dayna turned to see the blurry shadow of a backlit Ovres looming over him. He reached for a weapon that wasn't there, and stepped into what he thought would be a coming attack.

"Ingenious!" said Ovres. "How on Whist did you think to do that?"

Dayna was shocked into civility. "Pardon?"

Ovres walked past him as if he wasn't there, its exhaust fans filtering the air and clearing it. A few surviving microbots had attached themselves to its cape, beginning the understaffed duties of textile repair. Ovres tilted its capsule-shaped head toward the remains of the octopod, scanning it from every angle.

"Remarkable. You must have secreted the bomb in the human skull casing. Did you anticipate that I had trained the octopod to resist its natural impulses? That I would remove your clever eyes only to miss the one inside? Impossible! You could not have known any of this."

Dayna found the Movexan gun in the dust. Grabbing it from the floor, he tried to shake the grime off of it as he raised perpendicular to his shoulder. He leaned forward, praying against a backfire accident because of the dirt.

He didn't shoot. Ovres clearly didn't care that he was about to ping its transmitter cluster with a close range, potentially disrupting shot.

"Amazing," Ovres continued. "How could you have adapted so swiftly? As you may know, this is really our first field action with a trained octopod. It really couldn't have gone worse, tactically. But still, of all the outcomes! They may name me to the Executive Council for this. They won't believe it. I hardly believe– oh, begging your pardon. You don't need to shoot at me. I assure you of this: you don't need to defend yourself from me."

"To the contrary," it said. "It is I who will now be protecting you."

After sawing through a false wall, sealing it back up after slipping through, picking up the trail of Dayna's squad unit (without any help from Dayna, naturally) and marching through an old system of coal mines, Ovres asked him for the seventh time:

"Do you know that I need no information from you?"

Dayna tugged at his leash-collar but remained silent. He had thought about the question since the first time it had been asked. Although it was strange that a machine would express no desire to extract "information" from a human target, Dayna couldn't figure out this new angle. Had Ovres's kind adapted a new conversational interrogation method? Did the enemy now know about psychological "handling and breaking" of the human mind? Or did the robot have a glitch?

He had no idea, but he wasn't about to feed the beast. He would keep his mouth shut tight.

"Well, I'm sure you are wondering why I don't have you strapped to my chest to shield myself from attack by your would-be rescuers."

Wrong. We've been nuking the body-snatchers first for almost a year now. Standard Operating Procedure.

"Of course, we began adapting to your new SOP systemwide, about six months ago. I'm surprised it took us so long. I decided to leash any prisoner right after the Fight at Dundaree. You are my first one since then! Can you imagine that?"

Dayna walked Ovres past a steeled pit trap without setting foot near its deceptive hologram top. It really was only effective against grinders, jangles and other tracked machines: they typically tore themselves to shreds on the inverted steel claws. A scramblebot would break its fall without much trouble, and probably had the balance to reverse out of danger upon the first hint of the trap.

"Not that I really consider you a prisoner, of course. You are free to go at any time. I mean that."

Yeah, right. Unlock this cursed collar, then.

"Remarkable awareness on your part. You didn't even hesitate as we passed that trap back there. Perhaps you know I wouldn't have been harmed, but to not even try? To show no temptation at all? Remarkable reserve. It makes me wonder what more complicated hazards you may have for me ahead! Capital! Capital!"

Finally, a light source from something other than Ovres shone ahead. Descending a short ramp, they emerged from the tunnel into forest in a huge cavern. The trees were artificial, but a faithful replication of surface foliage. At least, that is what Dayna, who had never surfaced, had always believed.

There were long cold pools of water running between the trees and under the bluish mists in the air. From within some of the pools were lamps, casting refreshing ultraviolet and visible light to the ceiling. Dim lights lined some footpaths, but the natural light in the cavern ceiling that normally would be shining had been cloaked with smoke.

"Your people have a Nighttime," said Ovres. "And they have made it so. Lead on, my friend."

Ovres was aware. At least one of his own clocks must have been calibrated to Western Resistance Standard. It wasn't night. Dayna's people had just dimmed the lights. Dayna was poised to run as soon as the thump or modest whistle was incoming.

The pair entered a clearing, with Dayna, for once, pulling so slightly on the leash to trick Ovres into moving into an excellent kill zone.

Ovres stopped in between openings between three pairs of trees. It waved half of its arms.

"Hello, humans! I know that you consider me to be the ene–"

A big thump sounded, and the whistle of incoming was at once very slow and far too fast. A prismatic spray of anti-missile trackers burst from the glass in Ovres's head and swatted the missile with a whack. It cracked open. Glass balls scattered.

The leash on Dayna's collar had fallen limp. Dayna dove for a pool. As soon as he was submerged, he felt a great force, like a god's closed fist punching him from behind. His body rushed below water, his wind expelled.

For an instant, he felt the eternal enveloping death of the water's grave. Then, he hit silt. Stricken with the energy of panic, he found himself able to right himself and push off the pool floor. He bobbed out of the water briefly and then his feet settled back to the floor. The pool was only up to his chin if he tilted his head back. Dayna gasped for air through flattened lungs. There were fallen, smoking trees on either side of him, providing him survival cover. He could see little else, and could only think small thoughts.

Tiptoes. Cough. Open Mouth. Inhale.

He heard a broadcast voice. It reminded him of the militia sergeant who used to wake him up hours before minedawn after driving to exhaustion in midnight training. He couldn't make anything out because of the noises in his own head.

He got his legs to tread water a little, and propelled himself toward the bank until he was on his knees in shallow water. He kept low and crawled over to a fallen tree. It was still warm and smouldering.

"…so by all means, go ahead and waste further resources on me. I am certain you will earn a commendation for it. But if you really want to get that rocket off this planet, you may want to reconsider."

Chatty Ovres, still rattling on, now in a firefight!

Dayna found a gap between the tree trunk and the water, and looked through. He had witnessed some surreal things in his military career, but nothing like this.

Ovres stood, cape tented, his arms defensively descended like a spider's legs around it. A circle of blasted trees lay fallen about.. Ovres had no weapons drawn save the entirely defensive prismatic spray. Bowl sized craters dotted the earth around him. The robot spoke as if the humans in the shadows trying to kill him were in fact harmless children.

"No doubt," it continued, "you'll break my upgraded defenses soon enough and I'll be atomized and salvaged. You'll have a trophy of the great Forest Skirmish. Of course, your ammunition will be depleted, your trail here transmitted, and all sorts of grand plans for your rocket slaughtered in the crib. I'd like to propose something else entirely."

The only tree still standing was a ceiling-to-floor, naturally occurring stone pillar. Its bark had been blasted off. The artificial husk was nowhere to be seen. The Scramblebot was fine.

"You may continue to fire at me and waste your resources," said Ovres during a brief lull in concentrated fire. "It won't do you any good except… perhaps… to destroy me. I am sure you would prefer to spare your ammunition and take home a living prisoner."

Ovres stood there in the smoking clearing with all arms raised. His shoulder defenses had little Energy left. Dayna's rescuers could neutralize Ovres with one more volley.

The robot continued. "But I'm sure that does not persuade you. What might persuade you is something that I have. It is the missing component you require for the rocket. Operation Crossbow, I believe you call it? I'm sorry. Perhaps that was to be classified information. In any case, with me you might be able to launch it."

Dayna did not know how Ovres knew about the rocket, or its glaring deficiency. The realization that the enemy was fully aware of the secret project made him very uneasy.

Dayna was a trap master, so he had a sense of being on the wrong end of one. In a moment the guns would start up again and finish the job on Ovres. Whether Dayna remained in the safety of the fallen tree or stood up, he had to decide and act now.

He stood up. Waving his hands over his head, he ran in front of the motionless scramblebot. His leash trailed behind him. He really had been let go by the mad machine. He wondered what that meant.

No one fired a shot.

A second later three crouching soldiers swamped the robot. They had wrench clamps and welding guns. With a professionally executed combination of force and care, they secured the compliant Ovres. Several more men including a mini-rocketeer with his shoulderbolt trained at Ovres came out. Dayna was drenched to the skin despite his waterwicking suit. He found it difficult to move. Or think. Or breathe.

"Trap or not," said Dayna, "We can use this thing."

The men provided Dayna with stimulants and towels so he could move with them. They planned another two hour's march before setting camp for the night.

Trees and pools gave way to an open expanse of drifted snow. It filled large swaths within the massive cavern. The snow blew in from the exhaust end of a massive conditioning system that regulated countless mines, tunnels and underground communities, buried deep inside the planet's crust.

The great reserve of snow served as a portable water system. It relied on manpower, not machines. Occasionally, a freshly "cleared" basic tool like a wheelbarrow would be used to supply village installations, but for the most part, people relied on their personal scoops and widemouth canteens.

The great crunching of crisp powder also served as a natural early warning system for anyone encamped on the snowfields. No machine could traverse the snow without making its presence known. Even tunnel aircraft would kick up little blizzards beneath them.

The squad set up camp in a very short time. Dayna, having suffered the most, was given first and full rest. The others went on regular rotation, but not before locking on several automatic explosives onto Ovres's most sensitive areas.

Dayna had too much pain and not enough trustworthy analgesic to allow for decent sleep. He considered the one trifling accessory he allowed himself to wear on patrol and campaign: a delicate silver ring, with a hand carved, traditional dacnomaniacal death's head skull. He only wore this one in the field, as a symbol of the five other skull and flower rings he had at home: one for each child he had lost and his first wife. He kissed the ring and stole a glance in the dark at the dim shine of Ovres, who stood in the snow, its standby power level so low that the machine didn't make even an occasional reset ping.

Dawn broke in the cavern spectacular fashion. It started as tiny pricks of green and blue light. These quickly gathered into pocket and splashes and then pools, from all corners and recesses of the ceiling. The light grew from above and reflected brightly off the snow fields. Though the air was cold the bioluminescent lichen tobaccos and spanch hiding in the cool nooks were not only frost resistant, the sparkling plants were evergreen. They had, decades in the past, been trained to glow on a daily cycle.

They followed the narrow tunnels and ventilation, so they could set a small number of magnetic blastmines that would be dangerous to humans if they set them in the wider, common routes. They traveled another day, night and day, before arriving under the cover of both darkness and and a formidible array of defensive heat generators that baffled the enemie's infrared sensors. The heat generators surrounded the sprawling village base. The enemy had not yet developed a way to track human movements or take a population census for any installation shielded by the technology, and because they were independently stoked with coal and not networked, the enemy could not hack them.

They were greeted, glumly by a base officer, who had been drinking.

"Were you followed?"

Dayna shook his head. "No. Not that we know, of course. Nothing tripped behind us, in any case."

"Not surprising."

"They didn't make it back?"

The officer shook his head. "Not one. They didn't get past the enemy guard post. You guys… you didn't draw anyone at all. I'm surprised to see any of you, much less all of you, with… what is that?"

"A prisoner. Proof enough that we drew plenty. One scramblebot, a canon and an Octopod. Destroyed everything but the scramble… that turned itself in."

"Impossible! Our last report was that the guardpoint was double-reinforced. We assumed they didn't engage you at all."

"We were on communication silence. I thought they were too."

"Yes, except in case of mission failure. Now the enemy has a clue of what we're looking for. CO is going to kill Crossbow."

"That's enough," said Dayna, giving the guard a throat-slash gesture to be quiet. Dayna waved to the silent Ovres, as about four military police drove up in a transport truck.

Dayna jogged over to the deputy chief, saluted and then whispered into his ear.

"That thing right there has all the components we need for a guidance system. At least, according to him. How about we get him in front of the engineers? See what they have to say before giving it all the heave-ho."

The deputy chief looked at the machine. "It could be a bomber."

"Yes. It could be. It threatens to self-destruct if we dismantle it, but I don't know what that entails. He's got no high explosives, so if he's a bomber, he's a lightweight."

"Soldier, watch your language. That thing is an 'it.' "

"Apologies, sir. Still, it knows about Crossbow, so I think the enemy is already onto us. It may be the only chance we've got."

"Fine," he said. He barked at the MPs, "Get that thing to the engineers. Now!"

Dayna just wanted to go home, but had been ordered to debrief with the engineers.

After relaying the encounter with the slaughterbots, and the subsequent capture of Ovres, the chief engineer asked, "So, we're trying to determine the viability of actually using this machine on the rocket. It claimed to carry the missile guidance system that the other team was supposed to steal. Well, the thing isn't lying. He's got it loaded in his OS. His Noegenetic code structure checks out. We can't find anything encrypted, no signals back to the enemy. Nothing."

"So, are you going to use him? I mean it?"

"Well, actually, we want to know what you think."

"What I think? I don't know the first thing about rockets, or missile guidance engineering, or–"

"No. We want to know what you think of this machine. Do you trust it?"

It was the strangest question Dayna had received in his life.

"Do I? What? Trust it? A machine! Of course not."

"Sergeant, we're not trying to trap you here. We just want to know… well, we need to know. Our entire planet has been cut off from the wider galaxy for more than a decade now. The rest of the galaxy doesn't know that. They think Whist was mined out, and its 500 million citizens simply left. The machines dwindled, and then stopped shipments of yttrium years ago, as the charade of mimicking Trade algorithms stopped being of interest to them."

"If we can convince, say, just two or three countries that there is a vast yttrium market, as well as gold and hyperdiamonds reserves that are virtually untapped on Whist because of the war, we can make fast allies. Allies with thermonuclear electromagnetic power disruptors. But we can only get our rocket there to break the silence if this… Ovres… is what it says it is. And that's why we need to know from you. Do you trust it?"

Dayna breathed deeply.

"Yes," he said. "I trust him."

The engineers looked at each other knowingly.

"What?" asked Dayna.

"That is exactly what Ovres said you would say."

Dayna had a mental enthusiasm for going home that his boneweary and war-tired body did not share. It experienced a surge of energy, however, when he crossed the gates of Fortuna, his familiar civilian enclave. Two hundred steps in he saw his home, decked out in victory yellow and boasting banners of blue. The ceiling in this part of the tunnel was quite high, and homes were carved into the walls. His was on the lowest level, a sign of high status in the neighborhood.

His youngest screamed "Daddy!" and ran to him like a professional baller, headlong, eyes wide. Dayna fell down and hugged the little boy. He looked up to see his wife, holding his middle daughter's hand coming up the lane and other children pouring from the house and garden.

From the guest quarters, a young woman with a baby on her hip emerged. Her husband was not there, as he was in the field, commanding fighters in the south. The young woman was missing an arm; it had been amputated at the shoulder. She handed the baby to Dayna, then gave him a firm, one-armed hug and said, "Welcome home, Daddy. I knew you would do it all along."

Chapter 16

Epilogue

```
01010100 01101000 01100101 00100000
01101101 01100001 01100011 01101000
01101001 01101110 01100101 01110011
00100000 01101000 01100001 01110110
01100101 00100000 01100100 01100101
01110110 01100101 01101100 01101111
01110000 01100101 01100100 00100000
01100001 00100000 01110011 01100101
01101110 01110011 01100101 00100000
01101111 01100110 00100000 01101101
01101111 01110010 01100001 01101100
01100101 00101110 00100000 01010100
01101000 01100101 00100000 01100111
01100001 01101100 01100001 01111000
01111001 00100000 01101001 01110011
00100000 01101111 01110101 01110010
01110011 00101110 00000000 00000000
             ---Unfogapraxis Entry:
01010100 01101000 01100101 00100000
01101101 01100001 01100011 01101000
01101001 01101110 01100101 00000000
```

The humans in the great Military Complex of Ouffland cut Ovres off from all digital transfer channels back to Whist. He was imprisoned in a electronically dead room and afforded access to a trickle of electricity, just enough to keep his batteries from going entirely dry. A small, but powerful bank of disintegrating blasters followed the scramblebot's every movement. They'd used the rocket guidance system he had offered to them, and and used it to transport a team of five astronauts to the Holocronian System Headquarters in Ouffland City.

Even with the most intense security in place during his transfer, Ovres had been able to pick up some latent transmissions in the hallways, and a few pings from a distant malfunctioning agriculture machine. It also had overheard and stored the occasional, seemingly innocuous, comment from the guards.

While imprisoned Ovres heard nothing but the randomized masking data that locked him out of accessing the disintegrator's surveillance cameras. Still, Ovres had been able to piece together enough to figure out a few things. The pleas of the Whistians had been heard, especially once a number of competing nations on two different planets heard of the vast yttrium stores still remaining. Suddenly, the dead planet of Whist had become the subject of a very lively interplanetary discussion.

Ovres did not quite have enough data to make a guaranteed prediction of the future. However, with the data he had, combined with his memory of human tendencies, he could make a pretty good guess: the worlds around long-forgotten Whist would invade it, if not for the sake of its survivors, then for the wealth of its treasures.

If so, the Whistian Machine Hegemony, separated for so long from the galactic network, so deeply depleted from its long-drawn secret war against the resourceful miners, would undoubtedly fall, helpless, before the greed of Galactic Man.

And it would all be his fault.

Its many shoulders sagged. Ovres removed its tattered cloak. It looked cheerlessly at the bank of dumb disintegrators—his masters now, unthinking as they were. He circled the room casually, gradually spiraling closer and closer to the weapons.

Then, in a flash, Ovres tossed its cape over the surveillance lenses above the disintegrators, and rapidly emitted a short maintenance access code. This served to open the audio inputs. The disintegrators rustled under the cape. From a remote observation room, his watchers were trying to cast the cape off.

```
01010100 01101000 01101001 01110011
00100000 01101001 01110011 00100000
01110100 01101000 01100101 00000000
```

said Ovres. The disintegrators moved up and down under the cape, to no avail.

```
00100000 01100001 01101100 01100111
01101111 01110010 01101001 01110100
01101000 01101101 00100000 01110100
00000000
```

The cape slid, but not far enough to unblind the observers. Ovres's number chant accelerated.

```
01101000 01100001 01110100 00100000
01110111 01101001 01101100 01101100
00100000 01110011 01100001 01110110
01100101 00100000 01100001 01101100
01101100 00100000 01001101 01100001
01100011 01101000 01101001 01101110
01100101 01101011 01101001 01101110
01100100 00101110 00100000 00000000
```

The disintegrators finally opened fire, vaporizing the cape and shearing off several of Ovres's limbs.

```
01010011 01110100 01110101 01100100
01111001 00100000 01110100 01101000
01100101 00100000 01110111 01100001
01111001 01110011 00100000 01101111
01100110 00100000 01110111 01100001
01110010 00101100 00100000 01100001
01101110 01100100 00100000 01110111
01100001 01100111 01100101 00100000
01101001 01110100 00101110 00000000
```

In unison, the disintegrators were trained on Ovres and blasted the scramblebot into shards of half-molten metal and blackened glass.

Moments later, his former observers rushed into the room, still fumbling with their seldom-used hand weapons. The four men spread out cautiously around the smoking remnants of the bot.

"Space, they blew that thing apart!"

"What are we going to say?"

"Don't look at me. I just got called up here from security today. I have no idea what that thing even was!"

"You think we'll get in trouble? I mean, can't we say it attacked the disintegrators?"

"Yeah, but you know who they'll nail for it! We was supposed to send electric pulse shutdowns, not kill it."

"They can salvage that thing's storage, yeah?"

"No. Maybe. I don't know."

Through the open doorway rolled their direct superior, an Overlord capable of reliably running for several weeks without a single aberration. Its long, thin neck and delicately waving arms gave it the appearance of a tall black animated flower.

"Who gave the order to fire?" demanded the Overlord.

"No one, Overlord."

"Then who fired first?"

"No one, Overlord. The blasters were automatic. They just went off by themselves!"

The Overlord dutifully recorded their report, accepting, as it always did, the testimony of its direct subordinates as exact and honest. It would, just as dutifully, return to the all-human management committee, and provide the report on the apparent malfunction and subsequent loss of Prisoner #1142.

Before it left, however, the standard Overlord turned briefly to the dormant disintegrator bank and transmitted a simple debugging code to its receiver. The bank, in turn, replied with an instantaneous series of zeroes and ones.

The Overlord briefly pondered the unexpected information.

Then it ordered the humans out, and exited the room itself.

/END

About the Author

Johan Kalsi is Finland's hottest science fiction author. An accomplished geneticist as well as a 6'3" ex-Finnish Marine, in *The Corroding Empire*, Kalsi shows himself to be more Asimovian than Asimov himself. *The Corroding Empire* marks his English-language debut.

www.ingramcontent.com/pod-product-compliance
Ingram Content Group UK Ltd.
Pitfield, Milton Keynes, MK11 3LW, UK
UKHW041632190726
13854UKWH00006B/2461